Len Deighton was born in London in 1929. He worked as a railway clerk before doing his N̲a̲t̲i̲o̲n̲a̲l̲ ̲service in the RAF as a photographer ̲a̲t̲t̲a̲c̲h̲e̲d̲ ̲t̲o̲ Special Investigation Branch.

After his dischar̲g̲e̲ ̲ ̲ ̲ ̲ ̲ ̲ ̲ ̲ ̲ ̲ ̲ ̲ ̲ ̲ ̲ – first to the St Martin's ̲ Royal College of Art on a ̲ ̲ ̲ ̲ ̲ ̲ ̲ ̲ ̲ ̲ ̲ ̲ ̲ ̲ ̲ ̲ ̲ng as a waiter in the eveni̲n̲g̲ ̲ ̲ ̲ ̲ ̲d̲e̲v̲eloped an interest in cookery – a subject he was later to make his own in an animated strip for the *Observer* and in two cookery books. He worked for a while as an illustrator in New York and as art director of an advertising agency in London.

Deciding it was time to settle down, Deighton moved to the Dordogne where he started work on his first book, *The Ipcress File*. Published in 1962, the book was an immediate and spectacular success. Since then he has published twenty-four books of fiction and non-fiction – including spy stories, and highly-researched war novels and histories – all of which have appeared to international acclaim.

1987 marks the twenty-fifth anniversary of the first publication of Len Deighton's THE IPCRESS FILE, the novel that simultaneously revolutionized the espionage-thriller genre and marked the arrival on the fiction scene of one of the most powerful narrative talents in Twentieth Century literature.

Grafton Books is proud to present special Silver Jubilee editions of the major works of Len Deighton to celebrate the first quarter-century of his spectacularly successful writing career. All the books in the Len Deighton Silver Jubilee collection carry special forewords by the author exclusive to these editions. Published only during 1987, these limited editions are a tribute to one of the most accomplished writers of our time.

SILVER JUBILEE EDITION

LEN DEIGHTON

Twinkle, Twinkle, Little Spy

TRIAD
GRAFTON BOOKS

LONDON GLASGOW
TORONTO SYDNEY AUCKLAND

Triad
Grafton Books
8 Grafton Street, London W1X 3LA

Published by Triad/Grafton 1977
Reprinted 1978 (twice), 1979, 1980, 1981,
1982 (twice), 1984 (twice), 1985
Silver Jubilee Edition 1987

Triad Paperbacks Ltd is an imprint of
Chatto, Bodley Head & Jonathan Cape Ltd and
Grafton Books, A Division of the Collins Publishing Group

First published in Great Britain by
Jonathan Cape Ltd 1976

ISBN 0-586-07407-4

Printed and bound in Great Britain by
Cox & Wyman Ltd, Reading

Set in Times

Preface

I'd never had any particular desire to go into the Sahara Desert. My dreams of exploring the lesser known parts of the globe have long since been satisfied. But I do find it interesting to see other people doing their jobs.

So when I heard that a very close friend of mine was organizing a motor car rally that would not only cover Europe but also cross the Sahara Desert twice (from Morocco to Nigeria and then back to Tunisia) I wanted to know more about it.

After some lobbying and pretending to know far more than I did, I was eventually permitted to be a member of one of the control parties who time, and check, the arrival and departure of the cars at the various stages of the rally. It meant going across the desert ahead of the first cars, setting up the control points, and then 'sweeping up' on our way to the next assigned control point. Sweeping up meant going along the route to talk to any competitor who'd broken down, (and on this rally there were plenty) so that there was a double-check and no danger of anyone being left in the desert unknown to the rescue teams.

Even though I've lived a life more than averagely eventful, my journey across the Sahara was memorable. It was awe inspiring to drive through the desert at night: it produces a curious optical illusion of being in a big tunnel. To find people alone in the middle of this waste-land is a surprise, and to find them selling ancient Roman arrowheads, dug from its sand, was enough to send me back to my history books.

As always, the people were even more captivating than the landscape. There was the American oil-prospector from Libya who regularly found relics, and even tracks, left by the World War Two armies which fought there. There was the tough little English girl singer who, when I said that Algeria must be a communist country because there were hammer and sickle signs on coins and posters, laughed as though I'd made the funniest joke she'd ever heard. More immediately there were the two other members of the team. I'd met fanatics before, thousands of them, people obsessed with anything from politics to postage stamps and I never met fanatics more dedicated than these two were, to motor cars.

My father was obsessed by motor cars and enjoyed nothing better than methodically and quietly taking one to pieces and reassembling it. But these two made my father seem well-adjusted. For those weeks in the desert the conversation was nothing but motor cars and if I didn't join in, that was just my bad luck. I listened of course and with motor cars to hand, and not much to collide with in the middle of the Sahara, I tried out what I learned.

And if those long evenings when just the three of us talked cars seemed obsessive, then what about the evenings when the rally drivers got together. As had happened so many times before, I had so much exciting material in my hands that it was spilling over my shoes. But would it make a book? Many times before I had found myself over-provided with the stuff of which books are not made!

The worst thing about writing books is the disappointment when exciting projects come to nothing. I have always been lucky with my supply of ideas. When people come up to me at parties – as they are inclined to come up to writers at parties – and say, 'I have this wonderful idea for a book. You write the book, and we'll split the proceeds fifty-fifty.' I usually reply that I have dozens of ideas for books. If they'd like to do the time-consuming business of research and the drudgery of the writing, I would gladly split fifty-fifty.

In fact, as Napoleon said of battles, it's only when you engage on the task that you find out what's possible. A trip to some exotic place doesn't make a book. An idea that seems fine in one's mind will not survive as a scribble on paper. Even a long outline can fail to warn of major problems that come to light only when a book is half-written. Once (with *SS-GB*) I completed three quarters of the typescript and had to start again from page one. I have a large collection of unfinished books. Twice I have put completed books aside as unsatisfactory.

I work slowly, a thousand words here, two thousand there, and a full wastepaper basket every night. So I have to nurse my babies for at least a year, sometimes much, much longer. I couldn't get up each morning and face a manuscript I hated, so my books have to be planned in advance. First and foremost I have to be sure that my enthusiasm will extend over the year, or years, that the writing will take.

But many books that writers just loved to write (like films that film-makers loved to make) are terrible. So I keep ideas on the back burner for a long time to see whether the first enthusiasm endures. And lastly must come an examination of one's motives. Any book that might win for the author an enhanced literary reputation, make a superb film or provide special secret amusements to his or her friends should on no account be published (written: maybe).

Research that one particularly enjoyed doing is similarly deceptive. Just because a writer enjoyed taking the controls of an F-4 jet fighter or kicking in the door of a Los Angeles narcotics dealer, or in this case responding to the mysterious attraction of vast desolate expanses, doesn't mean that it will prove possible to convey this excitement to the reader.

Even if you can do it, the danger of using too much research is ever present. Of the very best material gathered in any research trip, I doubt whether it's ever been possible for me to use more than five per cent of it in the final published work. As an economist said when looking at my work programme: writing is not only a labour-intensive business, it's damnably inefficient.

And that's just the way I like it, I told him.

Len Deighton, 1987

> *'I have loved the stars too fondly*
> *to be fearful of the night.'*

Epitaph on grave of unknown astronomer

1

'Smell that air,' said Major Mann.

I sniffed. 'I can't smell anything,' I said.

'That's what I mean,' said Mann. He scratched himself and grinned. 'Great, isn't it?'

There's not much to smell when you are one thousand miles into the Algerian Sahara; not much to smell, not much to do, not much to eat.

For those travellers who know the swimming-pools and air conditioning of the government hotels along the northern edge of the Sahara, Adrar comes as a shock. Here the hotel has no more than tightly drawn curtains to protect the tourist from the sun, and the staff have noisy arguments about who should siesta on the cold stone floor of the entrance hall. Only Europeans stayed awake all day, notably four bearded Austrians who, night and day, played cards in the shuttered dining-room. They were waiting for a replacement petrol pump for their truck. Between games they swigged sweet, warm cola drinks. There was no alcohol on sale, and smoking was frowned upon.

Even on this winter's evening the stones and the sand radiated the heat of the desert day.

There was no moon but the stars were so bright that we could easily see our vehicles piled high with stores and sextant and a sign that said 'Dempsey's Desert Tours'. They were parked on the huge main square of Adrar. Mann walked round the vehicles just to make

1

sure the supplies had not been plundered. It was unlikely, for they were outside the police station.

Mann stopped and leaned against the Landrover. He took out a packet of cheroots; there were only four left. 'Look at those stars,' he said.

'The Milky Way – I've never seen it so clearly. A spaceship travelling at 100,000 miles per hour would take 670 million years to cross the Milky Way,' I said. 'There's a hundred thousand million stars there.'

'How do you know?' said Mann. He put the cheroot in his mouth and chewed it.

'I read it in the *Reader's Digest Atlas*.'

Mann nodded. 'And do you know something else . . . the way they're going, in another few years there will be another million stars there – enough spy satellites to put both of us out of business.'

'Twinkle, twinkle, little spy,' I said.

Mann looked at me to see if I was being insubordinate. 'Let's go back inside,' he said finally. He decided not to light the cheroot. He put it away again. 'I'll buy you a bottle of Algerian lemonade.' He laughed. Mann was like a small, neatly dressed gorilla: the same heavy brow, deep-set eyes and long arms – and the same sense of humour.

The dining-room is large, and although the big fans no longer turned it was the coolest place for hundreds of miles. The walls are whitewashed light blue, and crudely woven striped rugs are tacked to floor and walls. Overhead, the wooden flooring rattled like jungle drums as someone moved. There was the sudden roar of the shower and the inevitable violent rapping of the ancient plumbing. We helped ourselves to soft drinks and left the money on the till.

'That Limey bastard takes a shower every five minutes.'

2

'Yes, about every five minutes,' I agreed. Major Mickey Mann, US Army Signal Corps, Retired, a CIA expert on Russian electronics and temporarily my boss, had showed no sign of discomfort during the heat of day in spite of his tightly knotted tie and long trousers. He watched me carefully, as he always did when offering criticism of my fellow countrymen. 'That particular Limey bastard,' I said quietly, 'is sixty-one years old, has a metal plate in his skull and a leg filled with German shrapnel.'

'Stash the gypsy violin, feller – you want to make me weep?'

'You treat old Dempsey as if he's simple-minded. I'm just reminding you that he did four years with the Long Range Desert Group. He's lived in Algeria for the best part of thirty years, he speaks Arabic with all the local dialects and if it comes to real trouble in the desert we'll need him to use that sextant.'

Mann sat down at the table and began toying with the Swiss army penknife that he'd bought in the souvenir shop at Geneva airport. 'If the wind starts up again tonight . . .' he balanced the knife on its end, 'sand will make that road south impassable. And I don't need your pal Percy to tell me that.'

'Even in the Landrover?'

'Did you see that three-tonner down to the axles?' He let go of the knife and it stayed perfectly balanced. 'Sand that bogs down a three-ton six by six will bury a Landrover.'

'They were gunning the motor,' I said. 'You bury yourself that way.'

'You've been reading the camping-in-the-desert section of the boy scout handbook,' said Mann. Again he banged the folding knife down on to the table, and again it balanced on its end. 'And in any case,' he added, 'how

3

do we know the Russkie will be able to steal a four-wheel drive? He might be trying to get here in a Moskvich sedan for all we know.'

'Is he stupid?'

'Professor Bekuv's intellect is not universally admired,' said Mann. 'During the time he was with the Russian scientific mission at the UN he wrote two papers about little men in flying saucers, and earned his reputation as a crank.'

'Defecting cranks don't get the department's OK,' I said.

'Looking for messages from little men in flying saucers probably motivated his work on masers,' said Mann. 'And Bekuv is one of the world's experts on masers.'

'I'm not even sure I know what a maser is,' I said.

'You read the Technical Brief.'

'Twice,' I said. 'But not so as to understand it.'

'Maser,' said Mann. 'It's an acronym – "m" for microwave, "a" for amplification, "s" for stimulated, "e" for emission, "r" for radiation.'

'Do you mind if I take notes?'

'Listen, dummy. It converts electromagnetic radiation – from a whole range of different frequencies – to a highly amplified, coherent microwave radiation.'

'Is it anything to do with a laser?'

'Well, a maser is a laser but a laser is not necessarily a maser.'

'Is it anything to do with that guy looking in a mirror who says "Brothers and sisters have I none"?'

'Now you're beginning to get the idea,' said Mann.

'Well, somebody must be very interested in masers,' I said, 'or they wouldn't have sent us two down here to provide Bekuv with a red-carpet reception.'

'Or interested in flying saucers,' said Mann.

4

'If this Russian is such an idiot, what makes anyone believe that he's capable of escaping from that Russian compound, stealing a roadworthy vehicle and getting all the way up here to meet us?'

'Don't get me wrong, pal. Bekuv is crazy like a fox. Maybe he is a flying-saucer freak, but when he was in New York with that UN scientific set-up he was reporting back to the KGB. He joined the 1924 Society – crackpots maybe, but they have some of the world's top scientists as members. Bekuv was only too keen to read them long papers about gabfests through the galactic plasma by Soviet scientists, but he was listening very carefully when they told him what kind of work they were doing with their radio telescopes and electromagnetic wave trans-missions.' Major Mann ran his fingers back through his wispy hair that each day went greyer, now that he'd used up the last of his dark rinse. Almost without being conscious of what he was doing, he pushed hair over the balding patch at the back of his head. 'Professor Bekuv was a spy. Don't ever forget that. No matter how you dress it up as being a free exchange of scientific know-how, Bekuv was skilfully digging out a whole lot more than rumours about flying saucers.'

I looked at Mann. I'd seen plenty of such men all the world over from the Shetlands to Alaska, and all the way through Communist Algeria too: foot-loose Americans, their linen clean and their livers tormented, soft accents blunted by a lifetime of travelling. It would have been easy to believe that this wiry fifty-year-old was one of those *condottieri* of the oil fields – and that's what was written in his nice new passport.

'Where did Bekuv go wrong?' I asked.

'To be sent down to Mali, as part of Soviet aid to under-developed African countries . . . deputy head of a

5

six-man team of Soviet scientists.' Major Mann reached for his hip-flask. He looked round the room to be sure he was not observed before putting a shot of whisky into his sweet, fizzy Algerian cola. 'Nobody knows for sure. The latest guess is that Bekuv's flying saucers began to be an embarrassment for the Soviet Academy and they sent him down here for a spell to concentrate his mind on political realities.'

'I thought the Soviet Academy were very enthusiastic about flying saucers,' I said. 'What about this big radio telescope they've built in the northern Caucasus – the RATAN-600?'

'Now you reveal the depths of your ignorance,' said Mann. 'There's a whole lot of difference between the respectable scientific work of searching deep space for signals from extra-terrestrial intelligence and the strictly infra dig. pastime of looking for unidentified flying objects, or what the sci-fi freaks call ufology.'

'Now, I'm glad you told me that,' I said waving away Mann's offer of the flask. 'And so Bekuv was kicked downstairs into the foreign aid programme, and that's why he decided to defect. Well, that all fits together very neatly.'

Mann swallowed his drink and gave a grim smile to acknowledge that such a verdict was seldom intended as a compliment in the circles in which we moved. 'Right,' he said.

'Last one in the shower is a cissy,' I said. As I got up from the table I noticed that his knife was not balanced there after all; he'd driven its short screwdriver right into the wood.

2

The Trans-Sahara Highway is a track that goes south, through In-Salah and Tam, to the Atlantic. But we were using another trans-Sahara highway; the lesser known route that runs parallel to it, and many miles to the west. This was the way to the least known parts of Africa. This was the way to Gao and to Bamako, the capital of land-locked Mali. This was the way to Timbuktu.

It was four fifteen the next morning when we left the hotel in Adrar. Mann and Percy were in the Landrover. I followed in the VW bus with Johnny, an extra driver from 'Dempsey's Desert Tours'. We drove through the market-place in the gloom of desert night. It was damned cold, and the drivers wore scarves and woolly hats. The big trucks that cross the desert in convoy, loaded with dried fish and oranges, were nearly ready to move off. One of the drivers waved us past. Desert travellers have survival in common; never knowing when you might need a friend.

We turned south. I followed the rear lights of the Landrover. The road was hard sand, and we maintained a good speed past the roughly painted signs that pointed to distant villages. In places, loose sand had drifted on to the track, and I braked each time the Landrover's rear lights bounced; but the drift had not yet built up into the humps that tear an axle in half.

The gun-metal sky lightened and glowed red along the horizon until, like a thermic lance, the sun tore a white-hot hole in it. This road skirted the edges of the Sahara's

7

largest sand-seas. To the west the horizon rolled like a storm-racked ocean, but to the east the land was flat and featureless, as grey and as hard as concrete. Sometimes we passed herds of moth-eaten camels, scratching for a bite of thorn-bush or a mouthful of scrub. The route south was marked by small cairns of stones. Often there was a solitary Arab riding astride some wretched beast, so small and bowed that the rider's feet almost touched the ground. Once an Arab family were rearranging the burdens upon the saddles of their three camels. We saw no motor traffic.

We were three hours out of Adrar by the time we reached the end of the track. Six dented oil-drums blocked the way, and a sun-bleached wooden sign indicated that we should follow the tyre tracks in a diversion from the marked route.

The Landrover bumped off the hard verge with a flurry of sand as the wheels slipped into a soft patch. My smooth tyres took hold and then followed slowly along the pattern of tracks. I kept close behind the others, lining up our vehicles to simplify the problems of winching, for there was little doubt that I would be the one who got stuck. Their four-wheel drive would get them out of this kind of sand.

The detour was marked each hundred metres or so by an old oil-drum. Some of them had been blown over, and rolled far away from their original positions. Two were almost buried in drifting sand. It was easier to watch the tyre tracks.

After about eight kilometres the Landrover stopped. Mann got out and walked back to me. It was fully light now and even with sun-glasses I found myself squinting into the light reflecting from the sand. It was still early morning, but now that we'd stopped I felt the heat of the sun and smelt the warm rubber, evaporating fuel and Mann's after-shave lotion.

'How far was that last drum?' asked Mann.

'A couple of hundred metres.'

'Right and I don't see another ahead. You stay here. I'll mosey around a little.'

'What about these tyre tracks?' I asked.

'Famous last words,' pronounced Mann. 'Tracks like those can lead you out there into that sand-sea, and finally you get to the place where they turn around and head back again.'

'Then why tracks?'

'An old disused camp for oil prospectors, or a dump for road gangs.' He kicked at one of the tyre marks.

'These tracks look fresh,' I said.

'Yeah,' said Mann. He kicked one of the ridges of impacted sand. It was as hard as concrete. 'So do the tank tracks you find in southern Libya – and they've been there since Rommel.'

I looked at my watch.

Mann said, 'I hope the diversion is well marked on the highway to the south of here, or that Russian cat will come wheeling past us while we're stuck out here in this egg-timer factory.'

It was then that Percy Dempsey got out of the Land-rover and limped back to join us. He was a curious figure in his floppy hat, cardigan, long baggy shorts and gaiters.

'Jesus!' said Mann. 'Here comes Miss Marple.'

'I say – old chap,' said the old man. He had difficulty remembering our names. Perhaps that was because we changed them so often. 'Mr Antony, I mean. Are you wondering about the road ahead?'

'Yes,' I said. My name was Antony; Frederick L. Antony, tourist.

Dempsey blinked. His face was soft and babyish as old men's faces sometimes are. Now that he had taken off his sun-glasses, his blue eyes became watery.

Mann said, 'Don't get nervous, Auntie. We'll dope it out.'

'The oil-drum markers continue along this track,' said the old man.

'How do you know that?' said Mann.

'I can see them,' said the old man.

'Yeah!' said Mann. 'So how come I can't see them, and my buddy here can't see them?'

'I used my binoculars,' said the old man apologetically.

'Why the hell didn't you say you had binoculars?' said Mann.

'I offered them to you just outside Oran. You said you weren't planning a trip to the opera.'

'Let's go,' said Mann. 'I want to make camp before the sun gets high. And we have to find a place where the Russkie can spot us from the main road.'

Dempsey's Desert Tours VW bus was equipped with two tent sides that expanded to provide a large area of shade. There was also a nylon sheet stretched across the roof, and held taut above it, which prevented the direct sunlight striking the top of the bus and so making it into the kind of oven that metal car bodies became.

The bright orange panels could be seen for miles. The Russian spotted them easily. He had driven non-stop from some prospecting site along the river Niger east of Timbuktu. It was a gruelling journey over poor tracks and open country, and he'd ended it in the fierce heat of early afternoon.

The Russian was a hatchet-faced man in his early forties.

He was tall and slim with cropped black hair that showed no sign of greying. His dark suit was baggy and stained, its jacket slung over his brawny shoulder. His red check shirt was equally dirty, and the gold pencil clipped into its pocket was conspicuous because of that. Pale blue eyes were almost sealed by fine desert sand, and his face was lined and bore the curious bruise-like marks that come with exhaustion. His arms were muscular and his skin was tanned very dark.

Major Mann opened the nylon flap and indicated the passenger seats of the VW bus and the table-top fixed between them. In spite of the tinted windows the plastic seat covering was hot to the touch. I sat opposite the Russian and watched him take off his sun-glasses, yawn and scratch the side of his nose with his car-key.

It was typical of Mann's cunning, and of his training, that he offered the Russian no chance to rest. Instead he pushed towards him a glass and a vacuum flask containing ice-cubes and water. There was a snap as Mann broke the cap on a half-bottle of whisky and poured a generous measure for our guest. The Russian looked at Mann and gave him a thin smile. He pushed the whisky aside and from the flask grabbed a handful of ice-cubes and rubbed them on his face.

'You got ID?' Mann asked. As if to save face he poured whisky for himself and for me.

'What are ID?'

'Identification. Passport, security pass or something.'

The Russian took a wallet from his hip pocket. From it he brought a dog-eared piece of brown cardboard with his photo attached. He passed it to Mann, who handed it to me. It was a pass into the military zone along the Mali frontier with Niger. It described the Russian's physical characteristics and named him as Professor Andrei

Mikhail Bekuv. Significantly the card was printed in Russian and Chinese as well as Arabic. I gave it back to him.

'You have the photo of my wife?'

'It would have been poor security to risk it,' said Mann. He sipped at his drink but when he set it down again the level seemed unchanged.

Professor Bekuv closed his eyes. 'It's fifteen months since I last saw her.'

Mann shifted uncomfortably in his seat. 'She will be in London by the time we get there.'

Bekuv spoke very quietly, as if trying to keep a terrible temper under control. 'Your people promised a photo of her – standing in Trafalgar Square.'

'It was . . .'

'That was the agreement,' said Bekuv, 'and you haven't kept to it.'

'She never left Copenhagen,' said Mann.

Bekuv was silent for a long time. 'Was she on the ship from Leningrad?' he said finally. 'Did you check the passenger list?'

'All we know is that they didn't come in on the plane to London,' said Mann.

'You lie,' said Bekuv. 'I know the sort of people you are. My country is filled with such men as you. You had men there waiting for her.'

'She will come,' said Mann.

'Without her I will not come with you.'

'She will come,' said Mann. 'She is probably there already.'

'No,' said Bekuv. He turned in his seat, to see the road that would take him a thousand miles back to the Russians in Timbuktu. In spite of the tinted windows, the sand was no more than a blinding glare. Bekuv picked up the battered sun-glasses that he'd left on the table alongside his car keys. He toyed with them for a moment and then put them into the pocket of his shirt. 'Without her I am nothing,' said Bekuv reflectively. 'Without her life is not worth living for me.'

Mann said, 'There is urgent work to be done, Professor Bekuv. Your chair of Interstellar Communication at New York University will give you access time on the Jodrell Bank radio telescope – and, as you well know, that has a 250-foot steerable paraboloid. The university is also arranging time on the 1,000-foot fixed radio telescope they've built in the Puerto Rican mountains near Arecibo.'

Bekuv didn't answer but he didn't leave either. I glanced at Mann and he gave me the sort of glare that was calculated to shrivel me to silent tissue. I realized now that Mann's joke about little men in flying saucers was no joke.

'There is no one else doing this kind of cosmology,' Mann said. 'Even if you fail to make contact with life in other solar systems, you'll be able to give it a definitive thumbs down.'

Bekuv looked at him scornfully. 'There is already enough – *proof* to satisfy any but the most stupid.'

'If you don't take this newly created chair of Interstellar Communication there will be another bitter fight . . . and next time the cynics might get their nominee into it. Professor Chataway or old Delahousse would jump at such an opportunity to prove that there was no life anywhere in outer space.'

'They are fools,' said Bekuv.

Mann pulled a face and shrugged.

Bekuv said, 'I have a beautiful wife who has remained faithful, a proud mother and a talented son who will soon

13

be at university. Nothing is more important than they are.'

Mann sipped some of his whisky and this time he really drank. 'Suppose you go back to Timbuktu and your wife is waiting in London? What then, eh?'

'I'll take that chance,' said Bekuv. He slid across the seat and stepped down from the VW into the sand. The light through the nylon side-panels coloured him bright orange.

Mann didn't move.

'You don't fool me,' said Mann. 'You're not going anywhere. You made your decision a long time ago and you're stuck with it. You go back now, and your comrades will stake you out in the sand, and toss stale piroshkis at you.'

Bekuv said nothing.

'Here, you forgot your car keys, buddy,' Mann taunted him.

Bekuv took the keys that Mann offered but he did not step out into the sunshine. The sudden buzzing of a fly sounded unnaturally.

'Professor Bekuv,' I said. 'It's in our mutual interests that your family should be with you.'

Bekuv took out his hankerchief and wiped sand from the corners of his eyes but he gave no sign of having heard me.

'I understand there is still work to be done, so you can bet that the American Government will do everything in their power to make sure you are happy in *every* respect.'

'In their power, yes . . .' said Bekuv sadly.

'There are ways,' I said. 'There are official swops as well as escapes. And what you never hear about are the *secret* deals that our governments do. The trade agreements, the loans, the grain sales . . . all these deals contain hundreds of secret clauses. Many of them involve people we exchange.'

Bekuv dug the toe of his high, laced boots into the sand and traced a pattern of criss-cross lines. Mann reached forward from his seat and rested a hand upon Bekuv's shoulder. The Russian twitched nervously.

'Look at it this way, Professor,' Mann said, in the sort of voice that he believed to be gentle and conciliatory. 'If your wife is free we'll bring her to you, so you might as well come with us.' Mann paused. 'If she's in prison . . . you'd be out of your mind to go back.' He tapped Bekuv's shoulder again. 'That's the way it goes, Professor Bekuv.'

'There was no letter from her this week,' said Bekuv.

Mann looked at him but said nothing.

I had seen it before: men like Bekuv are ill fitted for the conspiracy of defection, let alone years of conspiracy that threatened the safety of his family. His gruelling journey across the Sahara had exhausted him. But his worst mistake was in looking forward to the moment when it would all be over; professionals never do that. 'Oh Katinka!' whispered Bekuv. 'And my fine son. What have I done to you. What have I done.'

I didn't move, and neither did Mann, but Bekuv pushed the nylon flap aside and stepped out into the scorching sun. He stood there for a long time.

3

The next problem was how to lose Bekuv's vehicle. It was a GAZ 59A, a Russian four-wheel drive field-car. It was a conspicuous contraption – canvas top, angular bodywork and shiny metal springs showing through the seat covers. You couldn't bury it in sand, and setting it ablaze would probably attract just the sort of attention we were trying to avoid.

Mann took a big wrench and ripped the registration plates off it and defaced the RMM sign that would tell even an illiterate informer that it was from Mali.

Mann didn't trust Percy Dempsey out of his sight. And Mann certainly didn't trust Johnny, the ever-smiling Arab driver. Only because he couldn't come up with a better idea did he agree to Johnny heading back north with the GAZ, while we followed with Bekuv in the VW. And all the time he was turning to look at Bekuv, watching Percy in the Landrover behind us and telling me that Percy Dempsey wasn't half the man I'd cracked him up to be.

'It's damned hot,' I said.

Mann grunted and looked at Bekuv still asleep on the bench seat behind us. 'If we dump that GAZ anywhere here in the south, the cops will check it to make sure it's not someone dying of thirst. But the farther we go north, the more interest the cops are going to take in that funny-looking contraption.'

'We'll be all right.'

'We haven't seen one of those heaps in the whole of Algeria.'

'Stop worrying,' I said. 'Percy was doing this kind of thing out here in the desert when Rommel was in knee pants.'

'You Limeys always stick together.'

'Why don't you drive for a while, Major.'

When we stopped to change seats, we stayed there long enough to let Johnny get a few kilometres ahead. The GAZ was no record-breaker. It wasn't all that far advanced from the Model A Ford from which it evolved. There would be no problem catching up with it, even in the VW.

In fact, the old GAZ came into view within twenty-five minutes of us resuming the journey. We saw it surmounting the gentle slope of a dune and Mann flicked his headlights in greeting.

'We'll keep this kind of distance,' Mann said. There was about five hundred yards between the vehicles.

Behind us Percy came into view, driving the Landrover. 'Is Percy a fag?' said Mann.

'Queer?' I said. 'Percy and Johnny? I never gave it a thought.'

'Percy and Johnny,' said Mann. 'It sounds like some cosy little bar in Tangier.'

'Does that make it more likely that they are queers, or less likely?'

'As long as they do their job,' said Mann. 'That's all I ask.' He glanced in the mirror before taking a packet of Camels from his shirt pocket, extracting a cigarette and lighting up, without letting go of the wheel. He inhaled and blew smoke before speaking again. 'Just get us up to that goddamned airstrip, that's all I ask.' He thumped the steering-wheel with his bony fist. 'That's all I ask.'

I smiled. The first hint of Bekuv's possible defection had been made to a British scientist. That meant that

British Intelligence were going to cling to this one like a limpet. I was the nominated limpet, and Mann didn't like limpets.

'We should have moved by night,' I said, more to make conversation than because I'd thought about it very carefully.

'And what do we tell the cops, that we are photographing moths?'

'No explanation necessary,' I said. 'These roads probably have more traffic at night when it's cool. The danger is running into camels or people walking.'

'Look at tha – Jesus Christ!'

Mann was staring ahead but I could see nothing there, and by the time I realized he was looking in the rear-view mirror it was too late. Mann was wrenching the steering-wheel and we were jolting into the desert in a cloud of sand. There was a howl of fury as Bekuv was shaken off the back seat and hit the floor.

I heard the jet helicopter long before I caught sight of it. I was still staring at the GAZ, watching it disappear in a flurry of sand and white flashes. Then it became a big molten blob that swelled up, and, like a bright red balloon, the fuel exploded with a terrible bang.

The helicopter's whine turned to a thudding of rotor blades as it came back and flew over us with only a few feet clearance, its blades chopping Indian signals out of the smoke that drifted up from the GAZ.

The Plexiglas bubble flashed in the sun as it banked so close to the desert that the blade tips almost touched the dunes. It was out of sight for a moment and by the time I heard the engine again I was fifty yards from the track full length on my face and trying to bury my head in the sand.

The pilot turned tightly as he came to the roadway. He

circled the burning car and then came back again before he was satisfied about his task. He turned his nose eastwards. At that altitude he was out of sight within a second or two.

'How did you guess?' I asked Mann.

'The way he was sitting there above the road. I've seen gun-ships in Nam. I knew what he was going to pull.' He smacked the dust off his trousers. 'OK, Professor?'

Bekuv nodded grimly. Obviously it had removed any last thoughts he might have had about driving back to Mali to kiss and make up.

'Then let's get the hell out of here, before the cops arrive to mop up the mess.'

We slowed as we passed through the smoke and the stink of rubber and carbonized flesh. Bekuv and I both turned to make sure that there was no last chance that the boy could have survived it. Then Mann accelerated, but behind us we saw the Landrover stop.

Mann was looking in the rear-view mirror. He saw it too. 'What's the old fool stopping for?'

I didn't answer.

'You got cloth ears?'

'To bury the kid.'

'He can't be that dumb!'

'There are traditions in the desert,' I said.

'You mean that's what the dummy is going to tell the cops when they get here and find him carving a head-stone.'

'Probably.'

'They'll shake him,' said Mann. 'The cops will shake Percy Dempsey, and you know what will fall out of his pockets?'

'Nothing will.'

19

'We will!' said Mann, still watching in the mirror. 'Goddamned stupid fruit.'

'I make it twenty k.'s to the turn-off for the airstrip.'

'Unless our fly-boy was scared shitless by that gunship, and went back to Morocco again.'

'Our boy hasn't even faked his flight plan yet,' I said. 'He's only fifteen minutes' flying time away from here.'

'OK, OK, OK,' said Mann. 'I don't need any of that Dunkirk spirit crap.' For a long time we drove in silence.

'Watch for that cairn at the turn-off,' I said. 'It's no more than half a dozen stones, and the sand has drifted since we came down this road.'

'There's no spade in the Landrover,' said Mann. 'You don't think he'd bury him with his bare hands, do you.'

'Slow a little now,' I said. 'The cairn is on this side.'

An aircraft came dune-hopping in from the north-west. It was one of a fleet of Dornier Skyservant short-haul machines, contracted to take Moroccan civil servants, politicians and technicians down to the phosphate workings near the Algerian border. The world demand for phosphates had made the workings the most pampered industry in Morocco.

The pilot landed at the first approach. It was part of his job to be able to land on any treeless piece of hard dirt. The Dornier taxied over to us and flipped the throttle of the port engine, so that it turned on its own axis, and was ready to fly out again. 'Watch out for the prop-wash!' Mann warned me.

Mann's father had been an airline pilot, and Mann had a ten-year subscription to *Aviation Week*. Flying machines brought out the worst in him. He rapped the metal skin of this one before climbing through the door. 'Great ships, these Dorniers,' he told me. 'Ever see a Dornier before?'

'Yes,' I said. 'My uncle George shot one down in 1940.'

'Just make sure you lock the door,' said Mann.

'Let's go, let's go,' said the pilot, a young Swede with a droopy moustache and 'Elsa' tattooed on his bicep.

I pushed Bekuv ahead of me. There were a dozen or more seats in the cabin, and Mann had already planted himself nearest the door.

'Hurry!' said the pilot. 'I want to get back on to my flight plan.'

'Casablanca?' said Mann.

'And all the couscous you can eat,' said the pilot, and he opened the throttles even before I had locked the door.

The place from which the twin-engined Dornier climbed steeply was a disused site left by the road-builders. There were the usual piles of oil-drums, two tractor chassis and some stone markers. Everything else had been taken by the nomads. Now a bright new VW bus marked Dempsey Desert Tours was parked in the shallow depression of a wadi.

'That's screwed this one up for ever,' said Mann. 'When the cops find the VW they'll be watching this airstrip for ever.'

'Dempsey will collect it,' I said.

'He's a regular little Lawrence of Arabia, your pal Dempsey.'

'He could have done this job on his own,' I said. 'There was no need for us to come down here.'

'You're even dumber than you look.' Mann looked round to make sure that Bekuv couldn't hear.

'Why then . . . ?'

'Because if the prof yells loud enough for his spouse, someone is going to have to go in and get her.'

'They'll use one of the people in the field,' I said.

'They'll use someone who talked to the professor . . . and you know it! Someone who was here, who can talk to his old lady and make it sound convincing.'

'Bloody risky,' I said.

'Yep!' said Mann. 'If the Russkies are going to send gun-ships here and blast cars out of the desert, they are not going to let his old lady out of their clutches without a struggle.'

'Perhaps they'll write Bekuv off as dead,' I said.

Mann turned in his seat to look at the professor. His head was thrown back over the edge of the seat-back. His mouth was open and his eyes closed. 'Maybe,' said Mann.

Now I could see the mountains of the High Atlas. They were almost hidden behind the shimmer of heat that rose from the colourless desert below us, but above the heat haze I could distinguish the snow-capped tops of the highest peaks. Soon we'd see the Atlantic Ocean.

4

I never discovered whether New York University realized that they had acquired a chair of Interstellar Communication; certainly it was not mentioned in the press analysis. The house we used was on Washington Square, facing across the trees to the university buildings. It had been owned by the CIA – through a land-management front – for many years, and used for various clandestine purposes that included extra-marital exploits by certain senior members of the Operations Division.

Technically, Major Mann was responsible for Bekuv's safety – which was a polite way of saying custody, as Bekuv himself pointed out at least three times a day. But it was Mann's overt role of custodian that enabled Bekuv to believe that the interrogation team were the NYU academics that they pretended to be. The interrogators' first hurdle was to steer Bekuv away from pure administration. Perhaps it was inevitable that a Soviet academic would want to know the floor-area his department would occupy, spending restrictions, the secretarial staff he was entitled to, his voting power in the university, his access to printing, photography and computer and his priority for student and postgraduate enrolment.

The research team was becoming more and more fretful. The reported leakage of scientific information eastwards was reflected by the querulous memos that were piling up in my 'classified incoming'.

Pretending to be Professor Bekuv's assistants, the interrogators were hoping to recognize the character of the data he already knew, and hoping to trace the American sources from which it had been stolen. With this in mind, slightly modified data had been released to selected staff at various government labs. So far, none of this 'seeded' material had come back through Bekuv, and now, in spite of strenuous protests from his 'staff', Bekuv declared a beginning to the Christmas vacation. He imperiously dismissed his interrogators back to their homes and families. Bekuv was therefore free to spend all his days designing a million-dollar heap of electronic junk that was guaranteed to make contact with one of those super-civilizations that were sitting around in space waiting to be introduced.

By Thursday evening the trees in Washington Square were dusted with the winter's first snow, radio advertisers were counting Christmas shopping time in hours, and Mann was watching me shave in preparation for a Park Avenue party at the home of a senior security official of the United Nations. A hasty note on the bottom of the engraved invitation said 'and bring the tame Russkie'. It had sent Mann into a state of peripatetic anxiety. 'You say Tony Nowak sent your invite to the British Embassy in Washington?' he asked me for the fourth or fifth time.

'You know Tony,' I said. 'He's nothing if not tactful. That's his UN training.'

'Goddamned gab-factory.'

'You think he knows about this house on Washington Square?'

'We'll move Bekuv tomorrow,' said Mann.

'Tony can keep his mouth shut,' I said.

'I'm not worrying about Tony,' said Mann. 'But if he knows we're here, you can bet a dozen other UN people know.'

'What about California?' I suggested. 'UCLA.' I sorted

through my last clean linen. I was into my wash-and-wear shirts now, and the bath was brimming with them.

'And what about Sing Sing?' said Mann. 'The fact is that I'm beginning to think that Bekuv is stalling – deliberately – and will go on stalling until we produce his frau.'

'We both guessed that,' I said. I put on a white shirt and club tie. It was likely to be the sort of party where you were better off English.

'I'd tear the bastard's toenails out,' Mann growled.

'Now you don't mean that,' I said. 'That's just the kind of joke that gets you a bad reputation.'

I got a sick kind of pleasure from provoking Major Mann, and he rose to that one as I knew he would: he stubbed out his cigar and dumped it into his Jim Beam bourbon – and you have to know Mann to realize how near that is to suicide. Mann watched me combing my hair, and then looked at his watch. 'Maybe you should skip the false eyelashes,' he said, 'we're meeting Bessie at eight.'

Mann's wife Bessie looked about twenty years old but must have been nearer forty. She was tall and slim, with the fresh complexion that was the product of her childhood on a Wisconsin farm. If beautiful was going too far, she was certainly good-looking enough to turn all male heads as she entered the Park Avenue apartment where the party was being held.

Tony greeted us and adroitly took three glasses of champagne from the tray of a passing waiter. 'Now the party can really begin,' said Tony Nowak – or Nowak the Polack as he was called by certain acquaintances who had not admired his spike-booted climb from rags to riches. For Antoni Nowak's job in the United Nations Organization security unit didn't require him to be in the lobby wearing a peaked cap and running metal detectors over the hand baggage. Tony had a six-figure salary and a three-window office with a view of the East River, and a lot of people typing letters in triplicate for him. In UN terms he was a success.

'Now the party can really begin,' said Tony again. He kissed Bessie, took Mann's hat and punched my arm. 'Good to see you – and Jesus, what a tan you guys got in Miami.'

I nodded politely and Mann tried to smile, failed and put his nose into his champagne.

'The story is you're retiring, Tony,' said Bessie.

'I'm too young to retire, Bessie, you know that!' He winked at her.

'Steady up, Tony,' said Bessie, 'you want the old man to catch on to us?'

'He should never have left you behind on that Miami trip,' said Tony Nowak.

'It's a lamp,' said Mann. 'Bloomingdales Fifty-four ninety-nine, with three sets of dark goggles.'

'You could have fooled me,' said Tony Nowak, 'I thought it was a spray job.'

Behind us there were soft chiming sounds and a servant opened the door. Tony Nowak was still gripping Bessie's arm but as he caught sight of his new guests he relaxed his grip. 'These are the people from the Secretariat . . .' said Tony Nowak.

'Go look after your new arrivals,' said Mann. 'Looks like Liz Taylor needs rescuing from the Shah of Iran.'

'And ain't you the guy to do it,' said Tony Nowak. He smiled. It was the sort of joke he'd repeat between relating the names of big-shots who had really been there.

'It beats me why he asked us,' I told Mann.

Mann grunted.

26

'Are we here on business?' I asked.

'You want overtime?'

'I just like to know what's going on.'

From a dark corner of the lounge there came the hesitant sort of music that gives the pianist time for a gulp of martini between bars. When Mann got as far as the Chinese screen that divided this room from the dining-room, he stopped and lit a cheroot. He took his time doing it so that both of us could get a quick look round. 'A parley,' Mann said quietly.

'A parley with who?'

'Exactly,' said Mann. He inhaled on his cheroot, and took my arm in his iron grip while telling about all the people he recognized.

The dining-room had been rearranged to make room for six special backgammon tables at which silent players played for high stakes. The room was crowded with spectators, and there was an especially large group around the far table at which a middle-aged manufacturer of ultrasonic intruder alarms was doing battle with a spectacular redhead.

'Now that's the kind of girl I could go for,' said Mann.

Bessie punched him gently in the stomach. 'And don't think he's kidding,' she told me.

'Don't do that when I'm drinking French champagne,' said Mann.

'Is it OK when you're drinking domestic?' said Bessie.

Tony Nowak came past with a magnum of Heidsieck. He poured all our glasses brimful with champagne, hummed the melody line of 'Alligator Crawl' more adroitly than the pianist handled it, and then did a curious little step-dance before moving on to fill more glasses.

'Tony is in an attentive mood tonight,' I said.

'Tony is keeping an eye on you,' said Bessie. 'Tony is remembering that time when you two came here with those drunken musicians from the Village and turned Tony's party into a riot.'

'I still say it was Tony Nowak's rat-fink cousin Stefan who put the spaghetti in the piano,' said Mann.

Bessie smiled and pointed at me. 'The last time we talked about it, *you* were the guilty party,' she confided.

Mann pulled a vampire face, and tried to bite his wife's throat. 'Promises, promises,' said Bessie and turned to watch Tony Nowak moving among his guests. Mann walked into the dining-room and we followed him. It was all chinoiserie and high camp, with lanterns and gold-plated Buddhas, and miniature paintings of oriental pairs in acrobatic sexual couplings.

'It's Red Bancroft,' said Mann, still looking at the redhead. 'She's international standard – you watch this.'

I followed him as he elbowed his way to a view of the backgammon game. We watched in silence. If this girl was playing a delaying game, it was far, far beyond my sort of backgammon, where you hit any blot within range and race for home. This girl was even leaving the single men exposed. It could be a way of drawing her opponent out of her home board but she wasn't yet building up there. She was playing red, and her single pieces seemed scattered and vulnerable, and two of her men were out, waiting to come in. But for Mann's remark, I would have seen this as the muddled play of a beginner.

The redhead smiled as her middle-aged opponent reached for the bidding cube. He turned it in his fingers as if trying to find the odds he wanted and then set it down again. I heard a couple of surprised grunts behind me as the audience saw the bid. If the girl was surprised too she didn't show it. But when she smiled again, it was too broad a smile; and it lasted too long. Backgammon is as much a game of bluff as of skill and luck, and the redhead yawned and raised a hand to cover her mouth. It was a gesture that showed her figure to good advantage. She gave a nod of assent. The man rattled the dice longer than he'd done before, and I saw his lips move as if in prayer. He held his breath while they rolled. If it was a prayer, it was answered quickly and fully – double six! He looked up at the redhead. She smiled as if this was all part of her plan. The man took a long time looking at the board before he moved his men.

She picked up her dice, and threw them carelessly, but from this moment the game changed drastically. The man's home board was completely open, so she had no trouble in bringing in her two men. With her next throw she began to build up her home board, which had been littered with blots. A four and a three. It was all she needed to cover all six points. That locked her opponent. Now he could only use a high throw, and for this his prayers were unanswered. She had the game to herself for throw after throw. The man lit a cigar with studied care as he watched the game going against him, and could do nothing about it. Only after she began bearing-off did he get moving again.

Now the bidding cube was in her hands – and that too was a part of the strategy – she raised it. The man looked at the cube, and then up to the faces of his friends. There had been side wagers on his success. He smiled, and nodded his agreement to the new stakes, although he must have known that only a couple of high doubles could save him now. He picked up the dice and shook them as if they might explode. When they rolled to a standstill there was a five and a one on the upper side. He still hadn't got all his men into the home board. The girl threw a double five – with five men already beared-off, it ended the game.

He conceded. The redhead smiled as she tucked a thousand dollars in C notes into a crocodile-skin wallet with gold edges. The bystanders drifted away. The red-head looked up at Bessie and smiled, and then she smiled at Major Mann too.

But for that Irish colouring she might have been Oriental. Her cheekbones were high and flat and her mouth a little too wide. Her eyes were a little too far apart, and narrow – narrower still when she smiled. It was the smile that I was to remember long after everything else about her had faded in my memory. It was a strange, uncertain smile that sometimes mocked and sometimes chided but was nonetheless beguiling for that, as I was to find to my cost.

She wore an expensive knitted dress of striped autumnal colours and in her ears there were small jade earrings that exactly matched her eyes. Bessie brought her over to where I was standing, near the champagne, and the food.

When Bessie moved away, the girl said, 'Pizza is very fattening.'

'So is everything I like,' I said.

'Everything?' said the girl.

'Well . . . damn nearly everything,' I said. 'Congratulations on your win.'

She got out a packet of mentholated cigarettes and put one in her mouth. I lit it for her.

'Thank you kindly, sir. There was a moment when he had me worried though, I'll tell you that.'

'I know,' I said. 'When you yawned.'

'It's nerves – I try everything not to yawn.'

'Think yourself lucky,' I said. 'Some people *laugh* when they are nervous.'

'Do you mean *you* laugh when you are nervous?'

'I'm advised to reserve my defence,' I told her.

'Ah, how British of you! You want to know my weaknesses but you'll not confide any of your own.'

'Does that make me a male chauvinist pig?'

'It shortens the odds,' she said. Then she found herself stifling a yawn again. I laughed.

'How long have you known the Manns?' I asked.

'I met Bessie at a Yoga class, about four years back. She was trying to lose weight, I was trying to lose those yawns.'

'Now you're kidding.'

'Yes. I went to Yoga after . . .' She stopped. It was a painful memory. '. . . I got home early one night and found a couple of kids burglarizing my apartment. They gave me a bad beating and left me unconscious. When I left hospital I went to a Yoga farm to convalesce. That's how I met Bessie.'

'And the backgammon?'

'My father was a fire chief – Illinois semi-finalist in the backgammon championships one year. He was great. I almost paid my way through college on what I earned playing backgammon. Three years ago I went professional – you can travel the world from tournament to tournament, there's no season. Lots of money – it's a rich man's game.' She sighed. 'But that was three years ago. I've had a lousy year since then. And a lousy year in Seattle is a *really* lousy year, believe me! And what about you?'

'Nothing to tell.'

'Ah, Bessie told me a lot already,' she said.

'And I thought she was a friend.'

'Just the good bits – you're English . . .'

'How long has that been a "good bit" among the backgammon players of Illinois?'

31

'You work with Bessie's husband, in the analysis department of a downtown bank that I've never heard of. You –'

I put my fingers to her lips to stop her. 'That's enough,' I said. 'I can't stand it.'

'Are your family here in the city with you?' She was flirting. I'd almost forgotten how much I liked it.

'No,' I said.

'Are you going to join them for Christmas?'

'No.'

'But that's terrible.' Spontaneously she reached out to touch my arm.

'I have no immediate family,' I confessed.

She smiled. 'I didn't like to ask Bessie. She's always matchmaking.'

'Don't knock it,' I said.

'I'm not lucky in love,' she said. 'Just in backgammon.'

'And where is your home?'

'My home is a Samsonite two-suiter.'

'It's a well-known address,' I said. 'Why New York City?'

She smiled. Her very white teeth were just a fraction uneven. She sipped her drink. 'I'd had enough of Seattle,' she said. 'New York was the first place that came to mind.' She put the half-smoked cigarette into an ashtray and stubbed it out as if it was Seattle.

From the next room the piano player drifted into a sleepy version of 'How Long Has This Been Going On?' Red moved a little closer to me and continued to stare into her drink like a crystal-gazer seeking a fortune there.

The intruder alarm manufacturer passed us and smiled. Red took my arm and rested her head on my shoulder. When he was out of earshot she looked up at me. 'I hope you didn't mind,' she said. 'I told him my boy-friend was here; I wanted to reinforce that idea.'

'Any time.' I put my arm round her waist; she was soft and warm and her shiny red hair smelt fresh as I pressed close.

'Some of these people who lose money at the table think they might get recompense some other way,' she murmured.

'Now you've started my mind working,' I said.

She laughed.

'You're not supposed to laugh,' I said.

'I like you,' she said and laughed again. But now it was a nice throaty chuckle rather than the nervous teeth-baring grimace that I'd seen at the backgammon table.

'Yes, you guessed right,' she said. 'I ran from a lousy love-affair.' She moved away but not too far away.

'And now you're wondering if you did the right thing,' I said.

'He was a bastard,' she said. 'Other women . . . debts that I had to pay . . . drinking bouts . . . no, I'm not wondering if I did the right thing. I'm wondering why it took me so long.'

'And now he phones you every day asking you to come back.'

'How did you know.' She mumbled the words into my shoulder.

'That's the way it goes,' I said.

She gripped my arm. For a long time we stood in silence. I felt I'd known her all my life. The intruder alarm man passed again. He smiled at us. 'Let's get out of here,' she said.

There was nothing I would have liked better but Mann had disappeared from the room, and if he was engaged in the sort of parley he'd anticipated, he'd be counting on my standing right here with both eyes wide open.

'I'd better stay with the Manns,' I told her. She pursed her lips. And yet a moment later she smiled and there was no sign of the scarred ego.

'Sure,' she said. 'I understand,' but she didn't understand enough, for soon after that she saw some people she knew and beckoned them to join us.

'Do you play backgammon?' one of the newcomers asked.

'Not so that anyone would notice,' I said.

Red smiled at me but when she learned that two one-time champions were about to fight out a match in the next room she took my hand and dragged me along there.

Backgammon is more to my taste than chess. The dice add a large element of luck to every game, so that sometimes a novice beats a champion just as it goes in real life. Sometimes, however, a preponderance of luck makes a game boring to watch. This one was that – or perhaps I was just feeling bad about the way Red exchanged smiles and greetings with so many people round the table.

The two ex-champions were into the opening moves of their third game by the time that Bessie Mann plucked my sleeve to tell me that her husband wanted me.

I went down the hall to where Tony Nowak's driver was standing on guard outside the bedroom. He was scowling at the mirror and trying to look like a cop. I was expecting the scowl but not the quick rub down for firearms. I went inside. In spite of the dim lighting, I saw Tony Nowak perched on the dressing-table, his tie loosened and his brow shiny.

There was a smell of expensive cigars and after-shave

lotion. And seated in the best chair – his sneakers resting upon an embroidered footstool – there was Harvey Kane Greenwood. They had long ceased to refer to him as the up-and-coming young Senator: Greenwood had arrived. The long hair – hot-combed and tinted – the chinos and the batik shirt, open far enough to reveal the medallion on a gold neck-chain, were all part of the well-publicized image, and many of his aspirations could be recognized in Gerry Hart, the lean young assistant that he had recently engaged to help him with his work on the Scientific Development Sub-Committee of the Senate Committee of International Cooperation.

As my eyes grew accustomed to the darkness, I saw as far as the Hepplewhite sofa, upon which sat two balding heavyweights, comparing wrist-watches, and arguing quietly in Russian. They didn't notice me, and nor did Gerry Hart, who was drawing diagrams on a dinner napkin for his boss Greenwood, who was nodding.

I was only as far as the doorway, when Mann waved his hands, and had me backing-up past Nowak's sentry, and all the way along the corridor as far as the kitchen.

Piled up along the working surfaces there were plates of left-over party food, dirty ashtrays and plastic containers crammed with used cutlery. The remains of two turkeys were propped up on the open door of a wall oven, and as we entered, a cat jumped from there to the floor. Otherwise the brightly lit kitchen was unoccupied.

Major Mann opened the refrigerator and took a carton of buttermilk. He reached for tumblers from the shelf above and poured two glassfuls.

'You like buttermilk?'

'Not much,' I said.

He drank some of it and then tore a piece of paper from a kitchen-roll and wiped his mouth. All the while he held the refrigerator door wide open. Soon the compressor started to throb. This sound, combined with the interference of the fluorescent lights above our heads, gave us a little protection against even the most sophisticated bugging devices. 'This is a lulu,' said Mann quietly.

'In that case,' I said, 'I will have some buttermilk.'

'Do we want to take delivery of Mrs B?' He did not conceal his anger.

'Where?' I asked.

'Here!' said Mann indignantly. 'Right here in schlockville.'

I smiled. 'And this is an offer from gentleman-Jim Greenwood and our friend Hart?'

'And the two vodka salesmen from downtown Omsk.'

'KGB?'

'Big-ass pants, steel-tipped shoes, fifty-dollar manicures and big Cuban cigars – yes, my suspicions run that way.'

'Perhaps Hart got them through central casting.'

Mann shook his head. 'Heavy,' he said. 'I've been close to them. These two are really heavy.'

Mann had the mannerism of placing a hand over his heart, the thumb and forefinger fidgeting with his shirt-collar. He did it now. It was as if he was taking an oath about the two Russians.

'But why?'

'Good question,' said Mann. 'When Greenwood's goddamned committee is working so hard to give away all America's scientific secrets to any foreigner who wants them – who needs the KGB?'

'And they talked about B.?'

'I must be getting senile or something,' said Mann. 'Why didn't I think about those bastards on that Scientific Cooperation Committee – commie bastards the lot of them if you ask me.'

'But what are they after?'

Mann threw a hand into the air, and caught it, fingers splayed. 'Those guys – Greenwood and his sidekick – are lecturing me about freedom. Telling me that I'm just about to lead some kind of witch-hunt through the academic world . . .'

'And are we?'

'I'm sure going to sift through Bekuv's friends and acquaintances . . . and not Greenwood and all his pinko committeemen will stop me.'

'They didn't set up this meeting just to tell you not to start a witch-hunt,' I said.

'They can do our job better than we can,' said Mann bitterly. 'They say they can get Bekuv's wife out of the USSR by playing footsie with the Kremlin.'

'You mean they will get her a legal exit permit, providing we don't dig out anything that will embarrass the committee.'

'Right,' said Mann. 'Have some more buttermilk.' He poured some without waiting to ask if I wanted it.

'After all,' I said in an attempt to mollify his rage. 'It's what we want . . . I mean . . . Mrs B. It would make our task easier.'

'Just the break we've been waiting for,' said Mann sarcastically. 'Do you know, they really expected us to bring Bekuv here tonight. They are threatening to demand his appearance before the committee.'

'Why?'

'To make sure he came to the West of his own free will. How do you like that?'

'I don't like it very much,' I said. 'His photo in the *Daily News*, reporters pushing microphones into his mouth. The Russians would feel bound to respond to that. It could get very rough.'

Mann pulled a face and reached for the wall telephone extension. He capped the phone and listened for a moment to be sure the line was not in use. To me he said, 'I'm going back in there, to tug my forelock for ten minutes.' He dialled the number of the CIA garage on 82nd Street. 'Mann here. Send my number two car for back-up. I'm still at the same place.' He hung up. 'You get downstairs,' he told me. 'You go down and wait for the back-up car. Tell Charlie to tail the two Russian goons and give him the descriptions.'

'It won't be easy,' I warned. 'They are sure to be prepared for that.'

'Either way it will be interesting to see how they react.' Mann slammed the refrigerator door. The conversation was ended. I gave him a solemn salute, and went along the hall to get my coat.

Red Bancroft was there too: climbing into a fine military-styled suede coat, with leather facings and brass buttons and buckles. She winked as she tucked her long auburn hair into a crazy little knitted hat. 'And here he is,' she said to the intruder alarm manufacturer, who was watching himself in a mirror while a servant pulled at the collar of his camel-hair coat. He touched his moustache and nodded approval.

He was a tall wiry man, with hair that was greying the way it only does for tycoons and film stars.

'The little lady was looking everywhere for you,' said the intruder alarm man. 'I was trying to persuade her to ride up to Sixtieth Street with me.'

'I'll look after her,' I said.

'And I'll say good night,' he said. 'It was a real pleasure playing against you, Miss Bancroft. I just hope you'll give me a chance to get even sometime.'

Red Bancroft smiled and nodded, and then she smiled at me.

'Now let's get out of here,' I whispered.

She gripped my arm, and just as the man looked back at us, kissed my cheek. Whether it was nice timing, or just impulse, was too early to say but I took the opportunity to hold her tight and kiss her back. Tony Nowak's domestic servants found something needing their attention in the lounge.

'Have you been drinking buttermilk?' said Red.

It was a long time before we got out to the landing. The intruder alarm man was still there, fuming about the non-arrival of the elevator. It arrived almost at the same moment that we did.

'Everything goes right for those in love,' said the alarm man. I warmed to him.

'You have a car?' he asked. He bowed us into the elevator ahead of him.

'We do,' I said. He pressed the button for ground level and the numbers began to flicker.

'This is no city for moonlight walks,' he told me. 'Not even here in Park Avenue.'

We stopped and the elevator doors opened.

Like so many scenes of mortal danger, each constituent part of this one was very still. I saw everything, and yet my brain took some time to relate the elements in any meaningful way.

The entrance hall of the apartment block was brightly lit by indirect strip-lighting set into the ceiling. A huge vaseful of plastic flowers trembled from the vibration of some subterranean furnace, and a draught of cold wind from the glass entrance door carried with it a few errant flakes of snow. The dark brown floor carpet, chosen perhaps to hide dirty footmarks from the street, now revealed caked snow that had fallen from visitors' shoes.

The entrance hall was not empty. There were three men there, all wearing the sort of dark raincoats and peaked hats that are worn by uniformed drivers. One of them had his foot jammed into the plate-glass door at the entrance. He had his back to us and was looking towards the street. The nearest man was opposite the doors of the elevator. He had a big S & W Heavy-Duty .38 in his fist, and it was pointing at us.

'Freeze,' he said. 'Freeze, and nobody gets hurt. Slow now! Bring out your bill-fold.'

We froze. We froze so still that the elevator doors began to close on us. The man with the gun stamped a large boot into the door slot, and motioned us to step out. I stepped forward carefully keeping my hands raised and in sight.

'If it's money you want,' said the alarm manufacturer, 'take my wallet, and welcome to it.' He was frantically reaching into the breast pocket of his camel-hair overcoat.

The alarm manufacturer's voice was such a plaintive whine of terror that the man with the gun smiled. He turned his head so that the third gunman could see him smiling. And then his friend smiled too.

There were two shots: deafening thumps that echoed in the narrow lobby and left behind a whiff of burned powder. The man with the gun screeched. His eyes popped wide open, he gasped and coughed blood. There was a brief moment before the pistol hit the carpet with a thump, and its owner slid slowly down the wall, leaving a long smudge of blood. Red Bancroft gripped my arm so hard that it hurt. The second shot hit the man watching the stairs. It went in at the shoulder, and smashed his clavicle. He threw his gun down and grabbed his elbow.

They say that's the only way you can ease the pain of a fractured collar-bone. He couldn't run very fast with that sort of wound. That's why the alarm manufacturer had time enough to put his gun up to eye level. He got him in the spine with the third shot. It was enough to tumble him full length on to scattered particles of impacted snow and the plastic sheet that had been put down in the outer lobby to protect the carpet. He died with his head resting on the word 'Welcome'. There wasn't much blood.

It was the body of that second man that obstructed me as I opened the glass door. It had an electric solenoid lock. I had to push the override.

The intruder alarm man collided with me in the door-way but we both scrambled out into the street in time to see the third man running. He was hatless now and halfway across the avenue. I heard a car being started. The alarm man raised his gun for a shot at him but slid on the ice and lost his balance. He tumbled. There was a clatter and a curse as he fell against a parked car. I ran out into the empty roadway. On the far side of the avenue the door of a black Mercedes opened to receive the gunman. The Mercedes leapt forward while the door was still open. I saw a flurry of arms, and one leg trailed, and cut a pattern in the snow, before the man was inside and the door closed. As the Mercedes reached the cross-street intersection, the driver switched his lights on.

'Fulton County plate,' said the voice of the intruder alarm man. 'Did you see that? It was a car from Fulton County. Did you get the number?'

He was breathless from the tumble he'd taken, and I was breathless too.

'Three digits and FC,' I said. 'It was too dirty to get it.'

'Goddamned weather,' said the man. 'I would have

41

plinked him but for that damned patch of ice.' He turned and we walked back to the lobby.

'I think you would,' I said.

He slapped me on the back. 'Thanks for taking his attention, young feller,' he said.

'Is that what I did?'

'Raising your hands and acting scared . . . that took his attention. And that was cool.' He stepped over the body that was sprawled in the doorway. I followed him.

'Spread that around,' I said. 'But just between the two of us – I wasn't acting.'

The alarm man laughed. It was the strangled sort of laugh that releases a lot of suppressed tension. He toyed with the .38 revolver that was still in his hand. It was a blue-finish Colt Agent, with the hammer shroud that prevented it from snagging when drawn from a pocket. He must have thumb-cocked the hammer, for there had been no time for double action between the movement of his hand and the sound of his shots.

'I'd put that away,' I said. 'Put it out of sight before the cops arrive.'

'I've got a permit,' he said indignantly. 'In fact, I'm president of my local gun club.'

'They come down the street and see you standing over two corpses with a hot shooter in your hand they are likely to shoot first and check the permits afterwards.'

He put the gun away but not before bringing the next loaded chamber into position. He unbuttoned his overcoat and jacket, to place his gun into a highly decorative Berns-Martin spring-grip shoulder-holster. As we got back to the lobby Mann arrived with Tony Nowak.

'You stupid bastard,' said Mann to the alarm manufacturer although I had the feeling that some overfill was intended to splash on to me.

'What am I supposed to do,' said the alarm man, looking in a mirror and combing his hair, 'let those punks drill me? I'd be the laughing-stock of the whole intruder alarm business.'

'They're both dead,' said Mann. 'You shot to kill.'

The alarm man turned to look at Mann. Then he looked at the two corpses and back to Mann again. For a moment I thought he was going to express satisfaction at what he'd done but he knew too much about the law to do that. 'Well, that's something you'd better talk about with my lawyer,' he said finally. Some of the bubbly elation that always follows such danger was now fading, leaving him flat and a little frightened.

Mann caught my eye. 'No, I'm getting out of here,' he said.

'I'm not Wyatt Earp,' said the man. 'I can't shoot guns out of guys' hands.'

I took Red Bancroft's arm. 'I'd better get you home,' I said.

'The police will want to talk to me,' she said.

'No. Tony will fix that,' I said.

Tony Nowak nodded. 'You get along home, Red. My driver will take you. And don't lose any sleep about those guys . . . we've had a whole string of muggings here over the past month. These are rough customers. I know the Deputy Inspector – I'll get him to keep you out of it.'

I thought the girl was taking it all with a superhuman calmness. Now I realized that she was frozen with fear. Her face was colourless and as I put my arm round her, I felt her body twitch violently. 'Take it easy, Red,' I said. 'I'll have to stay on here.'

'They're both dead,' she said, and stepped high over the body of the man in the doorway, without looking down at him. Outside in the swirling snowstorm she stopped and wound her knitted scarf round her head. She reached up for me and planted a sisterly kiss on my lips. 'Could it work out to be something special . . . you and me?' she said.

'Yes,' I said. While we stood there a police car arrived, and then a car with a doctor's registration.

Tony Nowak's driver opened the door of the Lincoln for her. I waved, and stood there a long time until the car could no longer be seen. By the time I got back to the lobby the cops were there. They were stripping the dead gunmen naked, and putting the clothes into evidence bags.

5

Tony Nowak's apartment is in the seventeenth police precinct, but dead bodies from those plush addresses go down to the Twenty-First Street Morgue and are put in the chilled drawers alongside pushers from Times Square and Chinese laundrymen from the Tenderloin.

'Can we smoke?' I asked the attendant. The cold room had an eerie echo. He nodded and pulled the drawer open, and read silently from the police file. Apparently satisfied, he stepped back so that we could get a good look at the hold-up man. He came out feet-first with a printed tag on his toe. His face had been cleaned of blood and his hair combed, but nothing could be done about the open mouth that made him look as if he'd died of surprise.

'The bullet hit the windpipe,' said the attendant. 'He died gasping for air.' He closed the file. 'This has been a heavy night for us,' he explained. 'If it's OK with you guys, I'll go back to the office. Put him away when you're through with him.' He put the clip-board under his arm and took a look at his pocket-watch. It was 2.15 A.M. He yawned and heaved the big evidence bag on to the stainless steel table.

'Medical examiner had them stripped at the scene of the crime – just so Forensic can't say we lost anything.' He prodded the transparent bag that contained a peaked hat, dark raincoat, cheap denim suit and soiled underwear. 'You'll find your paperwork inside.' He twisted the identification tag that was on the dead man's toe so that

45

he could read from the UF6 card. 'Died on Park Avenue, eh. Now there's a goon with taste.' He looked back at the body. 'Don't turn him over until the photographer has finished with him.'

'OK,' I said.

'Your other one is in drawer number twenty-seven – we keep all the gunshot deaths together, at this end of the room. Anything else you want and I'll be in the ME's office through the autopsy room . . . .'

Mann opened the bag and found the shirt. There was a bullet nick in the collar.

'A marksman,' I said.

'A schmuck,' said Mann. 'A marksman would have been satisfied with the gun arm.'

'You think this hold-up might have a bearing on the Bekuv situation?' I said.

'Put a neat litle moustache on Bekuv and send him up to Saks Fifth Avenue for a 400-dollar suit, grey his temples a little and feed him enough chocolate sodas to put a few inches on his waistline, and what have you got?'

'Nothing,' I said. 'I've got nothing. What are you trying to say?'

'Mister snap-shooting goddamn intruder alarm – that's who you've got, stupid.'

I considered for a moment. There was a faint superficial resemblance between Bekuv and the intruder alarm man. 'It's not much,' I said.

'But it might be enough, if you were a trigger-happy gorilla, waiting in the lobby there – very nervous – and with just an ancient little snapshot of Bekuv to recognize him by.'

'Who'd think Bekuv would be with us at Tony Nowak's party?'

'Greenwood and Hart: those guys wanted him there,' said Mann.

I shook my head.

Mann said, 'And if I told you that thirty minutes after we left Washington Square last night Andrei Bekuv was in his tux and trying to tell the doorman that I had given him permission to go out on his own?'

'You think they got to him? You think they gave him a personal invitation to be there?'

'He wasn't duding-up to try his luck in the singles bars on Third Avenue,' said Mann.

'And you agreed?' I asked him. 'You told Hart and Greenwood and Nowak that you'd bring Bekuv to their party?'

'It's easy to be wise after the event,' said Mann defensively. He used his tongue to find a piece of tobacco that was in his teeth. 'Sure I agreed but I didn't do it.' He removed the strand of tobacco with a delicate deployment of his little finger. 'These guys in the lobby: they didn't ask for cash, wrist-watch or his gold tie-pin, they asked for his wallet. They wanted to check – they were nervous – they wanted to find something to prove he was really Bekuv.'

I shrugged. 'Wallet . . . bill-fold . . . a stick-up man is likely to ask for any of these things when he wants money. What about the Fulton County number plate?'

'Do you know how big Fulton County is?'

'On a black Mercedes?'

'Yes, well we're checking it. We've got the guy from the Department of Motor Vehicles out of his bed, if that makes you feel any better.'

'It does,' I said. 'But if we'd found that "ancient little snapshot of Bekuv" amongst these personal effects that would make me feel even better still. Until we've got

47

something to go on, this remains a simple old-fashioned New York hold-up.'

'Just a heist. But tomorrow, when we tell our pal Bekuv about it, I'm going to paint it to look like they are gunning for him.'

'Why?'

'We might learn something from him if he thinks he needs better protection. I'm going to tuck him away somewhere where no one's going to find him.'

'Where?'

'We'll get him out of here for Christmas, it's too dangerous here.'

'Miami? or the safe house in Boston?'

'Don't be a comedian. Send him to a CIA safe house! You might as well take a small-ad in *Pravda*.' Mann rolled the body back into the chilled case. The sound set my teeth on edge. 'You take the back-up car,' Mann told me. 'I'll drive myself.'

'Then where will you put Bekuv?'

'Don't make it too early in the morning.'

'You've got my sworn promise,' I said. I watched him as he marched through the rows and rows of cold slabs, his shoes clicking on the tiled floor and a curious squeaky noise that I later recognized as Mann whistling a tune.

I suppose Mann's insouciant exit attracted the attention of the mortuary attendant. 'What's going on, Harry?' He looked at me for a few seconds before realizing that I wasn't Harry. 'Are you the photographer?'

'No,' I said.

'Then who the hell are you?'

'Seventeenth Precinct know about me,' I said.

'And I'll bet they do,' he said. 'How did you get in here, buster?'

'Calm down. I saw your colleague.'

48

'You saw my colleague,' he mocked in shrill falsetto. 'Well, now you're seeing *me*.' I noticed his hands as he repeatedly gripped his fists and released them again. I had the feeling he wanted to provoke me, so that he had an excuse for taking a poke at me. I was keen to deprive him of that excuse.

'It's official,' I said.

'ID, feller,' he said and poked a finger at my chest.

'He's all right, Sammy.' We both turned. The other mortuary attendant had come in by the centre door. 'I talked to Charlie Kelly about him. Charlie says OK.'

'I don't like guys creeping around here without my permission,' said the pugnacious little man. Still murmuring abuse, he studied his clip-board and wandered back upstairs with that twitchy walk one sees in punchy old prize-fighters.

'Sorry about that,' said the first attendant. 'I should have told Sammy that you were here.'

'I thought he was going to put me on a slab,' I said.

'Sammy's all right,' he said. He looked at me before deciding that I should have a fuller explanation. 'Sammy and me were cops . . . we joined the force together, we were both wounded in a gun battle near Delancey, way back in the 'sixties. Neither of us was fit enough to go back into the force. He's a good guy.'

'You could have fooled me,' I said.

'Saw his fifteen-year-old kid brought in here one day – hit by a truck coming out of school – that happens to you once and you remember. You start getting dizzy every time you unzip a body bag.' He turned away. 'Anyway, it was all OK for you, was it? I hear you were right in the middle when the shells started flying.'

'I was lucky,' I said.

'And the third guy took off in a black Merc.' He was reading it all on the report. 'You get the plate number?'

'FC,' I said. 'They tell me that's a Fulton County registration.'

'Well, at least you didn't get suckered by the Fulton County plate.'

'What do you mean?'

'Well, any cop who's been in the force a few years will tell you the way those people from Fulton County used to come into the city and double-park all over Manhattan. And no cop would ever give them a ticket. Jesus, the number of times I saw cars . . . would you believe treble-parked on Madison, jamming the traffic . . . and I just walked on and forgot about it.'

'I don't get it.'

'Well you wouldn't, being from out of town, but a Fulton County plate is FC and then three numerals. Not many cops noticed any difference between that and three numbers followed by FC . . . I mean, a cop's got a lot on his mind, without getting into that kind of pizzazz.'

'And what is it about a car with a registration plate that has three numbers followed by FC? What is it that makes it OK for him to treble-park on Madison Avenue?'

The mortuary attendant looked at me sorrowfully. 'Yeah, well you've never been a patrolman, have you. Three digits FC, means a car belonging to a foreign consul . . . that's an official car with diplomatic immunity to arrest, and I mean including parking tickets. And that's what all those smart-ass drivers from Fulton County were betting on.'

'Got you,' I said.

He didn't hear me; he was staring into the 'sixties and watching one of those nice kids we all used to be. 'Midnight to eight,' he said. 'I liked that shift – no dependants, so what's the difference – and you make more money, overtime and payments for time in court. But it was a rough shift for a cop in those days.'

'In those days?' I said.

'This was an all-night city back in the early 'sixties – bars open right up to the legal 4 A.M . . . all-night groceries, all-night dancing, all-night you-name-it. But the city got rougher and rougher, so people stayed home and watched TV . . . You go out there now, and the streets are dark and empty.' He picked up a piece of cloth and wiped his hands. His hands looked very clean but he wiped them anyway. 'Streets are so empty that a perpetrator can take his time: no witnesses, no calls to the cops, no nothing. Midnight to eight used to be a tough shift for a cop . . .' He gave a humourless little laugh. 'Now it's a tough shift here at the morgue.' He threw the rag aside. 'You should see some of them when we get them here . . . kids and old ladies too . . . ahh! So you're from out of town, eh?'

'Yes,' I said. 'Three thousand miles out of town.'

'You got it made,' he said.

Outside the night was cold. The sky was mauve and the world slightly tilted. Around the access points for the city's steam supply the crust of snow had melted so that the roadway shone in the moonlight, and from the manhole covers steam drifted as far as the cross-street, before the wind whipped it away. A police car siren called somewhere on the far side of the city. It was a pitiful sound, like the repeated cries of a thrashed animal crawling away to die.

6

The Washington Square house is 'twinned' in the CIA style – divided vertically – so that the back of the house, shuttered against telescopes and double-glazed against focusing microphones, is all offices, while the front half provides apartments for the staff, and so presents all the outward appearance of domesticity.

I lived on the second floor. Bekuv lived above me. Bekuv's appearance had changed during those few days in New York City. His hair had been cut by some fancy barber, and he'd had enough sleep to put some colour back into his cheeks. His clothes were transformed too: tailored trousers, a blue lambswool shirt and bright canvas shoes. He was sitting on the floor, surrounded by loud-speakers, records, amplifier components, extra tweeters, a turntable, a soldering iron and hi-fi magazines. Bekuv looked despondent.

'Andrei was screwed,' Mann told me as I went in. I found it hard to believe that Mann was sorry about it.

'In what way?'

'Coffee on the warmer,' said Bekuv.

I poured myself a cup and took a blini.

'All this damned hi-fi junk,' said Mann.

Bekuv applied the pick-up to one of his records and suddenly the whole room was filled with music.

'Jesus Christ!' Mann shouted angrily.

Delicately Bekuv lifted the pick-up and the music ceased. 'Shostakovich,' he said to anyone who was seeking that information.

Mann said, 'Andrei spent nearly two thousand dollars on all this stuff, and now he's been reading the discount-house adverts.'

'I could have got it for five hundred dollars less,' Bekuv told me. I noticed that several of the hi-fi magazines were marked with red pentel, and there were little sums scribbled on the back of an envelope.

'Well, perhaps we can do something about that,' I said vaguely, while I drank my coffee and thought about something else.

'Andrei is not going downtown,' said Mann, 'and that's that.' I realized they had been arguing about whether Bekuv was allowed to go out on the street again.

'Now *this* loudspeaker is buzzing,' said Bekuv.

'Listen, dummy,' Mann told him, bending forward from his chair, so that he could speak close to Bekuv's ear. 'There are citizens out there waiting to ice you. Didn't you hear what I told you about the shooting last night? We spent the small hours downtown in the city morgue – I don't recommend it, not even for a stiff.'

'I'm not frightened,' said Bekuv. He put the pick-up arm back on the record. There was a loud hissing before he reduced the volume a little. It was still very loud. Mann leaned forward and lifted the pick-up off the record. 'I don't give a good goddamn whether you are frightened or not frightened,' he said. 'In fact I don't give a damn whether you are alive or dead, but I'm going to make sure it happens after you are moved out of here, and I've got a receipt for you.'

'Is that going to happen?' asked Bekuv. He began looking through his loose-leaf notebook.

'It might,' said Mann.

'I can't go anywhere for the time being,' said Bekuv. 'I have work to do.'

'What work?' I said.

Bekuv looked at me as if only just realizing that I was present. 'My work on interstellar communication,' he said, sarcastically. 'Have you forgotten that I have a chair at New York University?'

'No,' I said.

'I've calculated for the initial programme of transmissions. It would cost very little money, and it will focus attention on the work we are doing.'

'Transmissions?' said Mann.

'In space there are clouds of hydrogen. They vibrate to make a hum of radio noise. You pick it up on any radio set at 1,420 megacycles. My theory is that this would be the best frequency to use for our first messages to outer space. Other civilizations are certain to notice any change in that hum of hydrogen vibrations.'

'Sure to,' said Mann.

'Not on that exact wavelength,' added Bekuv. 'They would be obliterated. We must transmit *near* to the wavelength, not on it.'

'Near to it; not on it,' said Mann. He nodded.

'It would cost very little,' said Bekuv. 'And I could have it working inside six months.'

'That's well before the flying-saucer men go to summer camp,' said Mann.

Bekuv looked up at Mann. His voice was harsh, and it was as if he was answering a long list of unspoken questions when he shouted, 'Twice I have attended meetings of the 1924 Society. Only twice! The last time was nearly five years ago. Science is not the cosy little club you believe it is. Don't keep pressurizing me. I recognized no one, and we did not exchange names and addresses, for obvious reasons.'

'For obvious reasons,' said Mann. 'Because those sons

of bitches were betraying the whole of America's military electronics programme.'

'And will it get your secrets back if you keep me a prisoner here?' yelled Bekuv. 'Not allowed to go out . . . Not allowed to make phone calls.'

Mann walked quickly to the door, as if frightened he would lose his temper. He turned. 'You'll stay here as long as I think fit,' he said. 'Behave yourself and I'll send you a packet of phonograph needles and a subscription to *Little Green Men Monthly*.'

Bekuv spoke quietly. 'You don't like cosmology, you don't like high-fidelity, you don't like Shostakovich, you don't like blinis . . .' Bekuv smiled. I couldn't decide whether he was trying to needle Mann or not.

'I don't like Russians,' explained Mann. 'White Russians, Red Russians, Ukrainians, Muscovite liberals, ballet dancers or faggy poets – I just don't like any of them. Get the picture?'

'I get it,' said Bekuv sulkily. 'Is there anything more?'

'One thing more,' said Mann. 'I'm not an international expert on the design of electronic masers. All I know about them is that a maser is some kind of crystal gimmick that gets pumped up with electronic energy so that it amplifies the weakest of incoming radio signals. That way you get a big fat signal compared with the background of electronic static noise and interference.'

'That's right,' said Bekuv. It was the first time he'd shown any real interest.

'I was reading that your liquid helium bath technique, that keeps the maser at minus two hundred and sixty-eight degrees centigrade, will amplify a signal nearly two million times.'

Bekuv nodded.

'Now I see the day when every little two-bit transistor

could be using one of these gadgets and pulling in radio transmissions from anywhere in the world. Of course, we know that would just mean hearing a DJ spinning discs in Peking, instead of Pasadena, but a guy collecting a royalty on such a gadget could make a few million. Right, Professor?'

'I didn't defect for money,' said Bekuv.

Major Mann smiled.

'I didn't defect to make money,' shouted Bekuv. If Mann had been trying to make Bekuv very, very angry, he'd discovered an effective way to do it.

Mann took my arm and led me from the room, closing the door silently and with exaggerated care. I didn't speak as we both walked downstairs to my sitting-room. Mann took off his dark raincoat and bundled it up to throw it into a corner. From upstairs there came the sudden crash of Shostakovich. Mann closed the door to muffle it.

I walked over to the window, so that I could look down into Washington Square. It was sunny: the sort of New York City winter's day when the sun coaxes you out without your long underwear, so that the cross-town wind can slice you into freeze-dried salami. Even the quartet echo-singing under the Washington arch had the hoods of their parkas up. But no street sounds came through the double-glazing; just soft Shostakovich from upstairs. Mann sat in my most comfortable chair and picked up the carbon of my report. I could tell that he'd already been to his office and perused the overnights. He gave my report no more than a moment or two, then he lifted the lid of my pigskin document case and put a fingertip on the Hart and Greenwood files that had arrived by special messenger in the early hours. They were very thin files.

'The car had a foreign consul plate?'

'Yes,' I said.

'And you read that stuff on the telex?'

'The two Russians are staying in a house leased to the Second Secretary of the Soviet Trade Delegation . . . Yes, I read it, but that doesn't make them KGB or even diplomatic. They might just be visiting relatives, or subtenants or squatters or something.'

Mann said, 'I'd like to bring in the owners of that car and sweat them.'

'And what would you charge them with? Leaving the scene of an accident?'

'Very funny,' said Mann. 'But the foreign consul plate on that car ties them to the stick-up artists.'

'You mean KGB heavies lend their official car to three hoods?'

Mann pouted and shook his head slowly, as if denying a treat to a spoiled child. 'Not the way you'd arrange it, maybe,' he said. 'But there was no reason for them to think it would all foul up. They figured it would be a pushover, and the official car would provide them with the kind of getaway that no cop would dare stop. It was a good idea.'

'That went wrong.'

'That went wrong.' He ran his fingers through the urgent paperwork inside my document case. 'Are we going to get some of this junk down the chute today?'

'Does that "we" mean you're about to break the seal on a new box of paper-clips?'

Mann smiled.

I put the case beside me on the sofa and began to sort it into three piles: urgent, very urgent and phone.

Mann leaned over the sofa back. He lifted a corner of the neatly stacked documents, each one bearing a coloured marking slip that explained to me what I was signing. Mann sucked his teeth. 'Those typewriter commandos downstairs don't know a microdot from a *Playboy* centrefold but give them a chance to bury you in paperwork and – goddamn, what an avalanche!' He let the paperwork slip out of his hands with enough noise to illustrate this theory.

I moved the trayful of papers before Mann decided to repeat his demonstration; already the slips and paperclips were falling apart.

'Well, I'll leave you to it,' Mann said. 'I've got to catch an airplane. Anybody wants me tell them to try the Diplomat Hotel, Miami, Florida.'

'Don't use your right name,' I said.

'I won't even be there, bird-brain. That's just being set up.'

I reached for the first pile of paperwork.

'Before I go,' Mann said still standing in the doorway watching me, 'Bessie says will you spend Christmas with us.'

'Great,' I said without looking up from my desk work.

'I'd better warn you that Bessie is asking that girl Red Bancroft along . . . Bessie is a matchmaker . . .'

'You're checking out a place to hide Bekuv, aren't you?' I said.

Mann bared his teeth in the sort of fierce grimace that he believes is a warm and generous smile.

I worked on until about noon and then one of the I-Doc people looked in. 'Where's Major Mann?'

'Out.' I continued to go through the documents.

'Where did he go?'

'No idea,' I said without looking up.

'You must know.'

'Two little guys in white coats came in and dragged him out with his feet kicking.'

'There's a phone call,' said the man from downstairs. 'Someone asking for you.' He looked round the room to be sure I wasn't hiding Mann anywhere. 'I'll tell the switchboard to put it through.'

'There's a caller named Gerry Hart coming through on the Wall Street line,' the operator told me. 'Do you want us to patch it through to here, and connect you?'

'I'll take it,' I said. If it had taken Hart only twenty-four hours to winkle-out the phone number of the merchant bank in Wall Street that I was using as my prime cover, how long would it take to prise open the rest of it? I pushed the police documentation to one side. 'Let's have lunch,' suggested Hart. His voice had the sort of warm resonance contrived by men who spend all day speaking on the telephone.

'Why?'

'There's a development.'

'Talk to my boss.'

'Tried that, but he's in Miami.' Hart's tone of voice made it clear that he didn't believe that Mann was in Miami.

'You could just make that flight where they serve free champagne in tourist,' I suggested.

'You really in Wall Street? Or are they patching this to some number in Langley, Virginia?' He gave a little chuckle.

'What's on your mind, Gerry?'

'Listen! I wanted to avoid Mann. It's you I want to talk to. Spare me thirty minutes over a cream-cheese sandwich. You know the Cookery? – University Plaza? Say one o'clock? Don't tell Mann – just you alone.'

He had chosen a restaurant about as close to the CIA safe house in Washington Square as it was possible to get. It could have been a coincidence – the Cookery was

59

one of my favourite haunts, and Gerry Hart might well know that – but I had a feeling that he was trying to cut me down to size before hitting me with his proposition. 'OK,' I said.

'I wear a moustache nowadays. Will you be able to recognize me?' he said. 'I'll be reading today's *New York Times*.'

'You mean with two peep-holes cut in the front page?'

'Just make sure you don't bring Captain America with you,' said Hart and rang off.

Gerry Hart pinched his trousers at the knees, so that he wasn't putting any strain on his twelve-ounce wool-and-mohair suit. That done, he eased his shirt sleeves far enough to reveal his cufflinks, but not so far that his black-faced Pulsar wrist-watch was hidden. The file said he was an authority on New Orleans jazz. 'Can't be all bad,' Mann had remarked at the time.

'I'm in politics now,' Hart said. 'Did you know that?'

'I thought perhaps you were playing the horses.'

'You always had a great sense of humour.' He smiled for just a fraction of a second. 'I'm not so touchy as I used to be in the old days,' he said. He fingered his new moustache self-consciously. I noticed the manicured fingernails. He'd come a long way from that nervous, opinionated State Department clerk that I remembered from our first meeting.

The drinks came. I put extra Tabasco into my Bloody Mary and then offered the same to Gerry. He shook his head. 'Plain tomato juice doesn't need flavouring,' he said primly. 'And I'm certainly surprised you need it with all that vodka.'

'My analyst says it's a subconscious desire to wash my mouth out with disinfectant.'

Hart nodded. 'Well, you have a lot of politician in you,' he said.

'You mean I approach every problem with an open mouth,' I said. I drank quite a lot of my Bloody Mary. 'Yes, well, if I decide to run, I'll come and talk to you.'

I knew it would be foolish to upset Hart before I knew what was in his mind. His file said he was a 31-year-old lawyer from Connecticut. I regarded him as one of the first of that growing army of young men who had used a few years' service in the CIA as a stepping-stone to other ambitions, as at one time the British middle classes had used the Brigade of Guards.

Hart was short and saturnine, a handsome man with curly hair and the sort of dark circles under deep-set eyes that made you think he was sleepy. But Gerry Hart was a tough kid who didn't smoke and didn't drink, and if he was sleepy it was only because he stayed up late at night rewriting the inaugural address he'd deliver to Congress on the day he became President.

Hart sipped a little of his tomato juice, and wiped his mouth carefully before speaking. 'I handle more top-secret material now than I did when I was working for the company – would you believe that?'

'Yes,' I said. Gerry Hart liked to refer to the CIA as 'the company' to emphasize that he had been on the inside. His file didn't mention service in the CIA but that didn't mean a thing.

'Did you ever hear of the 1924 Society?' he asked me.

'I'd rather hear about it from you,' I said.

'Right,' said Hart.

The waitress came to the table with the menus. 'Don't go away,' he told her. He ran his eye quickly down the list. 'Club sandwich, mixed salad with French dressing, regular coffee, and I'll take the check. OK?'

'Yes, sir,' said the waitress.

'The same,' I said. That made Gerry Hart feel very secure, and I wanted him to feel very secure.

The waitress closed her pad and took the menus from us. She came back with our order almost immediately. Hart smiled at her.

'We have penetrated the 1924 Society. That's why we can do it,' Gerry Hart explained when she had gone.

'What's inside a club sandwich?' I said. 'Do what?'

'Bring Mrs Bekuv here.'

'Is it like a triple-deck sandwich?'

'Bring Mrs Bekuv out of the USSR, officially or unofficially.'

'How?'

'What do you care how?'

I took the top off my sandwich and examined the filling. 'We don't have club sandwiches in England,' I explained.

'Even Greenwood hasn't been told that this is a CIA operation,' Hart said. 'Sure, we'll try to get Bekuv's wife by asking the Russians through the Senate Scientific Development sub-committee but if they won't play, we'll make it work some other way.'

'Wait a minute,' I said. 'What is this CIA operation you're talking about?'

'The 1924 Society.'

'I don't even know what the 1924 Society is,' I said truthfully.

Hart smiled. 'In 1924 Mars came very close to Earth. Scientists said maybe Mars would try to communicate with Earth. It caused no end of a ruckus in the scientific press, and then the newspapers joined in the speculation. Even the US Army and Navy ordered all their radio

62

stations to reduce signals traffic and listen for extra-terrestrial messages. The 1924 Society was formed that year. Twelve eminent scientists decided to pool information about communications from outer space, and plan ways of sending messages back.'

'And it's still going strong, is it?'

'Now there are twenty-seven members – only three of them founder members – but a lot of people take it seriously. In 1965, when three Russian astronomers picked up radio waves on a hundred-day cycle from quasar CTA-102, the 1924 Society were considering the report even before the Soviet Academy got the news, and before the Kremlin ordered them to retract.'

'And the CIA has penetrated the 1924 Society?'

'How do you think we got the first indication that Bekuv was ready to defect?'

I polished my spectacles – people tell me I do that when I'm nervous – and gave the lenses undue care and attention. I needed a little time to look at Gerry Hart and decide that a man I'd always thought of as blowing the tuba was writing the orchestrations.

Gerry Hart said, 'This is a big operation, make no mistake. Bekuv is only a tiny part of it but we'll get Mrs Bekuv here if that's what you want.'

'But?'

He stabbed a fork into his sandwich and cut a small triangle of it ready to eat. 'But you'll have to prevent Mann from putting his stubby peasant fingers into the 1924 Society. His abrasive personality would really have them all running for dear life, just at a time when we've got it ticking along nicely.' He changed the fork over to his other hand and fed himself some sandwich.

I picked my sandwich up in my fist, and didn't reply until I had a big mouthful to talk round.

'You've been frank with me, Gerry,' I said, 'and I'll be frank with you. You think we are worrying ourselves sick about getting Mrs Bekuv here? I'll tell you, we don't give a damn where she is. Sure we have made the right sort of noises and let Bekuv think we are pushing hard on his behalf, but we prefer things the way they are.'

'You can't be serious,' said Hart.

'Never been more serious in my life, old pal.'

'I wish someone had told us this before,' he said irritably. 'We have spent a lot of money on this one already.'

'On what?'

'We've paid some money to a couple of Russian airline people . . . we have organized travel papers for Mrs Bekuv. There was talk of getting her here by Saturday week.'

'This is a good sandwich, Gerry. They call this a club sandwich, do they? I must remember that.'

'Is your pal Major Mickey Mouse really planning to tear the 1924 Society apart?'

'You know what he's like,' I said.

Gerry Hart forked through his salad to find the last pieces of cucumber. He dipped them into the salt and ate them before pushing the rest of the salad away. He wiped his mouth on his napkin. 'No one would believe that I was trying to help you guys,' he said. 'No one would believe that I was trying to solve one of your biggest headaches and trying to stop you giving me one.'

'Are you serious about being able to get Mrs Bekuv here . . . getting her here by next week, I mean?'

Hart brightened a little. He reached into his waistcoat pocket and got out a tiny chamois purse. He opened it with his fingertips and dropped the contents into the open palm I offered him. There were two gold rings. One of them was old, and burnished to a condition where the ornamentation was almost worn away. The newer one was simpler in style and inside, where there was an inscription in Russian, I could see the gold was only a thin plating.

Hart said, 'Bekuv's wife's rings: the plated one is their wedding band – with suitably euphoric Komsomol slogan – and the other one is Bekuv's mother's ring, inherited when she died.' He reached out and I returned the rings to him. 'Good enough for you?' he asked.

'A wonderful piece of foresightedness, Gerry.'

'I know it's all part of your technique,' said Hart. 'I know you are trying to irritate me but I'm not going to be irritated.'

'I'm delighted to hear that,' I said.

'But there is a time factor,' he said. 'And if you don't give me a tentative "yes", shortly followed by a suitable piece of paper, I'm getting to my feet and walking out of here.'

'Yes, well, don't forget to pay for the sandwiches,' I said.

'There's nothing in this for me personally,' said Gerry Hart. 'I'm trying to prevent a foul-up between two separate investigations.'

'Why don't you make an official report?'

'You've got to be joking,' said Hart. 'It will take weeks to go through and at the end . . .' he shrugged.

'And at the end they might decide that Major Mann is right.'

'There's nothing in this for me,' said Hart again.

'You're too modest, Gerry. I'd say there was a lot in this for you. You tell me that Greenwood doesn't know you are up to the neck in a CIA investigation of the 1924 Society. You're too smart to hazard the main chance in search of a little career-garnish. I'd guess you keep your boss fully informed. And I'd say that you plan to come out the other side of this one having demonstrated what a powerful man you are, and what important connections you have with the CIA and how you can mangle its policies if you feel inclined. If Greenwood was impressed with that – and we both know that he might be – you could wind up in Congress, or maybe in the White House. Now don't tell me you didn't think of that possibility.'

'Don't you ever get depressed?' he asked. 'You always talk like everyone is on the make. Don't you ever get depressed?'

'I do, Gerry. Each time when I turn out to be right, which is practically always.'

'Do you hate me so much? Would you prevent Mrs Bekuv joining her husband just in case I get some political mileage out of it?'

'You're not talking to a junior cipher-clerk, Gerry. I've been there; and I know how the wheels go round, when jerks like you press the buttons . . .'

'Now, I've heard . . .'

'I've listened to you through a Bloody Mary, a club sandwich and a cup of coffee, Gerry. Now you listen to me. I'm not preventing Mrs Bekuv making a journey anywhere because I'll put my pension on an old under-wear button that Mrs Bekuv has already made her journey. She's in Manhattan, right, Gerry?'

'We've got a leak, have we?'

'No leak, Gerry,' I said. 'Agents in the Soviet Union – the ones that survive there – don't send messages to guys like Gerry Hart explaining what kind of travel arrangements they might be able to get for the Mrs Bekuvs of this world – they see an opportunity open up, they make a snap decision, they act on it, and disappear again.'

'I suppose so,' said Hart.

'And I picture Mrs Bekuv as a hard-nosed Party-worker, as smart as Stalin but only half as pretty. I see her pushing her absent-minded husband into his high-paid, top-secret job, in spite of his theories about flying saucers. I don't picture her as the sort of woman who hands over her wedding rings to some strange creep who might be a KGB man who likes a little hard evidence. No. But she might loan them out . . . for an hour or two.'

Gerry Hart didn't answer. He poured cream into the last little drop of his coffee and drank it slowly.

'We'll take her off your hands, Gerry,' I said. 'But no pieces of paper, and I can only *advise* Mann about the 1924 Society: no promises.'

'Do what you can,' he said. For a moment the bottom had dropped out of his world but, even as I watched him, I saw him coming up at me again as only soft rubber balls and politicians know how to bounce. 'But you're wrong about Mrs Bekuv,' he said. 'Wait until you see her.'

'Which of you asked for the check?' the waitress said.

'My friend asked for it,' I said.

7

Gerry Hart and I were both right. He delivered Mrs Bekuv to us within five days and had to be content with Major Mann's worthless assurance that any investigation of the 1924 Society would be conducted by men wearing velvet gloves. But I was wrong about Mrs Bekuv. She was in her middle thirties, a cheerful strawberry blonde with a curvacious figure that no one would ever persuade me to classify as plump. It required a superhuman faith in departmental files to believe that she'd been an earnest fourteen-year-old Young Communist, and had spent eight years touring the Soviet Union lecturing on fruit-crop infections. Gerry Hart was right – Mrs Bekuv was quite a surprise.

Elena Katerina, like her husband Andrei, had prepared her shopping-list long before her arrival in New York. She was complete with a caseful of Elizabeth Arden creams and lotions, and a complete range of Gucci matching luggage containing a wardrobe that would cope with any climate and a long time between laundries.

Sitting up front in Mann's Plymouth station-wagon, in suede pants-suit and white silk roll-neck, her blonde hair gleaming in the lights of the oncoming traffic, she looked more American than Bessie Mann or Red Bancroft sitting at the back each side of me.

Mrs Bekuv was wide awake but her husband's head had tilted until it was resting on her shoulder. Mann had left it too late to avoid the Christmas Eve traffic build-up and now it seemed likely that we would arrive late.

'Should we call them, honey . . . tell them to save some dinner?' said Bessie.

'They know we're coming,' said Mann. He pulled out and took advantage of a sudden movement in the fast lane. Bekuv had found a radio station in Baltimore that was playing Latin American music, but Mann reached over and turned the volume low.

'They say Virginia is like England,' said Red Bancroft trying to see into the darkness.

'I'll let you know, when it gets light,' I said.

'Anyone wants to drive,' offered Mann, irritably, 'and they've only got to say so.'

'And see where it gets them,' said Bessie Mann. She leaned forward and patted her husband on the head. 'We all have great faith in you, darling,' she cooed.

'Don't do that when I'm driving.'

'When shall I do it, then? It's the only time you turn your back.'

Red Bancroft said, 'Whenever my father asked my mother what she wanted for Christmas, she'd say she wanted to go away to a hotel until it was all over. But we never did spend Christmas in a hotel.' Red lit up one of the mentholated cigarettes she liked to smoke and blew smoke at me. I pulled a face.

'Because of all the work,' said Mann over his shoulder. 'She wanted to get away from all the cooking and the dishes.'

'Men see through us every time,' said Bessie Mann, feigning admiration.

'That's what she meant,' insisted Mann.

'Of course it is, darling,' she leaned forward to touch his cheek, and he took her fingers so that he could kiss the back of her hand.

'You two hide a torrid affair behind these harsh exchanges,' I said.

'Hold it, Bessie,' said Mann urgently. 'We've got two romantic kids in the back.'

'Why is it called Virginia?' said Mrs Bekuv suddenly. Her English was excellent, but she spoke it in a curiously prim voice and with poor pronunciation, like someone who had learned from a text-book.

'Named after England's virgin queen,' said Mann.

'Oh,' said Mrs Bekuv, not sure if she was being mocked.

Mann chortled, and changed down for the steep hill ahead.

It was certainly a remarkable hide-out: an old house set in four hundred acres of Virginia countryside. As we came up the potholed road our headlights startled rabbits and deer, and then through the trees we saw the hotel, its windows ablaze with yellow light and the façade strung with coloured bulbs like a child's Christmas tree.

Parked in the metalled space alongside the barn, there was a bus. It was a shiny metal monster, left over from the days before buses got tinted windows and air-conditioning. Alongside it there was another car, and as we came to a stop our headlights caught the shiny bodywork of a vintage Packard convertible, reconditioned by some enthusiast.

Mann switched off the lights and the radio. 'Well, here we are,' he said. 'Plenty of time for supper.'

'Eight twenty,' said Bessie Mann. Bekuv yawned, and his wife eased her shoes on and opened the car door.

'Happy Christmas,' I said, and Red kissed me on the ear.

'You'll love this place,' said Mann.

'We'd better,' said Bessie, 'or I'll never believe you again.'

As I climbed out of the warm car the cold of the open

70

countryside bit into me. 'Isn't that beautiful,' said Red. 'It's been snowing.'

'Is that like home, Professor Bekuv?' Bessie asked.

'I was born in the desert,' said Andrei Bekuv. 'I was born in a region more desolate than the Sahara – the USSR is a big place, Mrs Mann.'

'Is your home in the desert too, Katerina?' said Mrs Mann.

Mrs Bekuv wrapped herself in a long red cape and pulled the hood up over her head to protect her from the chilly wind. 'America is my home now, Bessie,' she said. 'I loved New York. I will never leave America.'

Mann was locking the doors of the car and I caught his glance. Any fears we'd had about Mrs Bekuv's conversion to capitalism seemed unfounded.

'Just take your pocket-books, and the cameras,' Mann told anyone who was listening. 'They'll send someone out for the baggage.'

'You always lock the car,' said Bessie Mann. 'He's so suspicious,' she announced to a world that already knew.

We went into the lobby of the hotel and I thought for a moment that Mann must have chosen it to make the Bekuvs feel at home. The furniture was massive and there were old-fashioned floral cushions and cracked lino on the stairs. Behind the reception counter there was a framed photo of Franklin Roosevelt and a litho reproduction of US Marines raising the flag on Iwo. The receptionist might have been chosen to match: she was a cheerful little woman with carefully waved grey hair and a chintzy dress. 'There's still time to catch the second half of the movie,' she said.

Mann picked up the menu from the desk. 'I think we'd rather eat,' he said.

'He changes the reel at the half-hour. The lights go on; you'll not disturb the show.'

'You want to send some food up to the rooms?'

'Whatever you say,' agreed the old lady.

'The home-made soup and steak – rare – and salad,' said Mann. 'And give us a bottle of Scotch and a bottle of vodka and a few mixes and ice.'

'I'll do it right away. Everyone the same?' she smiled. 'There's an ice-box in your rooms.'

We mumbled agreement, except for Mrs Bekuv who wanted her steak well done.

'The best steak this side of Texas,' said the old lady. 'That's what they all tell me.'

The two single rooms, booked for Red and me, were at the far end of the corridor. One had a shower and the other a bathroom. 'Shower or bath?' I asked as we looked into the rooms.

'I hate showers,' she said going into the room that was equipped with it. 'Especially these tin-sided contraptions. They make such a racket.'

She went over to the single bed and prodded it to see if it was soft. Then she pulled the blanket back and pummelled the pillows. 'No,' she said coming back to where I was standing and putting her arm through mine. 'I think we'll use the room with the tub.' She took me to the other room.

She sat on the bed and pulled off the silly little woollen hat she liked to wear. Then she undid the buttons of her dress. Her long red hair tumbled down over her pale shoulders. She smiled. She was the most beautiful creature I'd ever seen and her happiness warmed me. She kicked off her shoes. I picked up the phone. 'Can I have a bottle of champagne? Yes, French champagne. On second thoughts, better make that two bottles.'

72

It was a long time before we got back to the sitting-room that the Bekuvs shared with the Manns. There was a boy in starched apron and black bow-tie smoothing the tablecloth and setting out the cutlery.

'Thought you two were hungry enough to give dinner a miss,' said Mann archly.

'Mickey!' said his wife. 'You haven't ordered the wine.'

'You got red wine?' Mann asked the young waiter.

'Only Californian,' said the boy.

'I like Californian,' said Major Mann. He put a flattened hand over his heart, as if swearing to it.

The proprietor's wife had fixed dinner. The home-made soup was clam chowder and the steaks were delicious. Mann praised the buttered corn. 'You can keep all that lousy French chow,' Mann offered. 'You give me American cooking every time.'

Mrs Mann said, 'You like it; you got it.' The Bekuvs smiled but said nothing.

From downstairs the louder parts of the film's sound-track were sometimes audible. We heard exploding bombs and wartime melodies.

I suppose Bekuv must have been anticipating the pep-talk that Mann decided was due. When Mann produced a box of cigars and suggested that we smoke them down the hall, rather than wake up to the aroma of stale tobacco, Bekuv readily agreed, and I went with them.

The lounge was furnished in the same down-beat way that the lobby had been. There were several large sepia photographs of men with goggles, standing round old racing cars and grinning at each other. I guessed that Pierce, the proprietor, was a vintage-car freak, and probably owned the finely preserved Packard outside, and maybe the vintage bus, too.

Bekuv chose the dilapidated sofa. Mann leaned over

him to light his cigar. 'There have been a lot of new developments since you arrived Stateside,' said Mann.

'What kind of developments?' said Bekuv cautiously.

'At first we were asking you to tell us about the scientific data you were handling before you defected.'

'And I did that,' said Bekuv.

'Up to a point you did it,' said Mann. 'But you must have realized that there was another motive too.'

'No,' said Bekuv, drawing on his cigar and facing Mann quite calmly.

'For God's sake, Bekuv! You must see by now that our work on masers is way ahead of anything being done in the Soviet Union. We don't need you to tell us about masers.'

Bekuv had no intention of admitting anything like that. 'Then why ask me?'

'No one can be as dumb as you pretend to be at times,' said Mann.

I interrupted them before Mann blew his top. 'We know that American scientific data is being betrayed to the Soviet Union.'

Bekuv turned to look at me. He frowned and then gave a despairing shrug. 'I don't understand,' he said. 'You will have to explain.'

'We are hoping to recognize the form in which you recall the material. It might help us to trace the source of it. We might be able to find where it's coming from.'

'Much of it came from published work,' said Bekuv.

'Now don't get smart,' said Mann. He stood up, and there was a moment when I thought I was going to have to step between them. 'We are not talking about the kind of stuff that Greenwood and his committee are giving away. We are talking about military stuff.'

'What began as a scientific leak has now become a

flood of material,' I said. 'Some of it is intelligence data. There is British material too, which is why I am involved.'

'I wondered about that,' said Bekuv.

'I'm being squeezed,' said Mann, 'and when I get squeezed, you go through the wringer.'

'I'm giving you the material as fast as I can recall it,' said Bekuv.

'And that's not fast enough,' said Mann. There was an element of threat there.

'I can't go any faster,' said Bekuv. I watched his face. Perhaps this was the time he started to realize that his assistants at NYU had been trying to interrogate him.

Mann straightened and threw his head back. He held the cigar to his lips and put the other hand in the small of his back. It was a gesture both reflective and Napoleonic, until he scratched his behind. He strode slowly across the carpet in front of the log fire, staring all the time at the ceiling and puffing smoke. 'It was July of 'seventy-one. Berlin was stinking hot . . . you know the way it can get in that town. We'd included one of our kids in a party of trade union officials who were being given the treatment: that apartment block on the Allee that they pretend is full of workers' families, and the crèche near the Wannsee and the banquet where they drink the dudes under the table with endless toasts to the unity of the proletariat. Silly to put one of our boys into a scrum like that. It was an American trade union lawyer from Pittsburgh who reported him to the Russians. When we got him back, his arse was raw with untreated cigarette burns, and his bloodstream was full of pentathol. We flew him back to the best surgeon in the States but he never got the full use of his right hand again . . .' Mann smiled one of his cold smiles at Bekuv.

Bekuv had never taken his eyes off Mann as he paced

up and down. Now he said, 'It's not so simple to recall the details.'

'I was trying to help,' said Mann.

'I need more time,' said Bekuv.

Mann smiled again. He consulted his watch. 'Just look at the time. We'd better finish these cigars and join the ladies.' He threw his cigar away and ushered us out.

'It's a beautiful place,' said Red Bancroft. She was looking out of the window, cupping her hands to keep out the reflections. 'The moon is coming out. It is a wonderful evening for a walk.'

'It's freezing,' I said.

'Wrap up well, Pop,' she said scornfully. 'You can put on that nice new leather overcoat.'

I nodded my agreement, and I saw Red and Mrs Mann exchange the sort of knowing look with which women greet the downfall of a male.

The film show ended at ten minutes past ten. Red and I were walking through the cobbled yard at the rear of the house to get a closer look at the vintage bus and the old Packard. We'd heard 'Smoke Gets in Your Eyes' and 'Change Partners' coming faintly through the heavily curtained room where the movie was playing. As the finale music swelled, the back door opened, and some men came out into the cold air. One of them coughed and another slapped his back helpfully. Two more of the men lit cigarettes.

'London!' said one of the men. 'That's where I first saw that movie. I was a gunner, nineteen – youngest top-kick in the group – and I'd met this shy English kid. We went to a movie with her mother; can you imagine . . . with her mother! I was crazy about her.'

'What was her mother like?' said a second man. The first man laughed politely.

'I saw it with my Daddy and Ma,' said another voice. 'I was a shavetail, just out of pilot training. I was on leave before joining a bomb group in England. My folks just smiled and listened to me tell them how I couldn't wait to get into the fighting . . . and all the time they were figuring the odds against my getting killed . . . it's only now, when I've got kids of my own, that I understand what that cost them.'

'We all came back,' said another man. 'Sometimes I wonder why.'

'Not all of us,' said the man who'd been in pilot training. 'I lost a lot of real good buddies.'

'They shipped the squadron from England to France without warning,' said the first man. 'I forgot how to find the house in Manchester where she lived, and I never took down the address. I went back twice and walked the streets . . . but it was no use.'

'Wartime romance,' said the second man.

'It was more than that,' said the first man. 'I still think about her. Every week or so I remember her. That proves it, doesn't it.'

The door opened again and some women came out into the yard. 'What are you doing out here?' one of them asked shrilly. 'It's so cold!'

A second woman said, 'Telling dirty stories; I know what they were doing. Admit it now, Norm, you were telling dirty stories.'

'That's right,' said the man from pilot training. 'That's what we were doing.'

The proprietor's son was taking down the shutters from the room in which they'd been watching the film. As he did so, the light from inside lit up the yard. It was bright enough to see the men and women standing there. They were all in their late forties or early fifties. The women wore old-fashioned party dresses, and the men were in army uniforms. But the uniforms were not those of the modern army, they were the pink trousers, olive-drab jackets and soft-topped flyers' caps of the US Army Air Force, circa 1943.

8

It was breakfast-time on Christmas Eve. Low-angled winter-morning sunshine made slatted patterns on the wallpaper. 'Nostalgia isn't what it used to be,' pronounced Mann. He'd been reading aloud from the brochure that was included on our breakfast-table in the sitting-room. 'Nostalgia Inn' said the headline and there was a photograph of the hotel taken the previous summer when a vintage-car club used it for a convention. The furnishings, the recorded music, the film shows and even the menus had been chosen to give the clientele a chance to wallow in their memories and their illusions.

'This month and next month is the World War Two period,' Mann said. 'But last Christmas they did a 1914 week, and I hear it was terrific.' He was wearing a tweed jacket, white roll-neck sweater and khaki cotton trousers. It would do for World War Two.

'All we're saying,' repeated Bessie Mann patiently, 'is that you should have told us.'

'And had you buying special gowns and hair-dos.'

'Well, why not?' said Bessie.

'It would have loused up the security,' said Major Mann. 'This is supposed to be a way for our Russian friends to stay incognito. You telling every store clerk in Bloomingdales about it would have blown us all wide open.'

'You never trust me,' said Bessie Mann.

'Damn right,' agreed Mann cheerfully.

'Give me the car keys,' she said.

'Where are you going?' said Mann.

'I'm getting a 1940 hair-do and a party dress.'

'Don't curb those new radials,' said Mann. Bessie Mann aimed a playful blow at her husband's head. He ducked and grinned.

Red touched my hand across the table. 'Shall I go too? I need cigarettes.'

'Buy a dress and give me the bill,' I said. 'Happy Christmas.'

Red leaned over and kissed me.

'Break it up, you two,' said Mrs Mann.

'Listen, honey,' said Mann. 'Take a cab into town just in case I need the car.'

Soon after Mrs Mann and Red departed to go to town, Mrs Bekuv emerged through the connecting door. She was dressed in a blue silk pants-suit. It was a little flashy for my taste but it showed her blonde hair, and full figure, to advantage. Major Mann poured coffee for her, and offered her the butter. Only two warm rolls remained under the starched cloth in the basket. Mrs Bekuv broke one of them open and chewed a piece of its crust. She was still looking down at the plate as she spoke. 'You'll never get anywhere with my husband by threats, Major Mann.'

Mann put his coffee down and turned on his full unabated charm. 'Threats?' he said as if encountering the word for the first time. 'Is that what he told you, Mrs Bekuv? Perhaps he misunderstood. A long drive . . . all the strain of the last few days . . . he is looking a little tired.'

'Neither of us likes threats, Major Mann,' she said. She buttered her roll.

Mann nodded his agreement. 'No one does, Mrs Bekuv. No one I've ever met.'

'That's why we left the Soviet Union.'

Mann raised his hand as if to shield his eyes from a bright light. 'Now that's not quite true, Mrs Bekuv. You *know* it's not quite true. Your husband defected because he'd been passed over for promotion on four successive occasions, and because he was finally posted to that lousy little job in Mali, where he didn't get along with his boss.'

'That boss,' said Mrs Bekuv with great distaste, 'was a junior assistant to my husband only five years ago.'

'Exactly,' said Mann. 'And that's why your husband defected – nothing to do with living in a police state, or being threatened, or wanting to read Solzhenitsyn in the original Swiss.'

'You have my husband's defection all worked out, Major,' said Mrs Bekuv. 'So what about me? Why do you think I defected?'

'I'm not sure,' said Mann warily. 'But you certainly look like a million dollars in that Saks Fifth Avenue pants-suit, and Tiffany's gold wrist-watch and bangle.'

'You were having me followed?' She seemed very surprised.

She turned to see him better. The sunlight made her screw up her eyes, but even squinting into the light she was still a shapely and beautiful woman.

'Just making sure you weren't accosted by any strange men, Mrs Bekuv.' Mann leaned over and moved the slats a fraction to close the sun's rays out.

'Men from the Soviet Government, you mean?'

'Any kind of men, Mrs Bekuv.'

'It's not *me* you need to watch,' she said. She drank her coffee and put butter on the last piece of roll as if to signal that the conversation had ended.

'You mean I should be watching your husband?'

'He will not respond to pressure, Major Mann. Andrei

is a gentle person. If you bully him, he will run from you.'

'You're asking me to do business through you, Mrs Bekuv?' Mann had hit it, and she was disconcerted.

'It would be worth trying,' she said.

'Well, you must get your husband to co-operate, Mrs Bekuv.'

'But he already writes millions of words for you.'

'He has given us a great deal of scientific material – as close to verbatim as his memory will allow – but that's not what I call real co-operation, Mrs Bekuv.'

'What more do you want?'

'A man like your husband can get a lot of information from the style of the report and the procedure of the experiments and analysis. He knows which of the world's labs are concerned with the development of masers, and could probably name the men working in them – I think he knows where the leaks are coming from.'

Mrs Bekuv drank some coffee.

Mann continued his thesis. 'No Soviet scientist has been allowed more freedom than your husband has over the last few years. He has attended nearly thirty scientific conferences, lectures, seminars and symposiums, outside the Soviet Union – now that's unusual, Mrs Bekuv, you must admit. It's tempting to guess that he's been getting a lot of his material on a person-to-person basis, while talking with other scientists at these international conferences.'

'I'll talk to Andrei,' she promised.

'Me and my friend here,' said Mann pointing at me with his spoon as I poured another cup of coffee. 'We are an easy-going couple of kids. You know we are. But we've got to start scribbling a few picture postcards for the fellows in the front office. Otherwise they are going to start wondering if we are on some sort of fun-fest down here. They'll assign us to permanent night duty guarding the Lincoln Memorial. You get me, Mrs Bekuv?'

From the floor below us someone switched on the radio to hear a Christmas carol service. 'While shepherds watched their flocks . . .' came softly to us at the breakfast-table.

'I get you, Major Mann,' she said. I watched her carefully, but the slight smile she gave him revealed nothing but good-natured amusement. Mann picked up his orange juice and sipped some. 'You know something, Mrs Bekuv. It's getting so that freshly squeezed orange juice is just not available for love nor money. You'd be amazed at how many five-star hotels serve canned juice.'

'In the Soviet Union every hotel and restaurant serves freshly squeezed orange juice,' said Mrs Bekuv.

For a moment I thought Mann was going to challenge that contention but he smiled his most ingratiating smile and said, 'Is that so, honey. Well, I always knew there must be something good about that crummy wasteland.'

Mrs Bekuv pushed her cup aside and got to her feet.

'See you later,' said Mann affably.

Mrs Bekuv left the room without replying.

We were still sitting there when Bessie and Red phoned us from Waterbridge. They were almost through at the hairdressers, and the new dresses were gift-wrapped and ready for collection. All we had to do was to bring our chequebooks into town, and take them somewhere smart for lunch. To my surprise Mann readily agreed. He even invited the Bekuvs to go with us, but Andrei was going to record a Christmas concert on his Sony radio-recorder and Mrs Bekuv shook her head without looking up from *Dr Zhivago*.

Downstairs in the dining-room the hotel staff were

hanging ancient tin toys and celluloid dolls upon a Christmas tree. On the stage a ten-piece orchestra from Chicago were arguing with Mr Pierce about where the coloured spotlights should point.

Mann drove all the way to the end of the property and half-way up the hill before speaking. 'You don't approve of my little talk with Frau Bekuv?'

'I wouldn't put it into an anthology of psychological triumphs.'

'What did I do wrong?'

'Nothing,' I said. 'You obviously want her to put the finger on the 1924 Society, so that you've got an excuse to turn them over. Well, I'm sure she got the message and she will probably oblige you.'

'Why would that make you so mad?'

'If you are sure that the leak is through the crackpots on the 1924 Society, why not move in on them right away? If you are not sure, you are only confusing the situation by using Mrs Bekuv like a glove puppet.'

'Ah!' said Mann. 'Why not move in on the 1924 Society right away, you say. Well, I knew it was only a matter of time before you handed me a question I could answer.' He turned his eyes away from the road long enough to stare at me. 'The 1924 Society is a secret society, kiddo. No one's exactly sure who is a member of the 1924 Society.'

'Except the other members.'

'Like the Bekuvs. Yes, well now you're getting the idea, pal.'

'Suppose that, while we're all away, the Bekuvs call a cab and scram?'

Mann smiled as we pulled to a halt in a newly vacated parking-space in front of a pawnshop filled with saxophones and shotguns. I could see the hairdressers' a few doors away. 'You got a couple of quarters?' he said.

I gave him some change for the meter but he didn't get out of the car immediately. He said, 'I've put a couple of my boys to watch the back door.'

'You'd like them to skip,' I said accusingly.

'It would simplify things,' said Mann.

'Unless they succeeded,' I said.

Mann pulled a face and got out.

The Bekuvs were still in the hotel when we arrived back. Mozart's *Jupiter* was on the hi-fi. Andrei was still doing the calculations that would put messages into outer space and his wife was sleeping with *Dr Zhivago*. Mann dropped on to the sofa and heaved a sigh.

It's one of the many things I don't understand about women that the moment they return from some expensive hair-crimping parlour they stand in front of a mirror and comb the whole thing out again. Red and Bessie did that while Mrs Bekuv, evidently having decided that she'd missed out on a good thing, joined in the fun.

With seeming reluctance, she allowed herself to be persuaded into a new hair-style too. Red swept her hair up into a styling of the 'forties, and held it while they both admired it. Deftly Red pinned it into position and arranged the curls and the fringe with loving care.

Mann watched it all with interest, but his wife seemed strangely disquieted. It provided a revealing insight into Mrs Bekuv – and a portent of Red too, but I didn't see that at the time.

I ordered tea for all of us, but even before I'd put the phone down, Mann's autocratic manner told his wife that he wanted a private word with the Bekuvs. Bessie said she'd prefer to take her tea into her room, and even Red – no admirer of Mann's patriarchal moods – meekly agreed to do the same, even to the extent of leaving

85

Mrs Bekuv's hair-do unfinished. That didn't please the Russian lady, and after the others had gone she fixed Mann with a steely stare, told her husband to switch the music down, and said, 'Dr Henry Dean. He lives at a house called La Grange in the village of St Paul Chauvrac, Bretenoux, 46 Lot, France. Do you want to write that down?'

Mann said, 'Dr Henry Dean, La Grange, St Paul Chauvrac, Bretenoux, 46 Lot, France. No, I don't want to write it down.'

'He is not a scientist,' said Mrs Bekuv, 'not an important one, anyway. But he is the contact between the 1924 Society and Moscow.' She smiled and twisted a strand of blonde hair in her fingers. It was the artless gesture of the *ingénue*, inappropriate for this Rubenesque wife and mother, and yet she had more than enough charm to carry it off.

'That's fine,' said Mann tonelessly. He turned to me. 'Get on to that, will you.'

I looked at him closely. There was something in his voice that I could not recognize.

'I'll do what I can,' I said. I knew that my request to Langley for archive searches at five o'clock on a Christmas Eve would not be received with great enthusiasm.

'Don't try too hard,' said Mann. 'I wouldn't like to be ready to go by tomorrow morning.'

Mrs Bekuv looked from one to the other of us. 'You will go to France?'

'Dr Henry Dean, you say. Well, that's interesting,' said Mann. He said it in a louder voice. It was obviously intended to bring Andrei Bekuv into the conversation.

Andrei Bekuv nodded but did not turn round to meet Mann's eyes. He was toying with his new radio-recorder and trying to pretend he was nothing to do with the conversation.

Mrs Bekuv said, 'Andrei and I were talking about the investigation.'

'And I appreciate that,' said Mann.

She ignored his sarcasm. She went on. 'Our complete co-operation would not only be good for America, it would be very good for you too.'

'I'm not sure that I'm following your implications,' said Mann who was not only following the implications but well ahead of them. He pressed a splayed hand upon his heart. I saw now that what I had always thought was a spiritual gesture was done to check that his collar was buttoned down.

'Promotion and a better pay-scale, more power, a better posting . . . you know what I mean,' said Mrs Bekuv. 'This first name we give you freely but if you want more we must have a new agreement.'

Mann grinned. 'You mean you want *your* share of the prosperity – promotion, and pay-scale.'

'Otherwise,' said Mrs Bekuv, 'we will simply say nothing, until you are fired and a new team sent to work on us.'

'How do you know that I won't get out the rubber truncheons long before I get fired?'

Andrei Bekuv shifted uneasily and fiddled with the volume control so that a few chords of Mozart escaped and ran across the carpet. 'We'll have to take that risk,' said Mrs Bekuv.

'How much?'

'We didn't realize how expensive it is to live in New York,' said Mrs Bekuv immediately. 'With all those smart people at university, I'm going to have to look my best, you know.' She smiled as if we all shared some secret joke.

'I'll see what I can do,' said Mann.

'I couldn't resist all these new clothes, Major Mann,' she said. 'After all those years in the Soviet Union I was dazzled by the shop-windows, and Andrei insisted that I bought a whole new wardrobe, from shoes to underwear. He said it was all part of our starting our new life.'

'I understand,' said Major Mann.

'Forget what I said just now. With or without an increase in the money, we will both help you all we can.' Mrs Bekuv slapped a menu into *Dr Zhivago* and slammed the book closed. Then she stood up and smoothed her cornflower-blue silk dress, running her fingers down over hips and thighs in the sort of gesture used by nervous contenders in amateur beauty competitions. She smiled at both of us, and was still smiling as she leaned over her husband and kissed the top of his head.

The waiter arrived with a tray of tea and toast just as Mrs Bekuv went out of the room. Mann took the tray from him and began to pour the milk, and offer the home-made cherry cake. Andrei Bekuv took a slice of lemon in his tea and declined the cake. 'My wife gets very nervous, Major Mann,' he said. 'She misses the boy.'

'You knew your son would never join you. He'll be taking his exams next year . . . you wouldn't want us to try and bring him out against his will.'

'No, no, no,' said Andrei Bekuv. 'What you say is true . . . but it doesn't change the facts. My wife can't get used to the idea of never seeing her son again.' He looked away. 'And to tell you the truth, I can't either.'

'Sure,' said Mann. 'Sure.' He patted Bekuv's arm as one might try to calm an excited poodle.

Emboldened by this gesture of friendship, Bekuv opened his loose-leaf notebook. 'I have completely changed my work on interstellar communication.'

'Have you?' said Mann. 'That's good. No more humming hydrogen, you mean?'

Bekuv made some vague noises while pointing at the pages of closely written numbers. 'At first we were looking for some means of communicating through the galactic plasma without dispersion. Obviously this meant using electromagnetic waves. We knew X-rays were no good . . .'

'Why?' I said in an attempt to join in.

'They can't be focused,' said Bekuv, 'and gamma rays have too limited a range.'

'How limited?' I asked.

'About one hundred thousand miles,' said Bekuv. Mann pulled a face. Bekuv smiled and said, 'But now I am beginning to believe that we should abandon the idea of any sort of electromagnetic waves. After all, we will never be able to converse with another civilization, because each message will take twenty years getting there and another twenty to get back.'

'Sounds like the British telephone system,' said Mann.

'Now I believe we should simply seek to make a mark in the universe . . . a mark that some other civilization will detect and so know there is some kind of sophisticated life on planet Earth.'

'What kind of mark?' said Mann.

'Not ploughing patterns in fields. There has been a lot of talk about that but it is absurd. The canals on Mars that Schiaparelli reported in 1887 and the Mariner spacecraft revealed as a complete misinterpretation have ruled out that idea.' He turned the page to where there were diagrams and more calculations. 'I am thinking of a cloud of material that will absorb a chosen wavelength of light. This would leave a pattern – no more than a line perhaps – in the spectogram of a star's light. This would be enough to tell any civilization that there was scientific achievement here on Earth.'

I looked at Mann. He raised his eyebrows. 'What is the next step?' Mann asked, with trepidation evident.

'To put this before your Government,' said Bekuv. 'It will cost quite a lot of money.'

Mann was unable to completely suppress a sigh. 'Well, you'd better put this all to me in the form of a report. Then I will see what I can do.'

'I don't want it filed away and forgotten,' said Bekuv. 'I want to talk to someone about it. You have a Senate Committee on International Co-operation. Could I talk to them?'

'Perhaps,' said Mann, 'but you'll have to write it all down first.'

'One more thing,' said Bekuv. 'It's Christmas Eve, could I take my wife to the midnight mass tonight?'

'It doesn't say you are Catholics on the dossier,' said Mann. He was disconcerted, and slightly annoyed. Or perhaps he was feigning annoyance.

'We have lapsed in our church-going, but not in our faith,' said Bekuv. 'Christmas Eve has always been a special time for us.'

'Someone will have to go with you,' said Mann.

'I'll go,' I said.

Bekuv looked at Mann. Mann nodded.

'Thank you,' said Bekuv. 'I will go and tell Katinka. Thank you both.' He went away wagging his tail.

'Sometimes I don't know how I keep my hands off that jerk,' said Mann.

'And it shows,' I told him.

90

Mann sat down in the soft armchair and closed his eyes tight.

'Are you all right?' I asked.

'I'm all right,' said Mann but his face had gone grey, and he looked as if old age had overtaken him very suddenly. I waited for him to speak. I waited a long time.

'Henry Dean,' I reminded him of the name Mrs Bekuv had given us. 'Dr Henry Dean.'

'Hank Dean,' said Mann. He tightened his tie.

'You've heard of him?' I asked.

'Hank Dean: airline executive's son, born in Cottonwood, South Dakota. High school athlete; track star, truly great pitcher, tipped for pro baseball until he got injured.'

'How do you know so much about him?' I asked.

'We grew up together in a village just outside Cleveland. My dad was a pilot and his was sales manager for a tinpot airline; flying contract mail between Chicago and New York City. The airline families lived alongside the airfield, and the village kids beat shit out of us. The war came, we both went into the army. Hank was a bright kid, came out a captain in the airborne, but he'd done a few drops in civilian clothes. At the end of the war, the army kept him on, but sent him to MIT to get his masters. He wound up with a PhD before he got back into uniform. Next thing I heard he was working in Berlin for a little company that made high-voltage electrophoresis machines for medical labs . . . you're beginning to get the picture?'

'I get the picture,' I said. 'This little engineering company had a very lenient policy about employees who disappeared for long weekends, and came back with their hair slightly ruffled and a hole in the hat.'

'Yeah, a CIA front, and a very active one. Henry

Dean was making quite a name for himself. They switched him back into the army and gave him the police desk in Berlin. Then they began saying that Dean would be running Operations in Langley before he was thirty-five – that kind of crap, you know.'

'I know.'

'But Dean got into the juice. His old man was a lush, I remember. That's why his dad quit flying and went to sales. Hank was very close to his dad; he used to hide the bottles, argue with him, plead with him, but it was no use. Poor Hank – and Berlin is a bad place for a guy who is easily tempted.'

'Yes,' I said.

Mann passed a hand across his eyes as if trying to see into the past. When he spoke again it was the voice of a man half asleep. 'Got into the juice. There was some kind of foul-up . . . a row about some documents being given to the East Germans . . . there was an inquiry. I don't know the details but Dean was never the same again after that. They gave him a second chance. The next thing was a back-up assignment for a routine crossing. It was unlikely that he'd be needed, but suddenly he was, and they dug him out of a bar on the Ku-damm, stoned out of his mind. There was a lot of static from Langley, and a lot of promises from Dean. But it was the third time that ended his career.

'Berlin in the late 'fifties – it was heavy stuff, and two really good guys went that night. Those two had a lot of friends, and the friends blamed Hank Dean. He was finished for that kind of field-work. He went back to Washington but he couldn't handle a scene like that – it needs a light touch – Washington "A list" hostesses, all that muscle from the satellite embassies, too many whizzkids chasing your job. No, that wasn't Hank Dean.'

I tried to pour some tea. There was only a trickle left, and that was cold. There were no lights on in the sitting-room, and Mann was no more than a silhouette against the darkening sky. The silence lasted so long that when he spoke again it made me start.

'He stayed on the wagon for years,' said Mann. 'And then finally Special Services found something for him in Vietnam. They wanted me to sign a chit sponsoring him . . .' Mann sighed. 'I thought about it all day and all night. I was sure he'd foul up and spatter me with shit . . . so I said no.'

I tried to ease some of the guilt off his back. 'Hindsight reveals a wise decision,' I said.

It did nothing to cheer Mann. Against the wintry light from the window, I saw him pinch the bridge of his nose. He was slumped lower now, his chin almost on his chest. 'Can't be sure of that, can we?' he said. 'Maybe if I had signed it we wouldn't be running our pinkies down the Christmas airline schedules.'

'Maybe,' I agreed.

'There comes a time in your life when you have to do the human thing – make the decision the computer never makes – give your last few bucks to an old pal, find a job for a guy who deserves a break, or bend the rules because you don't like the rules.'

'Even in this job?'

'Especially in this job, or you end up as the kind of dispassionate robotic bastard that communism breeds.'

'Are you going to bring Dean back, or try to turn him?'

'I've embarrassed you, have I?' said Mann bitterly.

'Because if you are going to bring him back, there will be a lot of paperwork. I'll want to get started on it as soon as possible.'

'You like baseball?' Mann asked. 'He was second baseman. I saw the whole thing . . . a double play and this little fink put a set of sharpened cleats into his knee. He would have turned pro, I'm sure. He'd never have come into this lousy racket.'

'Turn Dean,' I said, 'and perhaps we could do without the Bekuvs.'

'Hank Dean . . . big noisy lummox . . . full of farts and funny stories . . . untrimmed beard, dirty dishes in the sink, rot-gut in flagons, and a sleeping-bag in the bathroom if you're too drunk to drive home. You'd never recognize him for this bright kid who got the sharpened cleats in his leg. Funny how a thing like that can change a man's whole life.'

'This is just a way of getting at you,' I said.

'It looks like it,' said Mann. 'I wonder how long ago they started working on it.'

'What are you going to do?'

'Poor old Hank. A KGB operation – I can smell it from here, can't you? Payments into his bank balance, witnesses who can identify him, microdots pasted into his copy of *Thunderball*, you know what they get up to. Jesus! – and I've got the choice of handing over to another investigating officer, the way the book tells it, or of bending the rules and try and make it easy on him.'

'If the KGB have set it up, they will have dotted every i and crossed every t. They dare not risk something like this blowing up in their faces.'

'They've not necessarily framed him,' said Mann calmly. 'They might have just offered him enough dough to get him working for them.'

'You don't believe that.'

'I don't *want* to believe it,' said Mann. 'Do you know something . . . for a moment there I wasn't even going to tell you that I knew Dean. I was just going to press on with the investigation and keep stumm.'

If the Russians wanted to compromise or discredit Mann, they'd chosen a racking dilemma for him. But they'd misjudged their target. Many would have folded under such pressure, most would have handed the file over to someone else, but not Mann. He was shaken, but not for long.

'Already it's working,' Mann said. 'Already there is a gap between us.'

The neon signs and the lights of the nearby town were turning the night sky fiery. 'No gap,' I said.

'No gap,' said Mann scornfully. 'Already you are getting nervous – worrying about your pension and trying to decide how much you can afford to play along with me.'

'No.'

'Why no?' he asked. 'Why no, Frederick Antony, old buddy?'

He deserved some warmer reassurance that reflected the times we'd had together. Something that told him I'd stake my life upon his judgment – be it good or bad. But I was too English for such extravagances. Coldly I said, 'Because I trust you more than I trust Mrs Bekuv. For all we know she could be planted by the KGB . . . acting on their instructions, and giving us the *spielmaterial* they want to feed to us.'

The phone rang but Mann made no attempt to answer it.

I said, 'That will be the girls reminding us about the dance they've dressed up for.'

Mann didn't move, and soon the phone ceased to ring. 'The side of his knee,' said Mann. 'His left leg, he still limps.'

95

9

That strange winter afternoon, Mann's soft voice in that darkened room, my lack of sleep, the infatuation for Red that was fast becoming love, the contrived nostalgia of the Christmas festivities, or perhaps those last three whisky-sours, accounted for the way I remember it as a hazy dream. A dream that became a nightmare.

The hotel management loaned us two old-fashioned tuxedos. My outfit included a shirt with a piqué front, as stiff as a board, and Mann's even had a wing-collar. The band played Glenn Miller arrangements with suitable verve and sweetness, and the brass stood up and swayed through the choruses.

The Manns were dancing to the tune of 'Sun Valley Serenade' when Red and I took the Bekuvs into town for the midnight mass. The Catholic church in Waterbridge was crowded, and an elaborate nativity scene occupied the entrance. The nave was lit by a thousand flickering candles. They made the interior warm and yellow, but the upper parts of the church were dark.

The Bekuvs sat close together, and we chose a seat behind them so that I could watch them without intruding upon their privacy. Long after the singing of the choir ended, my mind remained full of the candlelight and the resonant chords of the great organ. And, mixing with it, came the brassy riffs of the Glenn Miller arrangements and the soft whispered words of love from Red.

Outside, the first hours of Christmas Day were celebrated in an icy wind and scattered showers of sleet. At the exit people paused to wrap their scarfs tighter and button their thick overcoats. It was this that created a solid crush of worshippers at the door. We shuffled forward a step at a time.

It was exactly the right place for it.

I heard the strangled cry from Mrs Bekuv, and the scream of some other unidentified woman. Hands flailed and hats were knocked askew. A man began to shout. The Bekuvs were no more than five yards away from me but they might have been five miles for all the help I could give them.

I swore, and ripped at the crowd, tearing a way between the worshippers like a man demented.

By the time I got to the Bekuvs, the crowd had parted enough to let Mrs Bekuv sit on the stone steps. She was conscious but said nothing. She looked heavy and lifeless, the way soldiers do when their battle is done. Andrei Bekuv was bending over her. Both of them had blood on the front of their clothes. Andrei was pulling at his wife's sleeve so that blood ran down her arm to form a puddle on the step.

'They've killed Katinka,' said Andrei Bekuv.

I reached for her pulse and bloodied my hands.

'Get an ambulance, Red. Ask the church to phone.'

'They've killed my Katinka,' said Bekuv, 'and it's all my doing.'

I bound my handkerchief tightly round her arm but the blood still came. It marked the cuff of my borrowed tuxedo, and dribbled on to my new leather overcoat.

There were no shadows. Everything in the room was white, and the fluorescent tubes lit it with a cold, pitiless glare. My blood-encrusted handkerchief lay coiled and discarded on the trolley, like the scaly skin of some

97

terrible red serpent, and alongside it – carefully aligned – was the gold wrist-watch and bracelet that Bekuv had bought for his wife in New York.

My coffee was cold. I tore open a sachet of powdered cream, stirred the mixture and gulped it down. It was a hell of a lousy way to spend Christmas morning.

There was a rap at the door and Mann entered without waiting for a response. His eyes were bloodshot and his hair imperfectly parted.

'You talked with the surgeon?' He unbuttoned his trenchcoat to reveal a partly buttoned shirt, and a cardigan pulled down over his evening trousers.

'No arterial cuts. Her hands will be scarred for life – she grabbed at the switchblade – maybe scars on the abdomen too, but the thick coat saved her anything worse than superficial wounds. If the blade had entered her the way it was intended, she would have been dead before she hit the ground.'

Mann sniffed, walked over to the trolley and moved the wrist-watch and bangle with the tip of his finger, as if making a chess move. 'Description of the assailant?'

'At least a dozen,' I said. 'All of them different.'

'And our pal Andrei?'

'She stepped between them. It was meant for Andrei, but he wasn't scratched. He's taking it badly.'

'"My darling Katinka, what have I done to you?"'

'That's the kind of thing,' I agreed.

'No one could have known that the Bekuvs started talking,' said Mann, as much to convince himself as to convince me.

'There must be a few people in Washington suffering sleepless nights.'

'There will be a few people in the Kremlin suffering worse than sleepless nights if we break this one wide open,' said Mann. 'They don't set up Henry Dean situations unless it's really big.'

'We should have expected some attempt to kill them.'

'I *did* expect it. But not this soon. Who the hell could have known we'd brought them to this godforsaken hole.'

'Gerry Hart?'

Mann scratched his face. His was unshaved, and he touched his beard self-consciously. 'Yes, that little bastard is certainly kept well informed. Who might be leaking to him? Any ideas?'

I shook my head.

'Well, this is the way it's going to be from now onwards,' said Mann. 'We'd better get prepared for more of the same. We'd better move the Bekuvs out of here.'

I looked at my watch. 'Merry Christmas,' I said.

'The better the day, the better the deed. Isn't that what they say?'

'It might look damned funny to the local press boys.'

'A mugging?' said Mann. 'Nothing to leave the tree for.'

'Knifing at midnight mass,' I said. 'In Waterbridge that's a headline. They will go for it. You won't shake that one, Major.'

'And if I put a security guy at her bedside, it will look even more like a story.' Mann grabbed at his face and rubbed hard as if trying to wake up. 'And yet without a security guard they might try again.'

I tried to reassure him. 'It was an amateur kind of job,' I said. 'I never heard of the KGB using a shiv artist who hit the wrong target, and even then let them grab the knife away.'

'It damn nearly worked, and you know it,' said Mann. 'And there was nothing amateur about the way they found out where the Bekuvs would be last night.'

'They might have followed us all the way from New York City, and then staked out the hotel, waiting for an opportunity,' I suggested.

'You know nothing followed us,' said Mann. 'Even in the back seat with Red, you've got to know nothing followed us.'

I didn't answer. He was right, nothing had followed us down the highway and we'd had a helicopter to help check-out that fact.

'You get back to your girl-friend,' said Mann. 'Give me a call here in the morning. I'll have doped it out by then.'

Red was half asleep as I got into bed. She reached out for me in dreamy wantonness. Perhaps it was part of an attempt to forget the events of the previous evening that made us so abandoned. It seemed hours before either of us spoke a word.

'Is it going to be all right?' Red asked me in a whisper.

'She's not badly hurt. Andrei isn't even scratched.'

'I didn't mean that,' she said. 'I'm glad she's not badly hurt, but I didn't mean that.'

'What then?'

'This is all part of what you're doing, isn't it?'

'Yes,' I said.

'And it's going wrong?'

'It looks like it,' I admitted. 'Mrs Bekuv will have to be kept under surveillance and that will be more difficult now she needs medical attention.'

'In London,' said Red suddenly. 'What sort of house do you live in?'

'I don't have a whole house,' I said. 'I rent the top floor to a friend – a reporter – and his wife. It's a small Victorian terrace house, trying to look Georgian. The central heating is beginning to crack the place apart –

first thing I must do when I get back is to get some humidifiers.'

'Where is it?'

'That part of Fulham where people write Chelsea on their notepaper.'

'You said there was a garden.'

'It's more like a window-box that made it. But from the front you can see a square with trees and flower-beds – in summer it's pretty.'

'And what kind of view from the back windows?'

'I never look out of the back windows.'

'That bad?'

'A used-car dealer's yard.'

She pulled a face. 'I'll bet it's the most beautiful car dealer's yard in the world,' she said.

I kissed her. 'You can decide that when we get there,' I said.

'Do I get to change the drapes and the kitchen lay-out?'

'I'm serious, Red.'

'Yes, I know,' she said. She kissed me again. 'Don't let's be too serious though – give it time.'

'I love you, Red,' I said.

'I love you too – you know that. Do you want a cigarette?'

I shook my head. She reached across me to the bedside table and found her cigarettes and lighter. I couldn't resist the chance to hug her close to me, and she tossed the cigarettes aside and said, 'Well, if I can choose.' The cigarette-lighter slid down behind the mattress, and clattered to the floor. Red giggled. 'Will you always want me?' she said.

'Always,' I said.

'Not that, you fool,' she said.

She kissed me with opened mouth. Eventually I said, 'What then?'

'Would Major Mann let me stay with you?' she asked. 'I could make the coffee, and sweep the floor, and look after Mrs Bekuv.'

I said, 'I'll ask him tomorrow, if he's in a good mood.'

She kissed me again, more seriously this time. 'If he's in a good mood,' I repeated.

'Thanks,' she mumbled.

I reached for her. 'You chatter too much,' I said.

10

There was no sky, no sun, no earth: until a few hundred square miles of France appeared like a smear upon the lowest layer of cloud. And as suddenly it was gone again.

'I don't want to phone from the airport,' I told Mann, 'but I'll check that there is nothing for us on the telex.'

'Worry about something else,' Mann told me, as the stewardess removed the tray containing the dried-out chicken, shrivelled peas and brightly coloured pieces of tinned fruit. 'Worry about income tax. Worry about the inflatable life-rafts. Worry about pollution. Worry about ptomaine poisoning. Worry about youth. But quit worrying about Red Bancroft.'

'I've stopped worrying about Red Bancroft,' I said.

'She's been checked by the FBI, by the CIA and her hometown police department. That girl is OK. There is good security: she'll be safe. It will all be OK.'

'I've stopped worrying. I told you that.'

Mann turned in his seat so that he could see my face. He said finally, 'Bessie said you two were hitting it off, and I didn't believe her.' He leaned across and punched my arm so that my coffee spilled. 'That's just great,' he said.

'There's something wrong there,' I confided. 'She's a wonderful girl and I love her – at least I think I do – but there is something in her mind, something in her memory . . . something somewhere that I can't reach.'

Mann avoided my eyes as he pressed his call-button

and asked the stewardess to bring a bottle of champagne. 'We're getting awfully near Paris,' said the girl.

'Well, don't you worry your pretty little head about that, honey,' Mann told her. 'We'll gulp it down.'

I saw him touch the document case beside him. It contained the paperwork that we would need if Mann decided to drag Hank Dean, screaming and swearing, back to the New World. Mann caught my glance. 'I'm not looking forward to it,' he admitted. 'And that's a fact.'

'Perhaps he will talk,' I said.

'Perhaps he knows nothing,' said Mann.

The stewardess brought the champagne. Her uniform was one size too small, and the hair-do three sizes too big. 'We'll be going down in a minute or two,' she told us.

'All three of you?' said Mann. The stewardess departed. Mann poured the champagne, and said, 'I guess everything depends upon the way you look at it. Maybe if I'd been at college with Andrei Bekuv, I could even feel sorry for *that* schmendrik.'

'Everything depends upon the way you look at it,' I agreed. 'But I already feel a bit sorry for Andrei Bekuv.'

Mann made a noise like a man blowing a shred of tobacco from his lips. It was a sign of his disagreement.

'I feel sorry for him,' I said. 'He's crazy about his wife, but she's wrong for him.'

'Everybody is wrong for that jerk,' said Mann. 'Everybody and everything.' He picked up his champagne. 'Drink up,' he commanded.

'I don't feel like celebrating,' I said.

'Neither do I, my old English buddy, but we are pals enough to drink together in sorrow – right?'

'Right,' I said, and we both drank.

He said, 'Mrs Bekuv is the best thing that ever happened to that creep. She's one of the most beautiful broads I've ever seen – and I'm telling you, pal, if Bessie wasn't around, I'd be tempted. Bekuv doesn't deserve a doll like that. And she wet-nurses that guy: wipes his bottom, checks his haircuts, demands more dough from us. And she even takes a blade that's coming his way. No wonder he's in a constant sweat in case she kisses him goodbye.'

'Well, everything depends on the way you look at it,' I said.

'Don't tell me *you* haven't felt some stirring of carnal lust for Mrs Bekuv,' said Mann. 'Don't tell me you haven't fancied it.'

'I've got Red,' I said smugly.

Mann repeated his tobacco noise. 'You know something,' he said scornfully. 'You can be very, very British at times.'

I smiled, and pretended to think that it was a compliment. And I returned to him the Biographical Abstract I'd been reading. He locked it away in his case.

'Drink up. We'll be landing any minute,' he said. But, in fact, we joined the stack, somewhere over the great wooded region of Compiègne, and circled to await landing permission which did not come until forty minutes later.

It gave me time to think about Hank Dean. It was the new format BIO-AB, dressed up to look like a report from a particularly energetic personnel manager. This one was typed on onion-skin paper, carrying the logo of a small furniture factory in Memphis, Tennessee. Attached to it was an employee-record punchcard and a photo. It had been 'styled' to provide a cause-and-effect view of Hank Dean's life, instead of being, as the earlier sheets were, a list of dates and a terse summary.

And yet these sheets are always a poor substitute for sight and sound of the real person. What use was it to know that his middle name was Zacharias, and that some schoolfriends call him Zach. How many schoolfriends remain for a man who is nearly fifty years old? Dean had 'a drinking problem'. That had always struck me as an inappropriate euphemism to apply to people who had absolutely no problem in drinking. What Dean had was doubtless a sobriety problem. I wondered if that was anything to do with the break-up of his marriage. The wife was a New Yorker of German extraction, a few years younger than Dean. There was one child – Henry Hope Dean – who lived in Paris and spent his vacations fishing with his father.

I closed the file. Henry Zacharias Dean, PhD, 210 pounds at last dossier revision, soldier, company executive, failed CIA agent, failed husband but successful father . . . here we come. And won't you wish you were back in that village near Cleveland, getting punched in the head by the local kids.

'Did you say something?' asked Mann.

'The no-smiling sign is on,' I said.

Mann poured the last of the champagne into our glasses.

One Christmas – so many decades ago that I can't remember when exactly – an aunt gave me a book about some children who were captured by the crew of a pirate ship. The pirate captain was a huge man, with a hooked nose and a magnificent beard. He drank rum in copious amounts, and yet was never obviously drunk. His commands could be heard from fo'c's'le to crow's-nest, and yet his footsteps were as deft, and as silent, as a cat's. That pirate captain's mixture of bulk and dexterity, cruelty and kindness, shouts and whispers, drinking and sobriety were also the make-up of Hank Dean.

He would need only a Savile Row suit, some trimming of the beard and a glass of sherry in his hand to be mistaken for a wealthy gynaecologist or a stockbroker. And yet, in this shaggy sweater, that reached almost to his knees, denim trousers washed to palest blue, and swilling Cahors, the local wine, round and round in the plastic cup that had once contained Dijon mustard, he would have had trouble thumbing a ride to Souillac.

'Should have done it years ago. Should have done it when I was eighteen. We both should have done it, Mickey.' Hank Dean swigged his wine and poured more. He closed the typescript of his comic detective novel *Superdick*, put it into a manila envelope and shut it away in a drawer. 'That's just my excuse for staring into space,' he explained.

The heat from the big black iron stove disappeared up the huge chimney, or through the cracks and crevices that could be seen round the ill-fitting doors and windows. Only when Hank Dean threw some wax cartons and wrapping paper into the stove did it give a roar and a brief show of flame.

Dean lifted the frying-pan that was warming on the stove. 'Two eggs or three?'

'I'm not hungry,' said Mann. 'Give me a piece of that salami.' He picked up a slice of the sausage on his fork and chewed at it.

Dean said, 'Jesus Christ, of course you're hungry. You've come all the way down from Paris, haven't you. And this is the greatest food in the world. You're having an omelette with truffles – it would cost you a king's ransom in one of those phoney New York traps – and

107

that's not salami, goddamn it, it's pork sausage, smoked at the farm just up the hill there.'

Mann stopped eating the pork sausage and put his fork down.

'I miss the ball games,' said Dean. 'I'd be lying to you if I didn't admit to missing the ball games. But I can hear them on the radio sometimes.'

'Short-wave radio?' said Mann.

'And the Voice of America. On a good night, the Armed Forces Network from Germany. But I'm surrounded by high ground here, as you can see.'

'Sure,' said Mann.

I wondered how much of that exchange was about baseball, and how much was about short-wave radio reception – and maybe transmission too. I took some sausage, and tore a crusty piece of bread from the end of the loaf. It would all go on a long time yet, I decided. Mann and Dean would pretend to talk about old times, while talking about new times. And Mann would pace up and down, looking into cupboards and assessing the length of drawers and the thickness of walls to decide whether something could be concealed behind them. He would judge it all on a basis of infallibility, while hoping for a careless mistake.

'My kids went to camp this Christmas,' Mann told Dean. 'It cost me an arm and a leg. How I'm going to pay for them when they go to college, like your boy, sometimes scares the arse off me.'

Dean was cutting a large truffle into slices as thin as a razorblade. He was using a wooden-handled folding knife, of the type the Wehrmacht issued to special units that had to cut sentries' throats.

'Living here costs me practically nothing,' explained Dean. 'The company pays me five hundred bucks a month, and I'm still getting ten dollars a week for that ball-game injury back when we were kids. The team carried insurance and that was lucky for me.' He lifted the bread-board and carefully bulldozed the truffle slices into the beaten egg, then stood up and walked to the stove. There was a limp in his left leg. Whether this was for our benefit because he'd been thinking about it, or simply a result of sitting too long I could not be sure.

'But didn't you say your boy went to some kind of private college in Paris? Doesn't that really cost?'

Dean stirred the egg, and checked the heat of the frying-pan by tossing a scrap of bread into it. It went golden brown. He forked it out, blew on it and ate it before adding some salt and pepper to the egg mixture. Then he stood with the bowl of egg poised above the stove. 'You must have got it wrong, Mickey,' he said. 'The boy went to an ordinary French technical school. There were no fees.'

With a quick movement, and using only one hand, he closed the knife and slipped it back into the pocket of his jeans. He said, 'My old Renault will do more miles per gallon than any automobile I ever used. The running repairs I do myself. In fact, last month I changed the piston rings. Even with the present price of gas, I spend no more than the ten bucks a week that my injury provides – I figure I owe my leg that car.'

He turned round from the stove and smiled. 'As for the rest; that little restaurant next door sells me my lunch for about what I could buy the ingredients for. I don't know how they do it. In the evening I manage on a bit of charcuterie, eggs, bread and stuff. For special occasions, one of these twenty-franc truffles . . .' He smiled. 'Of course if my book hit the jackpot . . .'

'How often do you manage to get to the big city?'

Mann asked him. Dean tipped the egg mixture into the pan. The sudden splutter of the egg in the hot fat made Mann turn his head.

'Paris, you mean?' said Dean.

'Or New York,' said Mann. 'Or London, or Brussels – even Berlin.' He let the word hang in the air for a long time. 'Any big city where you can do some shopping and see a show.'

'I haven't seen a show – or even a movie – in a lot of years, Mickey,' said Dean. He dragged at the eggs with urgent movements of a wooden spoon, twisting and turning the pan, so that the uncooked egg would run on to the hot metal that he uncovered. 'No time, and no money, for those bourgeois pastimes.'

In another place, and at another time, such comment would have passed unnoticed but now Dean bent low to the pan, and watched the egg cooking with a concentration that was altogether unmerited, and I knew he could have bitten his tongue off.

Dean turned the pan up, so that the giant omelette rolled on to a serving-dish. He divided it into three equal parts and put it on our plates. Above the table the lamp was a curious old contraption of brass and weights and green shades. Dean pulled at the strings so that the lights came low over the dining-table.

We ate the meal in complete silence. Now that only the table was illuminated, it gave everything there an artificial importance. And the three sets of busy hands, under the harsh light, were like those of surgeons co-operating in some act of dissection. In spite of his protests about not being hungry, Mann gobbled the omelette. When there was no more than a few smears of uncooked egg on his plate, he took a piece of bread and wiped up

110

the egg with obsessional care before putting the bread into his mouth.

'The reason we came down here to see you, Hank . . .' Mann took another piece of bread, tore it into pieces and ate it piece by piece, as if trying to find reasons for not continuing.

'You need no reasons, old buddy,' said Dean. 'Nor your friend either. Hank Dean – open house. You know that by now, don't you? In the old days, I've had parties where they've slept under the table, and even in the bath.'

'Yeah, I know,' said Mann.

'And done a few other things under the table and in the bath,' said Dean. He let out a whoop of laughter and refilled the glasses. 'Cahors – black wine they call it here. Drink up!'

'We're squeezing a couple of Russkies,' said Mann. Again his tone of voice made it sound as if he'd stopped in the middle of a sentence.

'Defectors?' said Dean, helping himself to a slice of goat cheese, and pushing the plate nearer to me. 'Try the tiny round one, that's local,' he said.

'Defectors,' said Mann.

'I guess I always felt a bit sorry for those kids that came over the wall, back in my time,' said Dean. 'They'd toy with their goddamn transistor radios, and admire their snazzy new clothes in front of a full-length mirror. And they'd come along each day, and I'd write down the sentry details or the factory output or whatever kind of crap they thought was worth reporting to us. Then, one day, they'd feel like eating Sunday lunch with Mom and Pop, and suddenly they'd realize there were going to be no more of those Sundays. They'd come over the wall;

111

there would be no more nothing with any of their relatives, or their buddies, or their girls. And they would take it real bad.'

'Is that right,' said Mann.

'And I'd wonder whether it was worth it,' said Dean. 'They were going to get some lousy job in a plastics factory, not unlike the lousy job they had back with the commies. Maybe they would be stacking away a little more bread and listening to their pop groups – but should we have encouraged those kids? Well, I don't know.'

'That's the way you see it, is it?' said Mann.

'That's the way I see it,' said Dean.

'No wonder you were such a lousy field-man.'

'Now you know I was pretty good,' said Dean. 'You know I was.'

Mann didn't answer but I knew he'd signed a few reports that said that Dean had been very good indeed. One of them helped to earn Dean a medal.

'These defectors of ours,' said Mann, 'aren't sitting on sentry-duty timetables, or plastic toilet-seat outputs. This one could slice some balls in Washington, DC.' Mann moved his hand to indicate me. 'My friend here has been heard to express the opinion that it will carve a hole in the hierarchy at Langley, Virginia.'

'You don't mean that someone as high as CIA Special Projects might be involved?'

'They don't call it Special Projects any more,' Mann told him. 'But apart from that, you catch the exact nuance of my colleague's stated belief.'

'Jesus,' said Dean.

The kettle boiled and Dean poured the water on to the coffee. He put milk into a saucepan and lit a flame under it. Without turning round he said, 'I'm really glad, Mickey. Really pleased.'

'What are you talking about?' said Mann.

'This could give you a Class A station, Mickey. Paris maybe. Romp home with this between your teeth, and you'll never look back. Hell, you could get a Division even.'

Dean sat down and watched the coffee dripping through the paper filter. He looked up and smiled at Mann. It was difficult to understand what was going on between the two men. I wondered if Dean guessed the purpose of our visit, and if he thought Mann was going to turn the investigation into a witch hunt through the CIA, with the ultimate aim of securing a high position in it.

'These two commie defectors are stalling,' said Mann.

'There is always that initial inertia,' said Dean. 'In the good ones, anyway. It is only the hustlers who come in talking.'

'Your name cropped up,' said Mann.

Dean watched the milk as it started to bubble and then poured it into a jug. 'I drink it black, like the French do,' he explained. 'But I guess you foreigners might like milk in your coffee. My name what?' He poured coffee into the thick, brown coffee-cups of the sort they use in restaurants because they are so difficult to break.

'Your name was given in connection with the 1924 Society. Your name was offered to us by one of the Russkie defectors. They say you are working for Moscow.'

'Common enough trick,' said Dean. He drank some of the strong coffee. 'Enough people know me as a one-time CIA agent. I guess the story of the foul-up that night in Berlin must be on KGB file.'

'It's probably a standard part of their instruction course,' said Mann bitterly.

'Perhaps it is,' said Dean. He laughed and stroked his beard. 'Well, there you are then.'

'No, there *you* are,' said Mann.

'Do you mean this is on the level, Mickey?'

'That's what I mean, Hank.'

'Working for Moscow . . . you guys must be out of your minds.'

'You haven't asked me what the 1924 Society is,' said Mann.

'I haven't asked you what it is, because I *know* what it is,' said Dean. 'In the early 'fifties I did a 150-page report on the 1924 Society. And don't tell me you didn't read up my file before you came here. I know you better than that.'

It was Mann's turn to look disconcerted. 'No mention of it in your file now,' he said.

'Well, what a coincidence,' said Dean sarcastically. 'It's been mislaid just about the time your Russkies fingered me. Now maybe you'll get your mind back into working condition again.'

'You mean because someone raided your file, we should write you off as innocent?' Mann asked incredulously.

'Right,' said Dean.

Mann dabbed a finger through the tobacco smoke. 'You've been too long with the birds and the bees, St Francis. When we find there's a chapter missing from someone's personal file, the *subject* is the prime suspect. Is it all coming back to you now?'

Hank Dean poured himself a large glass of 'black' wine but changed his mind about drinking it. In a gesture that Sigmund Freud would have appreciated, he pushed it far across the table, out of arm's reach.

'You're wrong,' said Dean. 'You're both making a big

114

mistake. It would be crazy for a man in my position to get involved in any such caper. I'm on French political file . . . probably on local police-records even. I'd have to be crazy to do it . . .' his voice trailed away disconsolately. 'But you don't scare me. You go away and dig up some evidence. Until then, I'll sit here drinking plonk and eating truffles.'

'Not a chance, Hank,' said Mann. 'Make it easy on yourself. Let's do a deal, while we still need a deal. Play hard to get, and I'll harass you until you weep.'

'For instance?' said Dean.

'Tell him,' Mann said.

'Your pension has already stopped,' I said. 'You'll get no cheque this month, unless Major Mann signs a chit for the financial director. The money from the insurance will go on for a few weeks but eventually the insurance company will have a medical report from one of our doctors. He'll certify that your injury is no longer twenty-five per cent debilitating. As you remember, there is no award if the injury is less than twenty-five per cent debilitating.'

'What is this guy,' roared Dean. 'Some kind of speak-your-weight machine?'

'Do you want me to continue?' I asked.

'Go ahead, go ahead,' said Dean.

'The State Department have given us permission to declare your passport void, and make this known to the French authorities in any way we choose. That is to say, we can either tell them that it is invalid, or request them to hold you for using false or forged travel documents.'

'What are you talking about? My passport is real, issued by the State Department only two years back.'

'If the State Department say a US passport is forged,

115

Mr Dean, I don't think you can hope that the French will argue with them.'

'So you'll try to get me Stateside?'

'What did you imagine would happen?' Mann asked him. Dean swivelled to face Mann, his eyes dilated and his teeth bared. He was like some kind of wild animal trapped in a cave, while two hunters prodded him with long sticks – and there was a picture of that in one of my children's books too.

'I'm innocent, goddamn it,' said Dean. He hammered his mighty fist down upon the table so that the crockery jumped high into the air and landed with a rattle.

'Then co-operate,' shouted Mann.

'What do you want me to do?' yelled Dean. 'Dream up some fairy stories for you?'

'It might be a step in the right direction,' Mann growled.

I held up my hands in a gesture of peace-making. 'Now boys, you know the rules,' I said. 'No butting, no kicking, no gouging, and nobody slugs the referee. We've had a skinful of Hank's wine, and he knows he can't get very far, with or without his passport. There's no phone here and by now he probably guesses that we have immobilized his car and ours . . .'

'And I don't mean removing the distributor arm,' said Mann.

'So let's get some shut-eye,' I suggested. I looked to the end of the table where stood the three wine bottles we'd emptied. 'In the morning we can talk some more, and perhaps to better purpose.'

Hank Dean's cottage was built in the three-level style typical of rural buildings in this part of France. The ground floor was a cellar that Hank had converted into a store-room and a primitive sort of bathroom and shower.

Stone steps led up to the front door and the living-room-kitchen-dining-room that opened from it. A creaking old wooden staircase led to the top floor where there were four cell-like bedrooms, with tiny dormer windows, fitted with the sort of bubbly glass that made it look as if the landscape was melting.

No matter what the scientists say, when the moon is full and low upon the horizon it is gigantic. This night, coloured by the earth's dust, the great golden orb looked as if it was about to collide with our planet. From the upstairs window I could see the snow on the hills that faced us across the valley. St Paul Chauvrac is a hamlet of a couple of dozen families, dominated by the houses and out-buildings of two middle-sized farms. Two cottages have fallen into ruin. One of them still has the pink lettering of a *boulangerie*, but that faded many years ago, and now the baker visits three times a week in a corrugated van. There was also a large house, which some hopefuls back in the 'thirties had converted to a hotel and restaurant. But nowadays the Hostellerie du Château provided no more than a clean bed and a wholesome meal. Its management did not strive for stars in the guidebooks they sold in Paris, or for the bright enamel plaques that promise elegance in three languages, but it was popular with travelling salesmen. There were still lights burning at the Hostellerie when we all retired to our respective bedrooms. They were the only lights in the village. I heard a rusty catch being unfastened, and the creak as the next room's window opened. I knew that a man of Hank Dean's girth could not get through it.

I didn't go to sleep. It was cold and I took a blanket from the bed and draped it round my shoulders. I heard the bed in Dean's room creak. He would not sleep; he would think things over and, if Mann's plan came to fruition, he would sit down to breakfast singing like a bird. Or perhaps that wasn't Mann's plan; perhaps that was simply the cosy piece of self-deception that had enabled Mann to jump so heavily upon his old friend's neck.

My eyes must have closed for a few minutes, for I looked at my watch after hearing the noise, and saw it was after 3 A.M. There were no lights in the Hostellerie du Château. The hamlet was in darkness and so was the whole landscape, for by now the moon was down. Again I heard the sound. This time it was not the creak of ancient woodwork but a metallic sound. No more than the slightest vibration, it was a deep chime, like that of an artillery shell being loaded into the breech of a siege gun.

I waited for a minute, wondering if it was the striking of some antique clock that I had not noticed in the house. I wondered if Mann had heard the sounds too. I even wondered whether Mann had made the sounds, and what sort of reaction he'd have if I made the wrong move – or no move at all. Finally I was prompted as much by my own curiosity as by reasoning. I had wedged the door with a piece of paper, instead of using the door-catch, and now I was able to get to the top of the stairs without a sound. But the staircase would defeat me. Dean would know each creaky step, and how to negotiate them but such an obstacle will always betray a stranger. I bent low, and tried to see into the room below. The room was dark but I could just make out the figure of a man standing with his backside resting against the edge of the table. There was a flicker of light from the stove and it lit Hank Dean's face. It was a haggard face and deeply drawn. He was bending low over the stove, as he had been last night cooking the omelette. Again there was a flicker of flame.

118

This time he replaced the circular metal top of the stove so that the flame was fanned by the draught from the chimney. That was the metallic sound that had awakened me.

I jumped down most of the short staircase, and stepped across the tiny room. Dean turned and raised his fist. He was a giant, and now he rose above me like the Statue of Liberty. I took the blow of his fist upon my arm. It hurt but it didn't prevent me wrenching the metal top from the stove. I stuck my right hand into the flames and found the stove filled with papers. There were bundles of papers tied so tight that they would not burn. I smelled paraffin, and, as I started to pull the great handfuls of paper from the stove, it all ignited. There was a 'woof' of flame that licked up round the saucepans and utensils hanging inside the chimney piece. I dropped the flaming bundle, and beat at the flames that were coming from my sleeve.

'You stupid bastard, Hank! Why didn't you tell me?' It was Mann's voice. He switched on the electric light, to help us see the gun he was holding. I beat out the flames on my sleeve, and stamped upon the last remains of the burning papers.

'Don't worry about rescuing that stuff,' Mann said. 'This whole goddamned house is full of it.' I could see now what I was stamping upon. The floor was covered in paper money. There were French francs, Swiss francs, German marks, US bills, sterling and even Lebanese and Australian money. Some of the notes were charred along the edges, some almost completely destroyed, some were crisp, new and undamaged, some were old and dog-eared. But all of them were of high denomination. There must have been one hundred thousand dollars' worth of currency on the floor of that kitchen, and we found at least as much again when we took up the floorboards.

'Get nothing out of a guy within three hours and you'll get nothing for three weeks.'

'If there's anything to get,' I reminded him. It was early. A couple of starlings were pecking at last night's breadcrumbs, and the cows in the next field were moving over to the gate ready to go to the milking shed.

'Do you believe the money arrived by parcel post two days ago?' Mann asked.

'Hank was poor – broke, in fact – naturally he'd try to hang on to it, and hope we'd go away.'

'I would have called CIA Langley within the hour,' said Mann with simple truth.

'You're not natural, and neither am I. And that's why we're investigating Dean, instead of him investigating us.'

'Yeah, well I was wondering about that,' said Mann, and was able to smile at the absurdity of having principles that might cost so much.

'Don't worry,' I said. 'There's no one in Moscow planning to send us a quarter of a million dollars in used paper money.'

'I'm more worried by the chance that Hank Dean will . . .'

'Try to do a deal with the French,' I completed it.

'He wants to stay here,' said Mann. 'And he wants that desperately.'

'Not much in it for the French,' I said. 'A probe into our way of working, a bit of I told you so, but they'd have to give it to us in the end.'

'In the end,' said Mann. 'Yeah, that's the place they'd give it to us. What's it going to cost them – one French passport.'

'And American goodwill.'

Mann made his tobacco noise. 'I hate leaving him down there with those French cops talking to him.'

'Well, let's take another look round this place,' I said. I moved the corner cupboard that was filled with Hank Dean's classical gramophone records. 'The CIA guy from the embassy should be here soon. Then we can go, and take Hank Dean with us, if that's the way you want to play it.'

Mann paced up and down. 'This is a guy who stays in all the time. We can guess that from the mileage clock in the car. He's not running round Europe like a courier.'

'At least not in that car,' I corrected him gently.

'Not in any car,' said Mann tartly. 'Look at him – face fungus, all that hair – he'd stand out like a sore thumb, any place he stopped.'

'I agree,' I said. Mann moved his thinking on a stage. 'So they come here. Same guy or different guy?'

'Same guy – no one knocking on doors asking for Dr Dean in a foreign accent late at night.'

'I buy that,' said Mann. He looked round the tiny room. 'You know something,' he said. 'This is just about the dirtiest, smelliest dump I've ever been in.' He looked at me to get my reaction.

'Well, you're always complaining about the crummy places you find yourself in,' I told him. 'If this is the worst, it must be something for the record books.'

Mann gave me a humourless little smile. 'Look at that frying-pan. It hasn't been cleaned in an age.'

'It's an omelette pan,' I explained. 'You never wash omelette pans, it spoils the surface for all time.'

'I should have known you'd find an excuse for filth,' said Mann. 'Now you're going to tell me the downstairs

121

toilet never has to be cleaned, in case it spoils the surface for all time.'

'I don't spend as much time in the toilet as you do,' I said. 'I get in and get out again, I don't spend a lot of time looking around.'

'Yuck,' said Mann.

'But you start me thinking,' I said.

'You mean you're going to start using laundries and showers, and take a haircut from time to time?'

'Suppose Hank Dean's courier felt the same way about this place that you do.'

'He'd arrive after lunch and take off at tea-time,' said Mann.

'Complicated material,' I said. 'You said it would need six or seven hours of explanation.'

'Well, I'll stick by that,' said Mann.

'So suppose the courier checked in to the Hostellerie.'

'Hostellerie du Château?' said Mann. 'This flea-pit at the end of the alley?'

'No other,' I said.

'You don't imagine he left a forwarding address, do you?'

'I'll take a look if you don't mind, Major,' I said.

'I'll come with you. What have we got to lose.'

The roadway was surfaced in loose gravel. This back road did not even qualify for a French map numeral. Not many cars came along here. Outside the Hostellerie, a battered van was parked, and a mangy dog tried to break from its chain and, having failed to do so, snarled at us. There were two people in the bar, both dressed in greasy black suits. Behind the bar there was a fragile-looking man, in a threadbare shirt and denim trousers. His hair was wispy and grey, and he peered myopically from behind thick, rimless spectacles.

'Two beers,' I said.

He reached behind him, opened a wood-faced refrigerator, found two Alsace lagers and slammed them on the counter. The men in black suits ended their conversation abruptly. The barman rinsed two glasses under the tap and pushed them towards us. 'Visiting the doctor,' he said. It was not a question.

'That's right,' I said. I had already discovered that all the villagers called Hank Dean the doctor. It was probably the way he was referred to on his pension envelope.

'Not many visitors at this time of year,' said the barman. If he had seen the policemen arrive to collect Dean, he was not admitting it.

'I want to talk to you about that,' I said. 'There is one particular friend of the doctor whom we must get in touch with.'

'Oh,' said the barman.

'Came every few weeks,' I said.

'Perhaps,' said the barman.

'Did he stay here?' Mann put the question too hurriedly.

'Are you the police?' said the man.

'Yes,' I said, but Mann had already said no. The barman looked from one to the other of us, and allowed himself that vacuous smile which peasants reserve for government officials. 'A sort of police,' I continued. 'A sort of American police.'

'The FBI?' offered one of the men in black.

'Exactly,' I said.

'What has the doctor done?' asked the barman.

I tried to see in his face whether he would prefer to see the doctor exonerated, pursuing criminals or taken away in a small black van. Unsure of myself I said, 'The doctor is accused of defrauding an American bank.' I turned to

Mann and raised an eyebrow as if seeking his permission to take the old man further into our confidence. Mann, playing along with the game, nodded sagely. I leaned across the counter and said, 'Now we are beginning to think he is innocent. We need to find this man who visited the house.'

'Why won't the doctor tell you?' the man asked.

It was a hell of a good question. 'That's a very good question,' I told him. 'But it's a rule of the underworld. Even when you can help yourself, you never help the police.'

'Of course,' said Mann hurriedly. 'That doesn't apply to citizens. It doesn't apply to people who obey the law, and suffer from the criminals. Especially,' he added archly, 'especially it doesn't apply to licensed innkeepers.'

'The man you seek is young and slim, with hair that covers his ears. He wears the sort of clothes they wear in the Riviera – fancy silk neckerchiefs, tightly tailored trousers that show everything, and cheap imitation-leather jackets of all shapes and sizes and colours.'

'Shut your mouth, you old fool.'

A young man had entered the bar from a door marked 'private'. He was about twenty years old, wearing a large black droopy moustache and dressed in a phoney UCLA sweat-shirt and faded jeans. Around his wrist he wore a studded leather support, of the sort that old prize-fighters sometimes need. 'Tell these people nothing,' he said. 'They are Americans, capitalist police spies . . .'

'Now hold it, son,' said Mann mildly.

I think it was the gentleness of Mann's tone that incensed the boy. Feeling that he was not being taken seriously, he called us pigs, reactionary oppressors and Gestapo. One of the old men at the other end of the bar smiled derisively. Perhaps he remembered the Gestapo.

The boy saw the old man smile. He grabbed my sleeve in an attempt to drag me from the bar. He was stronger than he looked, and I felt a seam give way under his grip.

'Pig, pig, pig,' said the boy as if the physical exertion had driven all reason, and vocabulary, from his head. All the while he was tearing at my coat, so that I must either move with him or watch it tear apart.

I hit him twice. The first punch did no more than position him, head down and off balance, for the hook that sent him flying across the room. It knocked the breath out of him, and he made that sort of whistling howl with which an express train acknowledges a country station. Two chairs toppled with him, and a table was dislodged, before the boy struck a pile of crates and collapsed to the floor.

'Paid cash,' said the barman continuing as if nothing had happened. 'Never cheque, or those fancy travellers' things; always money.'

'Stayed overnight?' I said. I straightened my clothes and sucked the blood off my grazed fist, which hurt like hell. The boy remained on the floor in the far corner. He was blinking and watching us and mouthing obscenities but he did not get to his feet.

'It varied,' said the barman. 'But he seldom had any baggage with him. Just shaving things.'

'Give me the car registration,' I said.

'I don't have that,' said the man.

'Come along,' I said. 'A hotelier who takes clients without baggage, and doesn't make a note of the car registration. I'm sure you'll find it somewhere. I'll pay you twenty francs for it.'

The man reached below the bar to get a battered hotel register. It was a mess of illegible signatures and unlikely addresses. Its pages were creased and ringed with the marks of wine and beer, and goodness knows what else. Hank Dean's guest had not entered his name here but the barman was able to find his own scribbled note of the car registration. He read the number aloud, and I wrote it into my notebook and passed him the twenty francs. He smoothed the note carefully and inspected both sides of it before putting it into his bulging wallet.

'Thank you,' I said.

'There are more,' he said.

'More registration numbers?' I asked.

'Certainly there are.'

'Different ones?'

He nodded.

'Goddamn rental cars,' said Mann.

'Ten francs each,' I bargained.

'Twenty was the price you yourself set,' said the barman.

I looked at Mann. 'But no duplicates,' Mann warned him.

'We'll have the duplicates too,' I contradicted. 'But we must have the dates for each number.'

Page by page the man went through the book until we had a list of dates and numbers going back nearly two years. We finished our beers and drank two more.

'The same registration!' said Mann excitedly. 'That makes four times the same number.' He drained his beer, wiped his mouth and then pulled a face. 'It could be that it's a small rental company, or that he asks for that particular car.'

'I don't think so,' I said. 'Rental companies usually unload their cars every year or two. Those dates are too far apart. Here it is back at the beginning, soon after Dean moved here, and then again last August.'

'Always at holiday times,' said Mann.

'Yes,' I said. 'Always at a time when rental companies might not have a car available. It must be his own car.'

'The first lucky break we've had,' said Mann.

'Mine host feels the same way about it,' I said as we watched the man tucking a small fortune into his wallet. The man looked up and smiled at us.

'Goodbye and thank you,' I said. 'I'm sorry about the boy.'

'My son had it coming to him,' said the barman. 'But there is eight francs to pay for your beers.'

11

It took forty-eight hours to trace the car registration. It belonged to a very old four-door Fiat that for over eight years had been owned by Madame Lucie Simone Valentin, a nurse, born in Le Puy in the Haute-Loire, now residing in Paris, at Porte de la Villette, across the canal from one of the biggest abattoirs in Europe.

This particular part of north-east Paris is not noted for its historical monuments, cathedrals or fine restaurants. Madame Valentin's home was in a nineteenth-century slum, with echoing staircases, broken light-fittings and an all-pervading smell of stale food. It was just beginning to snow when we got there. Across the street two yellow monsters were eating walls and snorting brick-dust. Number ninety-four was at the very top. It was a garret. Painted up, crowded with antique furniture and sited so as to overlook Notre Dame, it would have been the sort of place that Hollywood set-designers call Paris. But this apartment had no such view. It faced another block, twice as tall and three times as gloomy. There was no chance that Gene Kelly would answer the door.

'Yes?' She had been beautiful once. She wore a hand-made sweater that was less than perfectly knitted, and her hair was styled into the sort of permanent wave that you can do at home.

'We would like to talk to you about your car, Madame Valentin,' I said.

'I can explain about that,' she said. 'I thought it would need only new sparking plugs. By the end of the month it will all be paid.' She paused. From the floor below came the sound of tango music.

'We are not from the service station,' said Mann. 'We want to talk to you about Mr Henry Dean.'

'You are Americans?' She said it in good English.

'Chéri,' she called to someone behind her. 'Chéri, it is for you.' To us she said, 'Henry has to be at work at six o'clock.' She pronounced his name in the French manner: Henri.

The concierge had mentioned that a man lived with her. I had expected someone quite different to the pink-faced youngster who now smiled and offered his hand. He was dressed in a newly pressed set of working clothes, a Total badge sewn over the heart.

'I'm Major Mann, US Army, Retired. I work for the State Department in Washington. I'd like to come in and speak with you.'

'I know all about you,' said the boy. 'Dad sent a message. He said he's being held in custody by the police. He said it was all a misunderstanding, but that you guys were straight and you'd do the right thing by him.'

'You're Hank Dean's son?' said Mann.

'Yes, sir, I certainly am,' said the boy. He grinned. 'Henry Hope Dean. Do you want to see my passport?'

'That won't be necessary,' said Mann.

'Come in, come in,' said the boy. 'Lucie darling, get the bottle of Scotch whisky that we were saving for my birthday.'

The room was very clean, and almost unnaturally tidy, like a holiday cottage prepared for new arrivals. And, like such rented places, this was sparsely furnished with cheap bamboo chairs and unpainted cupboards. There were some Impressionist reproductions tacked to the

129

faded wallpaper and a lot of books piled on the floor in stacks.

The boy indicated which were the best chairs and got out his precious bottle of whisky. I sat down and wondered when I'd have enough strength to get up again. It was four nights since either of us had had a full night's sleep. I saw Mann sip his Scotch. I poured a lot of water into mine.

'Who would want to get your father into trouble?' Mann asked.

'Well, I don't know much about the work he once did for the Government.'

'We'll talk to other people about that,' said Mann. 'I mean, amongst the people you know, who would want to see your father in trouble, or in prison or even dead?'

'No one,' said the boy. 'You know Dad . . . he can be exasperating at times, he can be pretty outspoken, and stubborn with it. I suppose I could imagine him getting into a brawl – but not this kind of scrape. Dad was swell company . . . *is* swell company. No one would go to all the trouble of planting a quarter of a million dollars in cash. Why, that's just impossible?'

'It's supposed to look impossible,' said Mann. 'You send a man a bundle of money so big he can't bear to turn it in – then you tell the cops he's got it.' I watched Mann's face, trying to decide whether he already pronounced Hank Dean innocent. He saw me watching him, and turned away.

'Gee, a quarter of a million bucks,' said the boy. 'You'd have to be really sore at someone to leave that kind of bread in his mail box.'

Lucie Valentin came into the room with coffee for us. The cheap crockery was brightly polished and there was a crisply starched linen tray-cover. She put it on the bamboo table, and then sat on the arm of the chair the boy occupied. She put her arm around him in a maternal gesture. 'Perhaps you should go and see your father, darling,' she said. 'You can take the car.'

'If I may be personal,' I said to the woman. 'How did you get along with Hank Dean?'

'I met him only twice,' said Lucie Valentin.

'Lucie wanted to get the whole thing out in the open,' said the boy. 'Lucie and I are going to be married, and real soon, but I've got to make it OK with Dad.'

'And he objects to Lucie?'

'He liked her,' said the boy. 'I know he did, and still does.' He patted her arm, looked at her and smiled. 'But the truth is that Dad would like me to marry an American girl.'

'Really?' I said.

'Oh, sure, Dad comes on very strong about how cosmopolitan he is, but Dad is an American, his French marks him as an American, and he's very self-conscious about that.'

'And your French is fluent?'

'I've grown up here. Most of the people I work with think I am a Parisian. And I think like a Frenchman – it hurts Dad when I say that, but it's true – I could never be really happy in the United States . . . nor married to an American girl.'

He smiled. The way that he'd said 'girl' was a way of saying that he preferred a 'woman'. Lucie Valentin was a lot older than the boy; he didn't have to say that Hank Dean didn't like that either.

'And there is Lucie's divorce,' said the boy. 'That is the real difficulty. The Church doesn't recognize it' – he shrugged – 'and neither does Dad.'

'But your father divorced your mother,' I said.

131

For a moment I thought the boy was angry that I had mentioned it, but he smiled at Lucie, and then said to me, 'He wrote that he was divorced on all the official forms and stuff but the truth of it is that he's always refused to give my mother a divorce – that's what caused all the bad feeling.'

'On religious grounds?'

'Mom said it was easy for Dad to have religious scruples – he didn't want to get married again.'

'But your mother did?'

'They never got on. They separated too long ago for me to remember anything about it but I can never imagine them getting along together. Mom digs the high-life. This guy Reid-Kennedy is just rolling in money. He's always wanted me to take an allowance but I wouldn't feel right about that; after all, he's not even my stepfather.'

'What does he do for a living?'

'He's in electronics.'

I said, 'That can mean anything from repairing a broken TV to walking on the moon.'

'His factories make complicated junk for communications satellites. They did a lot of work for this one French TV use to get live news coverage from the States. And there are the weather satellites too . . . I guess it's not military secrets, if that's what you guys are thinking.'

'You'll be late for the hospital, chéri,' said the woman.

'I'll skip it today,' said the boy. 'I was due to give blood at the hospital on the Boulevard but I can easily do that tomorrow.'

Mann nodded. 'You keep in touch with your mother?'

'We write.'

'When was the last time you saw her?'

'One,' said the boy, 'no, what am I saying, two years ago.'

Lucie Valentin got up from the arm of the chair and walked over to the window and took a sudden interest in the falling snow.

'And she doesn't write or phone?' Mann persisted.

'A couple of times in this last year,' said the boy. 'She's beginning to accept the situation for what it is.'

Lucie Valentin walked back to him and slipped a hand into the pocket of the overalls he was wearing, took his cigarettes out and lit one. It was an intimate gesture and yet it lacked the spontaneity that such actions usually have. He felt it too. 'What's the matter, darling?'

She turned away from him and shrugged. She puffed the cigarette and said, 'Your mother was here yesterday.'

'Are you sure?' he said incredulously.

Lucie still didn't turn. 'Of course I'm sure. She came here looking for you. Of course I'm sure.'

'Take it easy, baby.'

'I'm sorry, darling,' she said in a voice that showed no sign of regret. 'She hasn't accepted anything. She's determined to part us. I dreamed about her last night.'

'You're being silly.'

Lucie Valentin rounded on him. 'I'm not being silly, and don't call me baby.' She opened the handbag that was on the window-sill and produced from it a slip of paper. 'Call her!' said Lucie. 'That's what you want to do, isn't it?'

He didn't take the slip of paper. 'I love you, Lucie.'

She shrugged and turned away.

It was Major Mann who took the slip of paper from her. He didn't pass it on to the boy. He read it himself. Neither of them were aware of us any more.

'You should have told me, Lucie.'

Lucie dabbed at her eyes with a tiny handkerchief. 'She only stayed in France for three hours. She was going

133

back to the airport again. It seemed silly to risk all we have when she was only here for a few minutes.'

'She didn't cross the Atlantic just to pay one short visit,' said the boy. He was flattered by the idea, and his voice betrayed it.'

'No,' she said. 'They are in Europe.'

'This is hotel stationery,' said Mann holding up the note. 'No message, just "Please phone" and the printed notepaper. The Gresham Hotel, Dublin. What would she be doing in Ireland, do you know?'

'No,' said the boy.

'Well, think about it!' said Mann angrily. The tension in the room had got to all of us, and now Mann became unreasonably impatient with the boy. 'Think about it. Is she interested in stud farms or shark fishing? What's she doing in Ireland in the depths of winter?'

The boy shook his head and Lucie Valentin answered on his behalf. 'His mother had come on the Irish Airlines direct flight: Dublin–Paris. She said not to tell her husband about the trip. He thought she was shopping in Dublin, and going to the theatre in the evening.'

'So where the hell was he?' said Mann. 'Crazy kind of vacation where you send your wife to a show alone.'

'She didn't say anything about that,' said Lucie Valentin.

Major Mann reached for his hat and buttoned his coat. 'You're not planning to leave town, are you?'

Neither of them answered but as we went through the door that Lucie held open for us, the boy said, 'She's not trying to part us, baby. Quit worrying about that. It's having secrets from each other . . . that's what does the damage,' and after the door closed they switched to a gabble of French.

From below there came the music of the same tango

that we'd heard when we arrived. Either the autochange was stuck, or they were learning to dance. Mann didn't talk as we went down the narrow stone stairs. Some of the light bulbs were missing and the ones that worked gave no more than a glimmer of light. There is a false gaiety to the tango: it's really a very melancholy rhythm.

It was late afternoon but the low clouds darkened the street so that some of the cars had their lights on. We walked until we got to our rented Mercedes. The thin layer of snow that had collected on it was coloured yellow by the brick-dust of the demolition, and someone had drawn a hammer and sickle in it. Mann defaced it before getting in. Then he operated the wipers to make a clear patch of glass but even as he did so there was a thunderous crash from a collapsing wall and a great cloud of dust enveloped us. We were tightly boxed but Mann shunted us clear and joined the traffic that sped along the rue de Flandres towards central Paris. We were in the Place de Stalingrad before Mann said anything. 'Suppose the kid really is the courier?' he said.

'I can't believe that was all an act. Those two weren't doing all that for us?'

'And the kid's mother?'

'When a professional network makes a mistake, it's always this kind of mistake,' I said. 'It's always a jealous lover or a suspicious wife.'

'Or a cast-off wife who wants to remarry. So you think the wife framed Hank?'

'It was a way of putting pressure on you,' I said. 'It was a way of making you vulnerable.'

'But was it intended to get us off Bekuv's tail? Or is this a red herring – this junk about Dublin?'

'A good question,' I said. He nodded. We both knew that we'd got to go to Dublin – an investigator follows his

135

lead, no matter how much he suspects it might be a false trail.

By the time we got back to the hotel, near the Ministry of the Interior, the snow was getting a grip upon the city. Major Mann strode into the hotel shaking the ice from his raincoat. There was a message awaiting him. It was via the French police. Someone had been trying to reach us urgently. There was a contact phone number. I recognized it as one of the accommodation numbers used by the CIA floor of the Paris embassy. Mann rang it, and the messenger arrived within ten minutes. It had been through the cipher machine but it was enigmatic enough to require explanation.

JONATHAN TO SHOESHINE TRIPLE STAR URGENT.
FABIAN REGRETS PROSPECT DEAN NAMED IN ERROR STOP HE NOW SAYS BETTERCAR CAR RENTALS OFFICE IS IN BOSTON MASSACHUSETTS STOP RED SENDS LOVE STOP BRING COGNAC SIGNATURE JONATHAN ENDS

Fabian was the code name for Andrei Bekuv, and Jonathan was the CIA man responsible for the safety of the two Russians while we were away. 'Bring cognac' was the check code that Mann had arranged with Jonathan personally (different for every message and committed to memory by the three of us). How Red had persuaded security to add a personal message of love was beyond my understanding.

'Did you decode Boston, Mass, for me?' Mann asked.

'Yes, sir,' said the courier. He was a diffident young man. 'I looked it up. It's a little town in Ireland – Drogheda, if that's the way you pronounce it.'

'Drogheda,' said Mann, and nodded. 'And I suppose the code for Boston, Mass, is Drogheda, Ireland.' The courier smiled politely. Mann took the message sheet, and a packet of matches, and made a thorough job of burning the paper to ash. Mann was like that: he liked a chance to show what a well-trained operator he was.

'Is there anything else?' said the courier.

'Henry Hope Dean; I want his blood group,' said Mann. 'He's a blood donor, so it shouldn't be difficult.'

'Drogheda in Ireland,' he said again when the courier had departed. 'Well, the Bekuvs are really talking.'

'Are you going to tell me what Bettercar is, or are we going to play secret agents all evening?'

'Easy baby,' he said, imitating Henry Hope Dean's anxious voice.

'I'm going to eat,' I said. 'See you later.'

'Bettercar Car Rentals is the agreed code for the 1924 Society,' said Mann, 'and I'm buying the drinks.'

12

You turn left out of Dublin Airport, following the Belfast road. Major Mann had arranged for an Irish Special Branch officer to meet us at Drogheda. It was only a twenty-mile drive from the airport and Mann promised to do it in as many minutes, but he didn't count on the narrow, meandering route, the pot-holed surface or on the gigantic articulated trucks that had to reduce speed to a snail's pace in getting through the narrow streets of the villages en route. Nor did he expect the thunderstorm that greeted us. He cursed and fumed all the way. Finally he let me drive.

Drogheda, a colourless town of stone and slate, shone under the steady downpour of rain that in Ireland is called 'a soft day'. A soldier with an automatic rifle and a policeman in a flak jacket sheltered from the rain in the bank doorway. On the wall alongside them there was white spray-can writing: 'No Extradition'.

The Special Branch police inspector was waiting for us with the politeness and patience with which Irishmen meet delay. He was a tall, thin man with fair hair, and was dressed in the sort of dark, plain clothes that policemen wear when they want you to know that they are policemen. He got into the car and sat silent for a moment, wiping the rain off his face with a handkerchief. He removed his hat so that rainwater did not drip into the document case that he now opened on his knees. He found the papers he wanted and tapped them reassuringly. There was a roll of thunder that echoed through the town like a cannonade.

'Mr and Mrs Reid-Kennedy checked into the Gresham Hotel in Dublin four nights ago. His wife stayed there to do some shopping. She checked out yesterday. It's not easy to be sure which nights your man was there with her – the double room was paid for all the time.' He referred to his papers again. 'Mr Reid-Kennedy hired a small van from a hire company in O'Connell Street. He went to a fishing-tackle and sporting-goods shop. They say he didn't buy a shot-gun or ammunition but we can never be sure of that, not in Ireland! He did buy a pair of thigh-length rubber boots. Waders – the sort anglers wear for river fishing. And a waterproof jacket.'

'Rod? Line? Flies?' Mann asked.

'Just the boots and jacket. Then he drove the van up here. He didn't stay at any of the hotels in Drogheda, but two people saw the van he'd hired. A farm labourer saw it being driven back towards town at seven o'clock yesterday morning. He thumbed it, but the van wouldn't stop.'

'Did he identify Reid-Kennedy?' Mann asked.

'Positively. He was disappointed. In this part of the world, people always stop for a hitch-hiker, especially a local man. And it was raining too. Yes, a positive identification.'

'The other?'

'The baker's delivery-man saw the empty van parked in the lane at the entrance to a farm – the O'Connor property. He had difficulty getting past, the lane is very narrow there.'

'Tell me about the farm,' said Mann. There was a sudden crackle of lightning that lit the whole street, freezing every movement with its cruel blue light.

'A syndicate of Germans own it,' said the policeman. 'A farm, beef cattle, about five hundred acres.'

139

There was another rumble of thunder. Down the street came tractors, stray dogs, schoolchildren, dilapidated cars and a religious procession; everyone braved the rain as if they did not notice it.

The policeman put his papers away and locked his case. 'The only thing that bothers me is the petrol. The hire company say he used enough to get as far north as Dundalk, or over the border even.'

Mann grunted and turned to watch a boy on a bicycle. The boy had a shoulder resting against a brick wall, and was flicking the pedals with his toe. 'Where is this O'Connor property?' Mann asked. 'Let's turn it over.'

The policeman looked at the rain. 'There's nothing hard and fast,' said the policeman. 'I'd better telephone Dublin if you want to search.'

'Nothing doing,' said Mann. 'These sort of people we're after could pay a thousand dollars for news about your phone call to Dublin.'

'I'm surprised you trust *me*,' said the policeman irritably.

'I *don't* trust you,' said Mann. 'Now let's get on with it – tell them we're looking for blue films or checking foot and mouth disease, or something.'

Condensation was steaming up the windscreen. The policeman produced a handkerchief and wiped a panel clear. 'Straight up this road,' he said eventually. I turned the ignition key, and after a couple of tries I got the car going. 'The next side road on the left,' said the policeman.

We turned off the main road, and climbed through silent villages and a lonely landscape. The rainwashed hilltops were shiny and unkempt in the afternoon light but the ruins of some long-forgotten abbey were only just visible in the gloomy folds of the valley floor. 'Tell me more about this farm,' said Mann.

'This might not be your man,' said the police inspector. 'This syndicate of Germans – Frankfurt, it was – bought the O'Connor farm about two years ago. There was talk of a stud, and then of flying lobsters to Paris but never did anything come of the talk. People called Gerding live there now – man, wife and grown-up son – people come to see them regularly . . . described as shareholders in the syndicate: well-dressed foreigners come, not just Germans: Americans, a Dutchman, some Swedes and a man who said he was from the Argentine – according to what the taxi-drivers tell us.'

Mann sniffed. 'Sounds like what we're looking for,' he said.

'No neighbours for miles around,' said the police inspector. 'The Gerdings are Protestants – keep themselves to themselves. Hard-working people, the neighbours say. They go into the village for petrol and bread and milk, and into Drogheda once a week for groceries.' He tapped my shoulder. 'We'd better leave the car by the gate. We'll get her stuck in the mud if we try the lane in this sort of weather. Have you got raincoats?'

The farmhouse was on the brow of a hill, with the out-buildings forming a rectangle on the shallower slope to the east of it. The track that was too muddy for our car followed the ridge of the hill. There was a magnificent view from here for anyone prepared to look into the blinding rainstorm. But in spite of the noise of the wind, the dogs heard us. Their barks turned to howls as Mann struggled with the rusty bolt on the farmyard gate.

'Not exactly what the Lufthansa ads would lead us to expect,' said Mann. He clawed at the bolt angrily and its sharp edge took the skin off his thumb. He swore.

The yard was also lacking that sort of orderliness that one expects from a syndicate registered in Frankfurt.

The uneven cobblestones were strewn with spilled feed, matted hay, and puddles of rainwater over blocked drains. The farmhouse door was locked.

'The birds have flown,' said the police inspector, but he unbuttoned his coat and loosened his jacket. It was the sort of thing a man might do if he was reassuring himself about the availability of his pistol.

I tried the window and slid it up without difficulty.

'Hullo there,' shouted the policeman through the open window. The wind blew the net curtain so that it billowed over his face. There was no sound from within the farmhouse but the dogs barked as if in response to the call. I tugged at the skirt of my raincoat so that I could get one leg over the window-sill. The policeman pushed me gently to one side. 'This is my patch,' he said. 'I'm used to the kind of things that might be about to happen.' He smiled.

I suppose all three of us had done that kind of thing before. I covered him. Mann remained outside. We went through every room and inevitably there was the silly feeling when you look under the beds. 'No one at all,' said the policeman as he opened the last cupboard and rapped its wooden interior to make sure there were no hollow sounds. I went over to the window, raised it and called down to Mann in the yard to tell him the house was empty. By that time he'd taken a quick look around the out-buildings. They too were empty. The rain had almost stopped now and from this upstairs window I could see miles across the flat countryside of Kells, to where a dying sun was making a pink sky above the lakes of Meath. I saw the farm dogs too. They were wet and miserable, sitting on the manure heap behind the stables. 'Look at this,' called the policeman from downstairs. I went down to find Mann there too. They were both sifting through the ashes that buried the hearth. They had found some pieces of stiff plastic, about the size of a postcard. A dozen or more of them had fused together into a hard plastic brick. That had prevented their destruction in the flames. Mann picked a small white block from the ashes. 'What's this?'

'A fire lighter,' said the inspector. 'A compound of paraffin wax. They are used to start domestic fires. They'll get the coal or peat going without the need of paper or wood.'

'Is that right,' said Mann. He sniffed it. 'Well this baby didn't ignite. If it had done, we wouldn't have found anything at all.'

'Well, now, you can tell me something,' said the inspector. 'What is this laminated plastic?'

'Microfiche,' said Mann. 'Microfilm's little brother. Microfilm is on reels, and just dandy for someone who goes to a public library to read *War and Peace* but if you want to select your material these are far better.' He prised one of the plastic postcards away from the rest, and held it up to the light so that the policeman could see the fingernail-sized pages of photographed data.

'I'll want to take some of this with me,' said Mann. 'Just a sample. OK?'

'As long as you leave enough for the lab to tell us what kind of material it is.'

'This is all classified material from US Government sources,' said Mann.

'Why here?' said the policeman.

'The Irish Republic is accessible – your passport checks are perfunctory, and now the Russkies have got an embassy here the place is crawling with agents. With Ireland in the EEC, there are few restrictions on Europeans entering. From the United Kingdom, there's no check at all. Come on, feller, you know why.'

'I suppose you are right,' said the police inspector.

'Yes, I am,' said Mann. He put a couple of microfiche cards into his wallet.

'Will you hear those dogs,' the policeman said to me. 'I was brought up on a farm. My father would have sold dogs that fled when strangers entered the house, and howled their lungs out behind the raspberries.'

I got to my feet without answering, and went to the front hall. I picked up the phone, to be sure it was connected, and put it down again. Then I unbolted the massive front door. It must have been a century old and designed to withstand a siege. I stood in the porch and stared out across the fields. Cow dung had been spread across the grassy fields, and a few rooks were striding about and pecking it over. They were fine big birds, as big as vultures, with a shiny blue sheen on their black feathers. But most of the birds were in the sky – hundreds of them – starlings for the most part, wheeling and sweeping, great whirlpools of birds, darkening the pink evening sky, chattering and calling and beating the air forcibly enough to make a constant whirr of noise.

'Phone up your people,' I said finally. 'Get a police doctor and some digging equipment. There will be three bodies, I imagine . . . the people who call themselves Gerding . . . buried where the dogs are baying.'

The policeman said, 'So that's why the dogs are howling out there in the rain. I should have guessed that, I've lived in the country. I'm sorry.'

'Forget it,' I said. 'I've never lived in the country but I know the kind of bastards we're dealing with.'

'This man Reid-Kennedy?' said the policeman.

'Panel truck to move the microfiche machine . . . waders and waterproof jacket to shield his clothes from blood splashes . . . two extra gallons of gas to burn papers, and God knows what other material.'

'But why leave the telephone connected?'

'We're not dealing with teeny-boppers,' I said. 'He didn't want the telephone engineers arriving in the middle of his shenanigans.'

The Irish police inspector said, 'Then your man is a foreigner; an American most likely. Our lads have learned better than to fear interception at the hands of over-prompt telephone engineers.'

Mann looked at him to see whether he was being sarcastic but, having failed to decide, gave no more than a grunt, and turned back to his microfiche. Almost as suddenly as they had begun, the starlings swooped, settled and went silent. Now there was only the sound of the dogs.

13

From the air, it looks like a clutter of fancy boxes, washed up on to a tropical shore. But Miami's ocean was blue and inviting and its sky cloudless. Regardless of all those jokes about the Bahamas being where Florida's rich people spend the winter, arrive in Miami straight from an Irish January and you begin to realize that the oranges are not so stupid.

Downtown Miami may be the usual gridiron of office blocks, shopping plazas, city hall and war memorial. Downtown Miami may be like that, if you ever find it amongst the tower hotels. But the Reid-Kennedys didn't live in downtown Miami, and they didn't live in any of the hotel towers either. They enjoyed a five-acre spread of waterfront, with a Spanish-style eight-bedroom house – and an appropriate number of Spanish-style retainers to keep it polished – a garden filled with tropical flowers and a place to moor the fifty-foot motor cruiser. And if it was the right sort of conversation they needed, they could summon the light-blue Rolls-Royce with the uniformed driver, and go to the Yacht Club which was about one hundred and fifty yards along the waterfront. Mr Reid-Kennedy was still 'on business in Europe' but Mann decided to spread some alarm and despondency through the household.

'If you are a friend of Henry-Hope, we are just delighted to see you,' said his mother. She called her son Henry-Hope. If he'd come back to live with them, he would have become Henry Hope Reid-Kennedy, which sounds like a good reason for staying in Paris.

There was soft music playing and the woman reached behind her to a fluffy pink toy dog and the music went very quiet. I wondered whether that was a product of the Reid-Kennedy radio company. She smiled at us. She was in her middle forties, but a lot of expensive facials, lotions, massages and steambaths had been devoted to keeping her thirty-nine. It had almost succeeded. For some people, middle age brought a softening of the features, but her skin was tight rather than flabby, and there were white lines along the bone of her nose and her jaw. Yet there was no mistaking the beauty that she had once been, and her imperious manner suggested that she hadn't forgotten it either. She stroked the head of a white poodle she was nursing. 'Yes, if you are friends of Henry-Hope, we are just delighted to see you.'

She said it in such a way that we knew that if it turned out that we were not friends of her son, she would arrange for us to be roasted in hell: very slowly. She smiled again as she looked at the heavy woollen suits that Major Mann and I had chosen for a Christmas in Virginia, and at the shapeless tweed hat that Mann had bought at Dublin Airport. She was wearing pale-pink silk lounging pyjamas, with a Dior label twisted to face outwards. The poodle's collar was Gucci.

'You were a major in the American army?' She took a delicate sip at the bright red drink that was in a cocktail glass at her elbow.

'Signal Corps, Ma'am.'

'Oh, Signal Corps,' said the woman as if that explained everything. It was about this time that the servant decided that we were not borrowing money or selling encyclopedias. She departed silently.

147

'Although we have met your son and talked with him, it would be falsely representing ourselves unless I told you that we are here to make inquiries about your husband,' said Mann. He held his hat in both hands and turned it like a steering-wheel.

'About my husband?' she said. There was a note of alarm in a voice that seldom betrayed alarm. She reached for a pink shawl and tossed it round her shoulders in a way that made me feel that we had brought the temperature down.

'Dr Henry Dean,' said Mann.

'Ah, you mean my ex-husband,' said Mrs Reid-Kennedy. She began stroking the poodle, with urgent little movements, quite unlike the measured voice and relaxed smile that she was giving us. 'Do put your hat down, and be seated.' She had that *Gone with the Wind* Dixieland accent, but the low voice made her sound more like Clark Gable than Vivien Leigh.

Mann looked at her full in the eyes for a moment, and then said, 'That's what I meant, Mrs Reid-Kennedy. About Dr Henry Dean, your ex-husband.' He didn't sit down, and he didn't let go of his hat.

'Is he in some sort of trouble?' she asked.

'Yes, he is,' said Mann.

'I'm so sorry,' she said. She frowned, but didn't break down and weep about it.

Mann said, 'He had a lot of currency with him. So far he's not been able to account for it,' Mann shrugged. 'It could all mean nothing – on the other hand it could be serious.'

'And you are from?'

'The Internal Revenue Service,' said Mann. 'I thought I told you that already.'

148

'No,' she said. She wasn't sure whether to be more relaxed or more anxious. 'And what do you do?'

'Are you kidding?' said Mann with a smile. 'You know what the IRS do, Ma'am, we're modern Robin Hoods: we rob the rich and give it to the poor.'

'I mean you personally,' she said. She reached for a box with a coloured photo of kittens on its lid. The label said 'Hand-coated chocolate-covered brandied cherries'. She took a bite out of one so that she could see the inside, and then read the label again. Without looking up, she repeated the question. 'What do you do personally?'

'Now, I'd have to claim the Fifth Amendment on that one, lady, on account of the way I might incriminate myself.' He leered at her, but she gave no sign of having understood. 'In an inquiry like this one . . .' Mann paused, hoping that she would look up at him but she didn't. He continued, '. . . there's a whole lot of purely routine material to be filed. In the normal way of things, I suppose we would have extended the investigation into the business affairs of people associated with Dr Dean. But personally, Mrs Reid-Kennedy, I don't like probing into people's private affairs . . .'

She looked up and waited for him to continue but he didn't continue. She turned to glance through the huge Spanish-style picture window to where the palm trees cut jagged patterns into the blue water of the bay. Then she gave her whole attention to eating the chocolate-coated cherry and waited and waited.

'What kind of business is your husband in?' Mann asked suddenly.

'Electronics,' she said. I had the feeling that she was going to phone her lawyer and say nothing more until he arrived, but if that was in her mind she must have changed it.

149

'Has he always been in electronics?' Mann asked.

'How do I know you are on official business?' she said.

He didn't answer. Finally she said, 'He inherited the business from his father – Reid-Kennedy Radio Components, Inc. It was Douglas who saw the possibilities in electronics. The Chicago factory still manufactures pocket calculators and desk models but most of our business is concerned with very advanced electronic equipment.' She stopped stroking the dog long enough to sip at her drink.

'I appreciate your very complete answer, Mrs Reid-Kennedy,' Mann told her. 'Can I take it that neither you nor your husband have any connections, business or social, with this man Henry Dean?'

This man – that was a good touch. She brightened considerably at that and fluttered her eyelashes. 'None whatsoever, Major,' she said. She frowned as if trying to scrape the very bottom of her memory barrel for us. 'I believe my son, Henry-Hope, has kept in touch with Mr Dean from time to time, but neither myself nor my husband have contacted him personally since the divorce.'

'Since 1955, you mean.' He walked to her.

'Yes, since 1955,' she said and frowned again.

'Have you got a recent photo of Mr Douglas Reid-Kennedy?' Mann asked. He picked up a small photo in a leather frame and looked at it. It was an old sepia-tinted photo of a man in a wing collar and a boy in Bavarian-style shorts and top.

'Where did you get that?' she said.

'Right off your table there,' said Mann.

'It's my husband and his father, a photo taken before the war – he usually takes it with him. It's a sort of lucky piece.'

'Well, looks like this time his luck ran out,' said Mann.

'But anyway I want something recent. A passport shot would do.'

'He hates having his photo taken,' she said.

'Is that right,' said Mann. 'Maybe he was bitten by a little birdie.'

She took the photo from Mann and replaced it on the table. 'Yes, I expect that was it,' she said.

Mann smiled. 'Well, stay loose,' he said, 'we'll maybe be back again.'

'Will you?' she said.

'Just tying up a few routine odds and ends,' said Mann.

She smiled doubtfully, and got to her feet to show us out.

'Thank you again for all your kindness,' said Mann, waving an arm vaguely in the direction of the coffee table which was still as empty as it had been when we arrived, just as the drinks cabinet and cigarette box were no less full.

'It's just too bad we can't get out of this dinner at the White House,' said Mann, walking to the door.

Mrs Reid-Kennedy frowned at him. He stopped, turned and twisted the Irish tweed hat in his hands until she looked at it. Then he turned it inside out, to show her the irregular stitches that held the lining. Already it was coming loose. 'A more leisurely way of life over there,' said Mann. 'I bought that in Dublin yesterday, Mrs Reid-Kennedy.' He put the hat on and smiled.

Mrs Reid-Kennedy wet her lips nervously, and said, 'It's an Irish fishing hat, isn't it?'

Mann's smile came up slowly and beautifully, like the sun rising from the desert. 'Trouble was – that while I went there to do a little fishing, the guy I wanted to see was shooting.' Before she had a chance to reply, he doffed his hat solemnly, took my arm, and we departed.

A CIA courier was waiting at the airport. He'd brought a stage-one interim file on Reid-Kennedy, and another one designated Reid-Kennedy Inc. There was also a computer analysis of twelve years of tax returns – personal and corporate – with more to come. There was also time to feed two dollars into a jovial robot which dispensed cold cheeseburgers in warm Cellophane, and hot, watery coffee in dark-brown plastic cups. Mann wolfed it and said, 'Another one you don't approve, eh?'

'Of the way you handled the Reid-Kennedy woman?'

'You think she guessed what we were after, eh?' he grinned and bit into the cheeseburger.

'You should have unbuttoned your jumper and showed her your CIA teeshirt,' I told him.

'Crude Yankee wrassling, was it? Not the kind of cricket you play at Lords?'

'It might make them run: or it might make them destroy the evidence, shut their mouths and phone the lawyers.'

'Or she might not even mention it to her husband,' said Mann. 'Did you think of that possibility? Jesus, this coffee is terrible.'

He crushed the disposable cup, with the remains of the coffee still inside it. He lobbed it at the bin, so that it hit the swing-top and exploded softly. The wreckage steamed.

'Yes, I thought of that too,' I said.

Our gate number flashed on the indicator. Mann threw away the rest of his cheeseburger, wiped his hands on a paper towel and tossed that after it. 'You want a mint?' said Mann, reaching into his waistcoat pocket for his indigestion tablets.

'I'm getting too old for these formal dinners,' I said.

'I don't even know why you're heading north,' said

Mann. 'You should just stay here with all the senior citizens.'

On the plane we had the first-class accommodation to ourselves. I settled down with the Reid-Kennedy, Inc, file.

The Reid-Kennedy dossier was an American success story: local boy makes good by inheriting his father's factory. The sort of electronic equipment the Reid-Kennedy laboratories designed and made was not secret, they were on sale to anyone who wanted to buy. Included in the dossier there were some beautifully printed booklets that were sent to any potential purchaser, at home or abroad. I read the advertising carefully.

Telephone conversations – and a lot of other communication material – can be all jumbled together. One single wire can carry a hundred or more conversations simultaneously, providing that you have the 'time division multiplex switch' that Reid-Kennedy's laboratories designed (or, the brochure omitted to say, one from some rival manufacturer). These switches chopped the continuous transmissions into pieces one ten-thousandth of a second long, and then reassembled the pieces so that the human ear could not tell that it was receiving only 'tiny samples' of the voice at the other end.

Most of Reid-Kennedy's profits came from telephone users, and latterly from the commercial satellites that, on a 24-hour orbit 22,300 miles away from Earth, appear stationary. Hovering somewhere over Labrador, such satellites link London with Los Angeles. But the big breakthrough when it came would be from a 'time division multiplex switch' that could pack together the wider bands of frequencies that you need in order to transmit TV pictures. Phone users will endure a human voice that sounds like Donald Duck inside a biscuit-tin, but a flawed

TV picture is useless. R.-K., Inc, were working on it, promised the brochure.

'But no military secrets,' said Mann.

'Not that I can see,' I said.

'Does a guy with this kind of gravy moonlight as a hit man?' Mann held the photocopy at arm's length as if trying to discern something new there. 'Does he?'

'I left the ouija board in my other pants.'

'A man running a multi-million-dollar corporation takes a weekend in Europe in order to kill that family in Drogheda?'

'Don't go limp on me,' I said.

'A jury will need a lot of proof – better than an Irish hitch-hiker recognizing a rented car.'

'But you agree Reid-Kennedy must be the one who killed those people in Ireland?'

'You just bet your ass,' said Mann.

'You've a wonderful way with words, Major.'

14

The need for medical care, security and isolation were all met by moving the Bekuvs to the Commodore Perry US Navy Psychiatric Hospital, half an hour's drive out of Newport News, Virginia. There had been a hospital there before the word psychiatry was invented. It was an ugly sprawl of buildings on a desolate site near the water. The north wing was still used as a naval hospital, but all mentally disturbed sailors had been moved out of the inner compound that had been built to hold them. That was now a high security area, used by the CIA for debriefing American agents, interrogating enemy agents, and sometimes for deciding which were which.

A US Navy car met us at the airport. It came complete with uniformed driver and an 'official use only' sign stencilled on the door. Mann fumed, and at first refused to get into the car. 'Did you bring party hats and whistles, sailor?'

'There are no plain cars in the pool, sir,' said the driver. He was an elderly man with Second World War ribbons on his chest.

'Well, maybe we'll take a cab,' said Mann.

With commendable restraint, the sailor refrained from telling Mann that standing outside an airport building arguing with a uniformed sailor was more conspicuous than riding away in an official car. Instead, he nodded solemnly and said, 'The trouble with taking a cab is that they won't let you through the main gate without one of these stickers on the windshield. So you'd have to walk right through the hospital to the inner compound – it's about a mile.'

'OK, smart ass,' said Mann. 'Just as long as you don't use the flashing light and siren.' He got into the car. It didn't have a flashing light, and probably didn't have a siren either.

'You're a lousy loser,' I told him quietly as I got in beside him.

'Yeah,' agreed Mann. 'Well, I don't get as much practice as you do.'

We watched the scenery go past. Mann put his documents case on his knees as if about to do some paperwork, but then put it down again unopened. 'I should never have agreed to them putting the Bekuvs into this nut-house.'

'Calm down,' I said. 'You over-react.'

'How the hell do you know if I over-react – you don't even know what I'm reacting to.'

I decided to let him cool down, but I suppose he wanted to get it off his chest. 'We're losing control of this operation,' he said.

'Speaking personally,' I told him, 'I never had control of it – you did.'

'You know what I mean,' he said. 'I've got these Washington know-alls crawling all over me like bugs. You know what the PAD is?'

'Yes, I know,' I said. The Psychological Advisory Directorate was a cosy assembly of unemployed head-shrinkers who knew how to avoid every mistake that the CIA ever made, but unfortunately didn't tell anyone until afterwards. 'Twenty-twenty hindsight,' said Mann after one of their cryptic admonishments.

'PAD are moving in on Mrs Bekuv. They are taking her down to that farm near St Petersburg and Red

156

Bancroft will be with her.' He reached into his waistcoat, found some Bufferin tablets, and swallowed two without water. 'Headache,' he said. I knew it was that sort of headache that comes through official channels from Washington.

'Red Bancroft,' I said. I looked at him, waiting for some explanation.

'Red Bancroft works for the department – did you guess that?'

'No, I didn't guess that,' I said. 'And I don't remember any prompting from the studio audience.'

'Now don't get mad,' he said. 'I'm disobeying orders by telling you. I'm breaking orders because you're a buddy, and I don't want you caught in the mangle.'

'Why the hell didn't she tell me herself?' I said.

'Me and Bessie have known her a long time,' said Mann. 'She's had a lot of lousy breaks, and it's left her in a tangle – you know what I mean?'

'No.'

He leaned forward and gripped my arm. 'Stay loose. She's a nice girl and I'd like to see her settle down – but not with you.'

'Thanks.'

'For your sake,' he added hurriedly. 'She's a tough girl. She's a damned good operative and she can look after herself. Two years back she infiltrated a Marxist group in Montreal. She nearly got herself killed – she went into hospital for three months – but she put three conspirators into hospital too, and another five into jail. This is a very special kind of girl, and I love her very dearly – but do yourself a favour: move on.'

'She's working for PAD and going down to the farm with Mrs Bekuv?'

'Right,' said Mann. The car slowed as we got to the

157

main entrance of the naval hospital. A sentry checked our identity cards and waved us through to the inner compound where another sentry checked them all over again.

The car stopped outside the eight-storey building that had been designed to house violent patients. Still the faded signs and steel shutters could be seen on the lower floors. Inside there would be that depressing institutional look to it: hard floors, a lack of ornaments, doors that opened automatically and hissed like Japanese slaves, too much light and far too many bright red fire extinguishers. Even the art reproductions on the walls would have been chosen to dull the senses.

'I get out here,' said Mann. 'I'm in the duty-surgeon's accommodation, top floor. You're in the VIP block.'

I looked at him without bothering to conceal my anger. We had exchanged harsher words before, but we'd never come so close to a ding-dong row. I said, 'Which block is Miss Bancroft in?'

'I don't know,' said Mann.

'Then I shall have to phone the gate.'

'She left this morning,' said Mann. 'They moved Mrs Bekuv and Red went with her.'

My bad temper worsened. 'You deliberately moved her so that I wouldn't get a chance to talk with her.'

'Are you telling me I should schedule this caper to fit in with your private life?'

I didn't answer.

Mann said, 'I'll see you over here about nine in the morning. Maybe by that time you'll be in a mood to understand.'

'I understand already,' I said, 'I understand only too well. The PAD are moving in on you. And you are determined to put Professor Bekuv through the wringer and get results before the PAD get anything out of his wife. Yes, I understand. Red Bancroft is attached to PAD and you don't like the idea of me being that close to your opposition. You don't trust me, Major. Well, you've heard of self-fulfilling prophecies, haven't you?'

'Good night,' said Mann. He got out and closed the door.

I brought the window down. 'Do I get an answer?'

'Yes. Grow up,' said Mann. He buttoned up his coat and put on the silly-looking tweed hat, with the brim turned down at front and back. 'And stay away from Miss Bancroft – and that is an order.'

I watched him as he marched into the lighted entrance. The two sets of glass doors opened automatically, but beyond them I could see the newly painted graticule of prison bars, and an armoured booth for the doorman.

They'd provided me with the comparative luxury of a four-room house normally occupied by a US Navy captain, who was away on detachment to CINCLANT for a couple of months. His books and his furniture were still there. I had no doubt that this was the accommodation intended for Mann, until he swopped it for the cramped duty-surgeon's rooms that were so close to Bekuv.

I was tired, very tired. I thanked God for America, where even the poor-house probably has heated bathrooms. I opened my travelling bag and dumped my dirty linen into the laundry basket. Then I undressed and stepped into the shower. I stood there a long time, letting the hot water hammer at my muscles, and finished with water cold enough to make my teeth chatter. I grabbed the towel from the warm rack and wrapped it round myself before going into the kitchen. I set up a cup and saucer, filled the kettle and plugged in. While I waited for it to boil, I admired the captain's library. There were a lot of high-powered psychiatry books, papers and bound volumes. There were war memoirs, too, a Shorter Oxford Dictionary, and Dickens and Balzac, and a collection of very old volumes about chemistry.

I walked into the bedroom. It was a large room with a double bed. On one side of the room there were large wardrobes, the doors entirely covered by tinted glass. Standing in front of the mirror there was a tall slim woman; she was naked except for a triangular frill of black silk. It was Red Bancroft and she smiled, pleased that her joke had worked so well. Her smile became a different sort of smile as she watched me examining her nakedness. She was beautiful. I began to tell her so but she came towards me and put her fingers to my lips. With the other hand she loosened the damp towel from my waist and let it drop to the floor. She flinched as we embraced and she felt the cold water against her skin. My wet hair cascaded droplets over her face. We kissed, and she tightened her arms round me. I could not resist a glance at our reflection as we began our lovemaking.

Hardly had we started than there was a shrill scream. Red struggled under me but I held her. 'It's the kettle,' I said. 'It's sure to have a safety switch.' She sank back across the bed smiling. And in due time there was the reassuring plop of the kettle's switch.

We exchanged no words, apart from incoherent cries and murmurs, and afterwards, when she got out of bed, I pulled the blanket over my shoulders and settled my head into the down pillows. I was almost asleep by the time she reappeared. I was amazed to see her fully dressed.

'What's going on?' I said.

She sat down on the bed and looked at me as if seeing me for the first time. 'I must go.'

'Go where?'

She looked at her watch. 'We are moving Mrs Bekuv. I must be ready.'

'Nice timing,' I said.

'Don't be bitter.'

'Do you have to go?'

'Do *you* have to do the job you do,' she retorted. 'This is my job and I'm damned good at it, so don't treat me like the little woman.'

'So why not tell me about your job?'

'Did you tell me about your job – no, you didn't, because you're a secret agent –'

'What's this all about?' I said. I sat up.

She stretched her hand and touched my shoulder. 'I'm telling you goodbye,' she said. She shivered as if in apprehension.

'Goodbye for now, you mean?'

'I mean goodbye, goodbye.'

'Just for the record,' I said. 'Am I using the wrong brand of toothpaste?'

'Nothing personal, my darling. For a time you really had me going. Bessie Mann was asking me how many kids we were going to have, and I found myself looking at recipe books and baby carriages.'

I looked at her, trying to decide what could account for this resolute farewell.

'Don't try to puzzle it out, darling,' she said, and leaned over and gave me a sisterly kiss on the forehead. 'I planned it that way.'

'Only a woman would plan to say goodbye in bed,' I said.

'Don't believe it, baby. I've had the kiss-off that way, more times than I care to remember.' She got to her feet, and opened the wardrobe to get her suede overcoat. For a moment I thought someone was standing inside the wardrobe; but there were only two naval captain's uniforms in cleaner's transparent covers. She put her coat on carefully, watching herself in the mirror as she buttoned it.

I got out of bed and pulled on one of the captain's dressing-gowns. It was a little too short for me, but at the time I didn't care. Red Bancroft went into the lounge and picked up a large suitcase, opened the front door and placed it outside. She turned back to me. 'Look, darling, forget what I said just now – let's not part this way.'

'Why don't you tell me what this is all about?'

'There isn't time.'

'I'll make time.'

'And I'm too mixed up to know myself. Let me take a rain-check.'

'On a love affair?' I said.

'Please.'

Before I could answer, there were voices at the door and two men barged in. They were a tough-looking couple, with longish hair and denim jackets. But the hair was recently washed and carefully parted, and the denims were cleaned and pressed, so that the men looked like the sort of college lecturers who smoke pot.

'Scram,' I told them.

They didn't spare me more than a glance. To Red Bancroft one of them said, 'Is that your only bag?'

She pointed to another large case and then turned to me. 'I've got to go.'

'Who are these creeps?'

One of the men turned to me and said, 'You sit down and shut up and you won't get hurt.'

'I see.' I said it as passively as I could, and waited until he bent down to pick up Red's case before lifting the back of his jacket with one hand, while the other hand snatched the pistol from the holster he wore on his belt. 'Now let's try all over again,' I said, as he dropped the case and swung round at me. I'd already stepped far enough back to avoid any such counter action, and while he was still off balance I stepped forward and kicked the side of his knee, hard enough to make him yell. Without waiting to see him massaging the graze, I steered the Magnum to where the other one was standing. Even before I said anything he raised his hands. 'High,' I told him. 'Keep those hands very, very high.'

I went round the back of him and found his gun too. 'You've got to be quicker than that, if you want to keep your gun that far round your belt,' I told them. 'Now let's see who you are.'

'You know who we are,' said the first one. 'What do you think we are doing in this security area?'

'Keep your hands in the air, fatty,' I said, 'or I'll come over there and give you a bruise in the other leg.'

'We're CIA,' said the second man. 'We're moving Mrs Bekuv.'

'Well, why didn't you say so,' I said sarcastically. 'And then I would have known that I was being threatened by goodies.'

He didn't answer.

'Let's have your social security cards,' I said. CIA men rarely carry identification papers but they are assigned a special batch of social security numbers that enable them to be identified by fellow operatives, and also by the social security computer if they are found floating in the harbour.

Reluctantly the two men reached for their wallets. They did it one at a time, and very, very slowly. All the time Red Bancroft watched the fiasco, but said nothing.

Neither did the expression on her face give an indication of her feelings, until she said, 'All right, children, you've all had your fun. Now let's get on with the job.'

'OK,' I said. I threw the Magnum back to its owner. His catch was so clumsy that he bared a knuckle on it. I noticed that he pulled the holster round to the front before putting the pistol back into it. 'Now beat it while I say good night to the lady.'

They went. They picked up the wallets from the table where I'd left them, walked over to the door and left, closing it behind them. There was the sudden noise of a helicopter engine. Red went across to the window. Over her shoulder I could see some lights and activity and then I heard the helicopter's rotors turning as the clutch was engaged. Red Bancroft said, 'Mrs Bekuv swims in the big indoor pool every morning before breakfast. This morning we'll put her in the chopper and be down in St Petersburg, Florida, before it's time for brunch.' She turned away from the window and put one arm round my waist and hugged me. 'Are you going to give me a second chance?' she asked.

I kissed her. She picked up her case and went to the door. I heard the voices of the two men and then the sound of a car engine. Soon after that the helicopter roared and lifted up over the roof tops. I still hadn't answered her.

15

Mann gave Mrs Bekuv no time to say goodbye to her husband: that was all part of his scheme. We sat in Mann's little office – originally intended for the duty nurse – and heard Andrei Bekuv walk down the corridor, calling his wife's name.

Mann sat hunched over a desk in the corner, watching the dark storm-clouds come racing in from the Atlantic. The rain beat upon the windows and the morning was so dark that Mann needed the desk light in order to read. He looked at me and winked as Andrei Bekuv came back.

'Here we go,' said Mann softly.

Andrei Bekuv was silhouetted against the brightness of the corridor lighting as he opened the door and looked in on us.

'Where is my wife, Major Mann? She wasn't at breakfast, and she's not swimming. Do you know where she has gone?'

'We've moved her to Baltimore,' said Mann without looking up from the papers he held under the desk light.

'When? When was this?' said Andrei Bekuv. He was jolted, and he scowled and looked at his watch. Bekuv was a creature of habit. Breakfast at seven, coffee at ten, a light lunch at one, dinner at seven thirty, in time for him to finish his meal and be in the armchair, with hi-fi tuned, ready for the evening concert. He insisted that the supply of vitamins in his medicine cabinet be replenished

without his having to ask for them, and he liked decaffei-
nated coffee, served demi-tasse, in the evening, with
fresh cream. And he liked to know where to find his
wife.

'When?' repeated Bekuv.

'Oh, some time early this morning.' Mann turned the
desk clock round to see it better. There was a barometer
fitted into it and Mann tapped that. 'They should be
there by now. Do you want to phone her?'

'Yes,' said Bekuv.

Mann picked up the phone and went through a panto-
mime of asking for a number in Baltimore. He thanked
someone at the other end. And then hung up. 'Seems
like we can't get through to Baltimore from here.'

'Why not?'

'I didn't think to ask. Do you want me to call the
operator again?'

Bekuv came into the room and sat down. 'What game
are you playing now, Major Mann?'

'I might ask you the same question, Professor Bekuv,'
said Mann. From the clutter of papers and objects on the
desk in front of him, Mann selected a large brown
envelope. It contained something lumpy. He passed the
envelope to Bekuv. 'Take a look at that, for example.'

Bekuv hesitated.

'Go ahead, take a look at it.'

Bekuv handled the envelope as if it might explode. I
wondered afterwards if he guessed what was inside it. If
he did, he was in no hurry to see it again. Finally, he
ripped the edge of the envelope far enough to slide the
contents out. There was a transparent plastic evidence
bag with some typewritten labels attached to it. Inside
the bag there was a flick-knife.

'The police sent that over here yesterday afternoon,

Professor Bekuv. It was found near the steps of the church, during a search made during the early hours of Christmas morning. You remember Christmas morning?'

'It's the one used to wound my wife,' said Bekuv. He didn't open the bag. He dropped it back into the envelope as if it might have carried traces of some fatal contagion. He tried to pass the envelope back to Mann but the major would not accept it from him.

'That's right,' said Mann.

'What's it supposed to mean?' Bekuv demanded.

'Supposed to mean?' said Mann. 'I'm glad you said supposed to mean, because there's often a world of difference between what things mean, and what they are supposed to mean. For instance,' said Mann, 'that's the knife that caused your wife's wounds. Whether she was trying to knife you with it, or preventing you knifing her with it, or whether you were both trying to cut each other, or even turn it on yourselves, I wouldn't be too sure.'

'A man assaulted us,' said Bekuv.

'Yes, sure, that's the other theory isn't it? Didn't I mention that one? Forgive me.'

Bekuv looked at his watch. Whether he was thinking about his wife arriving in Baltimore, about his ten o'clock coffee or simply indulging in displacement activity that helped him gather his wits, there was no way of telling.

Mann picked up some papers from his desk, read for a moment or two and then said, 'Those gloves your wife was wearing . . . a shop in Fifth Avenue sells them for twenty-eight dollars a pair and advertises them as real kid, but in fact they make them from the skin of sheep. Now, that's the kind of dishonesty I hate. How about you, Professor?'

The professor did not commit himself: he grunted.

Mann said, 'Sheepskin. To make a pair of gloves like that, the tanning process removes the epidermal layer . . .' Mann was reading from the paper '. . . to expose the corium minor or grain layer. It is the nature of this grain layer that enables a scientist to distinguish the age, sex and species of animal from which the skin originated.'

Professor Bekuv said, 'I'm not interested.'

'Hold on, Professor. I'm not through yet. It gets better. Did you know that the grain pattern from any piece of animal skin is as individual to that animal as a fingerprint is to one individual man?'

'What of it?'

'I'll tell you what of it,' said Mann. He put the papers back on his desk, turned to Bekuv and smiled. 'The police forensic lab took leather prints off that knife. They say it was wielded by your bride. They say her Fifth Avenue gloves left prints on that knife as clear and as evidential as if she'd used her bare hands.' Mann picked up another evidence bag that contained the gloves, and dropped it back on to the desk again. 'The police say your wife knifed herself, Professor. And they say they can prove it.'

Bekuv looked away.

'Anyway,' said Mann, breathing a sigh. 'The fact of the matter is that the investigation is closing as far as you are concerned. My people have lost interest in you – you've cost the American taxpayer too much money already. You'll be allowed to live wherever you like – within reason – but you'll have to find a place for yourself . . . the same goes for getting a job. No chair at NYU. You will have to read the vacancies in the papers. For the time being the two of you are being kept separate but that's for your own protection. My people say that there will be more chance of your KGB squads killing you if you are together. Next year, of course, the danger will have subsided a little. By then there will probably be no objection to your living under the same roof again.'

'Now wait a minute . . .' said Bekuv.

'Sorry it had to be this way, Professor. As your wife understood so well, this could have been a big one for us.' He smiled to show that he held no ill feelings. 'You'll be able to keep the hi-fi and the recordings and stuff of course.' He picked up papers from his desk and tapped them edge-down on the desk to tidy them.

It was only then that Bekuv seemed to become aware of my presence in the dark corner of the office. He turned to me. 'Is Miss Bancroft with my wife?' he asked.

'That's right,' I said. 'She'll be with her for a little while.'

'How long,' he said. 'I don't want my wife to be with Miss Bancroft.'

'No one tells me anything, Professor,' I said.

Mann said, 'Your wife wanted Miss Bancroft along for company.' Bekuv nodded. Mann had been making a great play of rummaging round his desk and, as Bekuv turned to leave, he suddenly produced a flimsy sheet of paper, waved it and said, 'Oh, this is something for you, Professor. It's a copy of a letter to your wife.'

He passed it to him. It was a carbon copy of a letter. There were a couple of official rubber stamps on it and a paper-clip. Bekuv took it without a word, and moved over to the window to read it by the grey morning light. He read it aloud in his careful English . . .

'Dear Mrs Bekuv, This is to confirm our conversation of yesterday. As promised, I have applied for the necessary documents in connection with your immigration and naturalization. You will appreciate that, although you have been admitted to the USA under the special provisions

169

granted to certain government agencies, your continued stay and permission to take up gainful employment must remain subject to the usual procedures. Yours truly . . .'

'Just a lot of legal evasions and doubletalk,' pronounced Bekuv when he finished reading.

'I quite agree,' said Mann, who had invented it and typed it.

Professor Bekuv put the flimsy copy back on to Mann's desk. Bekuv had been close to the security business long enough to understand such a message.

'You're going to send us back to Russia?' said Bekuv. He walked across the room and opened the door a fraction so that there was a bar of blue fluorescent light cutting him into two halves. 'Either we do exactly as you demand, or you will send us back to them.'

Mann didn't answer but he was watching Bekuv's every move.

'This letter is just the beginning,' said Bekuv. 'It is typical of you, Major Mann. You'll let your official government departments carry out the execution for you. Then you will be able to say you had no hand in it.'

'You've got it a little bit wrong haven't you, Professor? The US immigration department has no executioners on its payroll. These executions you want to make me responsible for will be carried out after you return. They'll be carried out by your little old KGB comrades. Remember the KGB, Professor? Those wonderful people who gave you the Gulag Archipelago.'

'You have never lived in the Soviet Union, or you would know how little choice a man has. The KGB ordered me to work for them – I did not volunteer to do so.'

'You're breaking my heart, Professor.'

Bekuv stood in the doorway, with the door to the

corridor open just an inch or two. Perhaps he wanted to let enough light into the room to be able to see the expressions on our faces.

'Is that all you have to say, Major Mann?'

'I can't think of anything else, Professor . . . except maybe farewell.'

Bekuv stood in the doorway for a long time. 'I should have told you about the place in Ireland . . . I should have told you earlier.'

'You jerk,' said Mann. 'Three people died.'

'I was with the trade delegation in London,' said Bekov. 'It was years ago. I had to meet a man from Dublin. I met him only once. It was at Waterloo Station in London. He had some documents. We used the copying machine on the station.'

'The maser programme?'

'We were falling behind,' said Bekuv. 'This man brought drawings and calculations.'

Mann pulled the desk light so that it shone on to a bright blue blotter. Under the light he arranged a row of photos. One of them was a passport picture of Reid-Kennedy. 'Do you want to come here a moment, Professor.' Mann's voice was precise and quiet, like that of a terrified parent coaxing a small child away from an electrified fence.

'He wasn't a scientist,' said Bekuv, 'but he understood the calculations.' He walked over to the desk and looked at the photos arranged neatly like winning tricks in a bridge game. Mann held his breath until Bekuv placed a finger on the face of Reid-Kennedy.

Mann shuffled the pictures together without commenting on Bekuv's choice. 'And the KGB were running the operation?'

'Entirely,' said Bekuv. 'When the maser programme

was given a shortened development target, the KGB became responsible. I'd been reporting to the KGB since my time in university and I was a senior man in the maser programme. It was natural that the KGB chose me. When the scientific material started to arrive from America, the KGB told me that I would get it first, and that the department would not be notified.'

'That gave you a chance to shine,' said Mann.

'It was the way the KGB always did such things. They wanted their own people promoted, and so they gave their own men the best of the foreign intelligence material.'

'And no one suspected? No one suspected when you went into the lab next morning and shouted eureka?'

'It would have been a reckless fool who voiced such suspicions,' said Bekuv.

'Jesus,' said Mann sourly, 'and you corrupt bastards have the nerve to criticize us.'

Bekuv didn't reply. The telephone rang. Mann picked it up and grunted into it for a minute or two before saying goodbye.

'Why don't you take a coffee break, Professor,' said Mann.

'I hope I've been of help,' said Bekuv.

'Like a good citizen,' said Mann.

'I will be happier,' Bekuv said, 'when I can read what those duties are, on the back of a US passport.' He didn't smile.

'We're going to get along just fine, Professor,' said Mann.

Neither Mann nor I spoke until we heard Bekuv go into his room and switch on the radio. Even then we observed all the usual precautions for not being overheard.

'It was her all the time,' said Mann. 'It was Mrs Bekuv.

172

We had it the wrong way round. We thought he was clamming-up.'

I said, 'Without his wife, he'll be singing his way through the hit parade by weekend.'

'Let's hope so,' said Mann. He went over to the light-switch and put the lights on. They were fluorescent tubes, and they flickered a dozen times before filling the room with light. Mann searched the drawers of his desk before finding the box of cigars his wife had given him at Christmas. 'Makes you wonder what kind of hold she had over him,' said Mann. He lit the cigar and offered the box to me. Already half the contents had been smoked – I declined.

'Perhaps he loves her,' I said. 'Perhaps it's one of those happy marriages you never read about.'

'I hate those two Russian bastards,' said Mann.

'Having his wife join him was the worst thing that happened to this investigation,' I said.

'Right,' agreed Mann. 'Just a little more help like that from Gerry Hart, and I fall down dead.'

I looked at my watch and said, 'If there's nothing else, I've got a call booked to London.'

Mann said, 'And it looks like another trip to Florida tomorrow.'

'Oh, no!' I said.

'That phone call just now – the CIA duty-officer at Miami Airport. Reid-Kennedy just got off the London direct flight. His chauffeur met him with the Rolls – looks like his old lady was expecting him.'

'What time do we leave?'

'Give the Reid-Kennedys a little time to talk together,' said Mann. 'What about the six A.M. plane tomorrow morning. Leave here at four thirty.'

16

It wasn't the same when we went back: it never is. The gardener was having trouble with the sprinklers, one of the cars had scraped the fencing and taken away a section of bougainvillaea. Crab grass was in the lawn, the humidity was high and there was haze over the sun.

'Mr and Mrs Reid-Kennedy are not at home,' said the Spanish lady slowly and firmly and for the third time.

'But that's not what we were asking,' explained Mann patiently. 'Are they in? Are they in?'

I suppose even the ladies who guard rich people's doors learn to recognize the ones who can't be stopped. She let Mann push her to one side but she failed to look as if she liked it.

'You know we're cops,' said Mann. 'Let's not fool about, shall we.'

'They are not here,' said the woman sullenly.

He looked at her as if seeing her for the first time. He ran his fingers up his cheeks as if trying to force himself to smile. 'Listen, did I ever tell you that I moonlight for the immigration department?' he said. 'You don't want us to run all through the house, checking out whether all these people have got permission to work in Florida. You don't want that, do you?'

The lady went as pale as an illegal Mexican immigrant without working papers can go, and then shut the door gently, behind us.

'Now, where are they?'

'On the *Sara Lee*,' said the woman pointing to the big

motor-boat that was moored to the jetty at the end of the enormous garden.

'*Sara Lee!*' said Mann very respectfully. 'And there's me been calling it the *Aunt Jemima* all the time.' He smiled at her and she forced a smile back at him. 'Well, you just make sure no one leaves the house, Duchess, or . . .'

We walked through the breakfast-room. It faced the lawn and the water. The remains of a breakfast were still on the white marble table. There were half a dozen different kinds of bread, a couple of uneaten boiled eggs and a silver dish loaded with crisp rashers. Mann picked up a piece of bacon and ate it. 'Still warm,' he said, 'they must be there.' He went out on the balcony and looked at the boat. There was no sign that it was about to depart. In the distance across the water I could see the Goodyear airship glinting silver against the clear blue sky.

'What the hell would they be doing down there in that boat,' muttered Mann. 'They aren't the kind of couple who enjoy decoking diesels together.'

I said, 'If you've got a dozen servants in the house, I guess you need a long garden, and a moored boat, to go and have an argument.'

I was opening the fly-screen that separates the polished oak balcony from the raked gravel back-drive, when I heard a woman shout. Then I saw Mrs Reid-Kennedy. She had already come down the gangway from the boat, and was hurrying towards us across the lawn. She was shouting.

'Hey there, what do you want? What do you want?' She almost tripped. She was wearing the same sort of silk lounging pyjamas that we'd seen her wearing last time, except that these were pale green, like the silk scarf she had tied round her head. But a lot of that Southern belle

175

had disappeared. That you-all eyelash fluttering, and help yourself to the candied-yams gesturing, had now been replaced by a nasal tone and shrillness that was saurbraten, schweinkotelett and sour cream, and all the way from Eighty-Second Street.

She was speechless when she reached us. She put a hand on her chest while she caught up on her breathing.

'You shouldn't run like that, Mrs Reid-Kennedy,' said Mann. 'A woman of your age could do herself a permanent injury running across the lawn like that.'

'You will have to come back,' she said. 'Come back another day. Any day you like. Phone me and we'll fix it.'

'Unless of course the kind of injury that you might do yourself by not running across the lawn is even more permanent. Then, of course, it would make sense.'

'We'll talk in the house,' she said. 'We'll have coffee.'

'That's mighty civil of you, Ma'am,' said Mann. 'That's right hospitable of you.' He touched his hat at the end of the peak. 'But I think I'm going to just nosey down to the levee there and see if I recognize anyone aboard the paddle-steamer. You see, I've always been a gambling man.'

'You're too late, Major Mann,' she said. Her voice was neither frightened nor boastful. She said it as if she was stating a fact that could not be argued, like the number of kilogrammes in a ton, or the weight of a cubic metre of water.

'You had better tell us about it, Mrs Reid-Kennedy.' His voice was gentle, and he took her arm, to support her weight.

'If I talk to you, will you promise that it is in confidence? Will you promise not to do anything . . . at least for the time being?'

176

'Well, I couldn't promise that, Mrs Reid-Kennedy. No one could. I mean, suppose you told us about a plot to assassinate the President of the United States. You think we could listen to you and keep a promise about doing nothing?'

'My husband was a good man, Major.' She looked up, into Mann's face. 'I mean Douglas was . . . Mr Reid-Kennedy.'

'I know that's who you mean,' said Mann. 'Go on.'

'He's in the boat,' she said. She didn't turn round far enough to see the twelve-ton cabin-cruiser, but she pointed vaguely at the waterfront. 'Douglas went down to the boat about half an hour ago. I thought something was wrong, so after the bacon was almost cold . . . Douglas loves bacon when it's crisp and warm but he never eats it when it's cold . . .'

'OK, Mrs Reid-Kennedy.' Mann patted her arm.

'And bacon is so expensive nowadays. The servants could have it, of course, but none of them eat it either.'

'Go on, about Douglas.'

'Well, that's all,' she said. 'I found him on the boat, just now. He's shot himself. He's lying there in the engine-room . . . the top of his head . . . I don't know who will clear it up. There's blood everywhere. Will the police know someone who will do it? I couldn't go down there again.'

'No need, Mrs Reid-Kennedy. No need to go down there again. My friend will take a look in the boat just to make sure that there are no valves open, or anything like that. While you and me go up to the house, and get you a stiff brandy.'

'Do you think I should, Major? It's not even eleven thirty yet.'

'I think you need one,' said Mann firmly.

She shivered. 'My, but it's turned cold suddenly,' she said.

'Yes it has,' agreed Mann, trying to look suddenly cold.

'It's telling the servants that's the real trouble,' she confided.

'Don't worry about that,' said Mann briskly. 'My friend will do that. He's British; they're terribly, terribly good at speaking to servants.'

Many American soldiers kept their guns after the war. It was bad luck for the woman who found him that one-time Master Sergeant Douglas Reid-Kennedy, US Army Military Police, had been equipped with the M 1911 automatic pistol. Even if you can't take it with you, a .45-inch bullet still makes an expensive way to blow your head apart.

He was a big man, and it was easy to imagine him as a military cop, in white helmet liner, swinging a stick. Now his body was twisted, face up, his arms spread as if to keep himself from falling into the oily bilges between the beautifully maintained twin diesels, where he now lay sprawled. The floral patterned Hawaiian shirt was open to reveal a tanned hairy chest. He wore smart canvas shoes with the yachtsman's grip-sole, and around his tailored shorts there was an ancient leather belt with a sailor's clasp-knife hanging from it.

The back of his skull had exploded, so that there was blood, brain and bone fragments everywhere, but most of his jaw was still there, complete with enough teeth to get a positive identification from his dental records. He must have been standing in the lounge at the fatal moment, with one hand on the stair-rail and the pistol in his mouth. The force of it had thrown him down the steps into the engine-room. I suppose he'd been taking a last look at the mansion, and the gardens, and perhaps at his wife breakfasting. I looked at the jetty and the lie of the land and tried to stop thinking of the different ways I could have come and killed him unobserved.

I went to the forward end and sorted through the radar and depth-sounding gear. It was all very new and there were screw-holes and paint-lines to show where previous models had once been. Owning the most modern electronics had now become more prestigious for a yachtsman than having a few extra feet of hull or even a uniformed crew, providing of course there was a distinctive aerial for it somewhere in view.

Douglas Reid-Kennedy had left his zipper jacket draped over the throttles. It was blue nylon, with an anchor design and the word 'captain' embroidered on the chest. And it had two special oilskin pockets, in case you were the sort of captain who fell overboard with the caviar in your pocket. In one of the pockets there was a briar pipe, with a metal windguard, and a plastic tobacco pouch with a Playboy bunny on it. In the other pocket there was a wallet containing credit cards, yacht-club membership cards, a weather forecast from the yacht club, dated the same day, a notebook with some scribbled notes, including radio wavelengths, and a bunch of keys.

Keys can be of many different shapes and sizes, from the large ones that wine waiters wear round their necks in pretentious restaurants, to the tiny slivers of serrated tin that are supplied with suitcases. The keys from Douglas Reid-Kennedy's yachting jacket were very serious keys. They were small, circular-sectioned keys, made from hard, bronzed metal, each with a number but without a manufacturer's name, so that only the owner knew where to apply for a replacement. It was one of

179

these keys that fitted into the writing-desk in the boat's large, carpeted lounge.

I sat down at the desk, and went through the contents carefully but he wasn't the sort of man who was likely to leave incriminating evidence in his writing-desk. There was a selection of papers that one might need for a short voyage. There were photostats of the insurance, and several licences and fishing permits. In a small, and rather battered, leather frame there was the sepia-coloured photograph that Mann had remarked upon during our previous visit. It was a glimpse of a world of long ago. Reid-Kennedy's father, dressed in a dark suit, with a gold pin through his tie, sat in front of a photographer's painted backdrop. One wrinkled hand rested upon the shoulder of a smiling child dressed in Lederhosen. I took the photograph from its frame. It was mounted on a stiff card that bore the flamboyant signature and address of a photo studio in New York City. It had the superb definition of a contact print; the sort of quality that disappeared with the coming of miniature cameras and high-speed films.

I looked at the photo for a long time. The informality of the child's clothes could not conceal the care and attention that had preceded this visit to the photographer. Nor could the stern expression on the face of the man conceal an immense pride in his handsome son. And yet the shutter had caught a moment of tension in the boy's face as he stiffened in the embrace of his autocratic father. There was an element of tragedy in the gulf between them and I wondered why this was the picture that the son had carried in his personal baggage for so many years.

There was a book-shelf above the desk. I flipped through the usual array of books about knots and flags, and 'vessels running free giving way to vessels that are close-hauled'. There was a visitors' book, too: a beautiful leather-bound volume, kept in neat handwriting and dutifully signed by the Reid-Kennedys' guests. Some of the pages had been roughly torn from it, and I noted those dates.

Then I replaced everything I'd moved, and wiped the things I'd touched, and walked back to the house where Mrs Reid-Kennedy was nursing a treble brandy, and Mann was pouring himself a soda-water on the rocks.

'I told Douglas,' she said.

'Told him what?' Mann asked.

'Hello,' she said to me. 'Told him not to go to Europe this time.'

'Why'd you tell him that?'

'I want to phone my lawyer. You've got no right to stop me.'

'No sense in phoning your lawyer,' said Mann. While she was looking at the phone, he caught my eye. I gave him the least amount of nod I could manage.

'Did you wipe your feet?' she asked me suddenly.

'Yes,' I said.

'When the sprinklers are on, the grass-marks tread in to the carpet,' she said. It was a tired voice that had explained that problem many times before.

'I know,' I said. I smiled. Perhaps that was a mistake.

'Maybe you could talk to your friend about coming back tomorrow or the next day,' she suggested to me. 'I don't want to offend you but a couple of days to recover would be worth so much to me.' I didn't answer, and Mann didn't say anything either.

'I'll phone my lawyer,' she said. She opened her handbag. It was made from a couple of yards of the Bayeux Tapestry, and had gold handles, and a leather strap that went over the shoulder. She searched through it to find a plastic smile but finally she closed the bag with a lot of sighs and tut-tutting. 'I'll phone the yacht-club, the people there will know a good lawyer.'

'Mrs Reid-Kennedy,' said Mann. 'A real good lawyer might be able to reduce the fifty-year sentence you are liable to get, by ten years. But I have the kind of authority that could leave you out of this investigation altogether . . .'

She misinterpreted Mann's offer. I suppose rich people have to develop sharp ears for subtle offers of corruption. She said, 'A couple of days to recover from . . .' she lifted a limp hand '. . . all this, would be worth anything to me. Let me send you away with some little gift for your wives. I have lovely things in the house – porcelain and gold, and all kinds of little things – your wife would probably love some little treasure like that to add to her collection. Wouldn't she?' She was looking at me now.

'To tell you the truth, Mrs Reid-Kennedy,' I said, 'my complete collection of porcelain and gold is here in my dental work. And right now, I don't have a wife.'

'You mind if I take this jacket off?' asked Mann. She didn't answer but he took it off anyway.

'My husband hated air-conditioning. He said he'd rather put up with the heat than have the endless noise of it.'

She went over to the small unit in the window and adjusted the controls.

Mann said, 'You'd better face up to it, Mrs Reid-Kennedy. There's not going to be any yacht-club lawyer who can get you off the hook. And if you don't spill it to us right now, there's not going to be any yacht-club. Not for you, anyway. Even yacht-club secretaries get sticky about espionage.'

She flinched at the word espionage but she didn't argue about it. She took a deep draught of her brandy and when she next spoke her voice was angry. 'Ask this one,' she said, jabbing a thumb at me. 'Ask him – he's been down to the boat, hasn't he. He can see what happened.'

'I wish you'd understand that I'm trying to help you,' Mann told her in his wanting-to-help-you voice. I recognized that voice, because he'd used it on me so often. 'Sure, my colleague can tell me a lot of the answers, because he's been down to the boat. But if you tell me the same thing, I'll be able to write it down as coming from you. I don't have to tell you how much that could help you, do I?'

'You're a couple of schnorrers,' she said bitterly, but it was the last of her resentment. She sighed. 'You ever been to Berlin?' she said.

Probably every life has a moment when it reaches its very lowest: for Mrs Marjorie Dean it was Berlin in the summer of 1955. Physically she had completely recovered from the miscarriage, but psychologically she was far from well. And Berlin made her feel rootless. Her fluent German made no difference to the way that Berliners regarded her, as a prosperous American of the occupying army. Yet the other Americans could not forget her German-born grandparents and were always reminding her that she should feel at home here. But Berlin was a claustrophobic city, 'the island' Berliners called it, a tiny bastion of capitalism in the vast ocean of Soviet Zone Germany. And for her, the wife of a senior intelligence official, there could be no jaunts into Berlin's Eastern Sector, and the long ride down the autobahn to the western half of Germany required the special permission of the commanding general.

And she hated this old house, it was far too big for just the two of them, and the Steiners who looked after the place lived in the guest house at the far end of the overgrown garden, with its dilapidated greenhouses, dark thickets and high hedges. It was easy to see why the US army had taken over the house as VIP accommodation, and then as a school for agents learning radio procedures before going over to the East, but it wasn't really suitable for housing Major Dean and his wife. The furniture was still the same as it had been when this was the home of a fashionable Nazi neurologist. The hall still had the paintings of men in Prussian uniforms, and, on the piano, there was a vignetted photograph of a woman wearing a tiara. The Deans had decided that it must have been the Nazi doctor's mother.

That Thursday, Marjorie Dean stayed in bed until almost noon. Her husband was away for a few days – these trips of his seemed to be getting more and more frequent – and there was nowhere to go until the ladies' bridge tournament at tea-time in the officers' club at Grunewald. But she bathed and put on her favourite linen dress because at one o'clock the courier would arrive from the barracks.

The coffee that Frau Steiner had brought her was now cold, but Marjorie sipped at it just the same, staring at herself as she applied make-up as slowly as she could to spin out the time. On the bedside table there was a tall pile of novels, about romance in America's deep South. She despised herself for reading such books but it helped to numb the mind that otherwise would think about the way the marriage was going, her husband's terrible disappointment at the miscarriage, and the all-pervading boredom.

Suddenly from the drawing-room she heard the piano.

184

Someone was playing an old German song about a farmer and a rich merchant. Her father used to sing it to her. She thought her mind was wandering until she remembered that she'd told the Steiners that their daughter could practise on the piano for an hour each morning. She could hear the Steiners talking. It was so hot that the kitchen window was open wide. She could also hear the voice of Steiner's brother-in-law. Marjorie hoped that the brother-in-law wouldn't stay too long. What had started out as only one weekend had now become frequent visits. He claimed to be a master book-binder from Coburg in Thuringia but Marjorie's ear for German accents put him in Saxony, now in the Russian Zone. The lilt was unmistakable and slightly ridiculous. As she heard him again through the open window, she could hardly suppress a smile. But as she listened more carefully to what was being said, the smile faded. The argument flared up, and the brother-in-law's voice was threatening and abusive. The tempo of his speech, the shrill Saxon accent and the use of much German soldier's slang made the conversation difficult for Marjorie to follow, but suddenly she was afraid. Her intuition told her this visitor was not a relative of the Steiners, and that his presence – and his anger – was in some awful way connected with her husband and the secret work he was engaged in. She heard the window being closed, and could hear no more. Marjorie put the matter from her mind. It was too easy to let one's imagination run away in a town like this.

The courier arrived at one o'clock every day, bringing classified paperwork in a locked metal case. He was always punctual. She looked forward to his visit, and she knew that he enjoyed it too. Usually he would find time to have coffee and a snack. He liked the old-fashioned

German *Süssgebäck*, and Frau Steiner was an expert at making a whole range of spice and honey breads and sometimes more intricate examples, with marzipan inside and a thick coating of toasted almonds. There is a tradition that *Lebkuchen* are exchanged by lovers, and although the relationship between Marjorie Dean and the young corporal was proper almost to the point of being staid, there was sometimes an element of tacit flirtation in the choice of these breads and cakes.

On this particular day, Frau Steiner had cooked hazelnut biscuits. There was a plate of them on the kitchen table, covered with a starched napkin. Alongside she had left the coffee and the percolator and a tray set with one of the antique lace tray-cloths that were on the inventory of this old house. Usually, she found Corporal Douglas Reid-Kennedy brought some new snippet of small-talk or rumour with him. Sometimes they would talk of their childhood in New York. They had both grown up there and Douglas insisted that he had noticed the pretty girl who sat always in the same church pew with two parents and a brother. Once he had told her all about himself and his family. His father was born in Hamburg. He'd emigrated to the USA in 1925, after losing everything in the inflation period. His father had changed the name to Reid-Kennedy after meeting some neighbours who didn't like Germans, and said so. And yet in the 'thirties it became an advantage to be German. The Jewish man from the US Army procurement office who in 1940 gave them a contract to manufacture radio tuners for B-17 bombers, assumed that they were refugees from Hitler.

The army contract brought a change in the fortunes of the Reid-Kennedys. His father rented more space and took on extra workers. From being a four-man radio component sub-contractor, they ended the war with a turn-over only a few hundred dollars short of two million. Douglas was sent to a swanky private school, and acquired a million-dollar accent but was still unable to pass the US Army officers' selection board. He'd been annoyed at the time but now he had decided they were probably right; he was too irresponsible and too lazy to be an officer. Look at Major Dean, for instance, he seemed to work twenty-four hours a day, and had no time for getting drunk, chasing women or mixing with the real Berliners.

Mixing with 'real Berliners' was one of Douglas's very favourite occupations. It was quite amazing the people he knew; a selection of German aristocracy, a Nazi film star, a professional lion-tamer, sculptors and painters, radical playwrights and ex-Gestapo officers with a price on their heads. And if you were after a new camera or some priceless antiques, Douglas knew where the newly impoverished sold their wares at knock-down prices. Douglas was young and amusing, he was a raconteur, a gambler who could lose a little money without crying too hard. He'd been too young for the war, he didn't give a hoot about politics, and for the army he did only what he had to do to stay out of trouble until the happy, happy day when he went back home. In short, Douglas was as different to Hank Dean as any man could get.

And so it was surprising to find this day a changed Corporal Reid-Kennedy who was serious and downcast. Even his clothes were different. His job with the army permitted him to wear civilian clothes and he liked to dress in the slightly ostentatious style of a newly rich Berliner. He chose silk shirts and soft leather jackets and the sort of hand-made hunting clothes that looked good in a silver Porsche. But today he was wearing a cheap blue suit, shiny on the elbows and baggy at the knees. And he wasn't wearing his gold wrist-watch, or the fraternity ring, or the heavy gold identity bangle. He looked like one of the Polish refugees, who went from door to door offering to do odd jobs in exchange for a meal.

He sat down in the kitchen and left the coffee and hazelnut biscuits untouched. He asked her if she could let him have a Scotch. Marjorie was amazed at such a suggestion but she tried not to show it. She put the bottle on the table and Douglas poured himself a treble measure and swallowed it down hastily. He looked up and asked her if she knew what Major Dean's job was in intelligence. Marjorie knew that Dean had 'the police desk' but she didn't know what a police desk was. She'd always assumed that he was a liaison officer between the US Army and the West Berlin police; getting drunken GIs out of jail and dealing with all those German girls who wanted to be a wife in the USA but found themselves alone in Berlin and pregnant. Douglas told her what the police desk really was: Major Dean assembled all the accumulating intelligence material to build a complete picture of the East German Volkspolizei. The trouble was that he'd become so interested in his work that he had gone across to the East for a first-hand look.

She drank some of the fresh coffee and tried the biscuits. Douglas let her have a few minutes to think about the situation before he spoke again. Marjorie, he said finally, you'd better understand that they are holding your husband in East Berlin, and the charge is spying. And they don't fool about over there, they could shoot him. He took her wrist across the table as he said it. It was a sudden change in the relationship. Until now he'd always called her Mrs Dean, and treated her with all the deference due to the wife of his major. But now the problem they shared, and the fact that they were very

188

nearly the same age, unified them, just as it separated them from the older man who was at the centre of the problem. Suddenly Marjorie began to cry, softly at first and then with the terrible racking sobs of hysteria.

The events that came after had been repressed and repressed until she no longer had a clear idea of the order in which they happened. Douglas made long telephone calls. People arrived at the house and departed. There was a chance, he said. The East German police had not transferred custody of Major Dean to the Russians at Berlin-Karlshorst. They offered to exchange Dean for a document stolen from the East Berlin police HQ the previous week. She hesitated. The safe was built into the wall and concealed at the back of the desk in the library. She told Douglas that she didn't have the key and didn't know the combination. Douglas didn't take her seriously. It's your *husband*, Mrs Dean! Eventually she opened the safe and got it. They looked through the document that the East Germans wanted. There were forty-nine pages of it; mimeographed on poor quality pulp paper, tinted pink. There had been file numbers on it but these were now obliterated with black ink. The edges of the paper had faded in the sunlight and Marjorie felt that it couldn't be all that secret if it had been lying around in the sun long enough to fade.

She wondered if she shouldn't telephone Dean's senior officer but Douglas reminded her of what he was like. Can you imagine him taking the responsibility? He wouldn't give the OK to hand over even a used Kleenex tissue to the East Germans. No, he'll shuffle the responsibility to Frankfurt, and we'll wait a week for an answer. By that time Major Dean will be in Moscow.

But how can you be certain that this document isn't of vital importance? Douglas laughed and said it was only of vital importance to the East German official who'd had it stolen from his safe. Now he wanted to get it back and forget the whole thing as soon as possible. These things happen all the time. Marjorie was still worried about how important it was. Look for yourself, said Douglas, but Marjorie couldn't understand the jargon-heavy officialese of his report on police organization in the Eastern Zone. Do you imagine that someone like your husband would keep any really important stuff in his safe at home? Marjorie didn't answer but she finally decided that it was unlikely.

Marjorie remembered Douglas making her go to a cinema. She sat through *Jolson Sings Again*. The dialogue was dubbed into German but the songs were the original recordings. She didn't get home until late. There was a glorious sunset behind the trees in the Grunewald. When she came through the garden to the front door she thought that the roses had bloomed. It was only when she went to look at them that she discovered that behind the rosebushes the whitewash had been spattered with blood. She became hysterical. She blundered through the back garden to the apartment the Steiners used but there was no answer to her rings at the doorbell. Then Douglas arrived in a black Opel Kapitän and persuaded her to spend the night in the VIP quarters at the barracks. He had arranged the necessary permission.

She didn't go back to the house until after Major Dean arrived from the East. The Volkspolizei had kept their word: as soon as the returned papers had been verified, Major Dean was brought to the crossing checkpoint. From there he took a taxi. She never again saw the Steiners. At her insistence the Deans moved to a smaller and more modern house in Spandau. Soon after that, Marjorie became pregnant, and for a time the marriage seemed to go very well but there was now an abyss separating Hank Dean and his young wife.

The perfunctory inquiry was held behind closed doors and its findings were never made public. It was agreed that the document passed to the Volkspolizei was a document originating from that East German force. It had already passed across the desk of Dean's analysers and was in any case of a grading no higher than confidential. Steiner's brother-in-law was found dead and floating in the River Spree, having suffered severe wounding 'by a person or persons unknown' prior to death. He was described on the record as 'a displaced person'. Mrs Dean's evidence about the man's argument with Steiner was rejected as 'inadmissible hearsay'. Major Dean was reprimanded for taking official documents home, and was removed from his job. Mrs Dean was totally exonerated. Corporal Douglas Reid-Kennedy took much of the blame. It was inevitable that he should face the inquiry's wrath, for he was a draftee. Reid-Kennedy had no military career at stake; he wasn't even an officer. However, his quiet acceptance of the findings was rewarded by a transfer to a US Army recruitment depot in New Jersey, promotion and an early release.

And yet, for Douglas Reid-Kennedy and the Deans, the events of that week in Berlin were traumatic. Hank Dean knew he would never again be given a job so important and so sensitive as the one he lost. A couple of times fellow officers snubbed him. He drank. When Hank Dean's drinking became bad enough for the army to send him to a special military hospital near Munich to dry out, Marjorie took the newly born son, Henry Hope, back to her parents in New York. She met Douglas. The first time it was by chance but eventually the relationship became serious and then permanent.

191

It seemed as if the nightmare were over, but in fact it was only just beginning. At college Douglas had been a heavyweight boxer of considerable skill. He had been well on the way to a State championship when by an unlucky blow he severely hurt a fellow contender. Douglas never went into the ring again. It was the same sort of bolo punch that he used to fell the Steiners' bogus brother-in-law. The fact that the man was a blackmailer and an East German spy persuaded the inquiry to skirt round that happening. But the Russians were not prepared to kiss and make up. Three years after the incidents in Berlin, Douglas was visited by a baby-faced young man who presented the card of a Polish company that made transistors. After the usual polite small-talk he said that through nominee holdings, the company for which he worked now owned 37 per cent of Douglas's company. He realized that 37 per cent was not 51 per cent – the baby-faced man smiled – but it was enough for them to have a real control over what was going to happen. They could pump money into the company, or turn it over to making razor-blades or tear it down and go into real estate. The young man reminded Douglas that he had killed one of their 'employees' and Douglas realized that his company was now owned by the KGB. They offered to pay Douglas off each year in his own shares, if he would work for them. They would tell him exactly which US Government electronics contracts to bid for, and their agents would be able to discover exactly what his business rivals were bidding. In return, they wanted a steady supply of technical information about the whole US electronics industry. If Douglas refused to work with them, the young man told him, they would bankrupt his company and 'execute' all of the people implicated in the events of that night: Marjorie, the Steiners, the Steiners' daughter and Douglas himself. Douglas asked for a week to think it over. They agreed. They knew the answer must be 'yes'.

As she finished her story, she poured herself another large brandy and sipped some. Major Mann went over to the air-conditioner and moved the control from medium to coldest. He stood there letting the cold air hit him. He turned round and gave her his most engaging smile. 'Well, it's great,' he said. 'I want you to know I think it's just great. Of course, you've had about twenty years to goose it up, and work in some interesting details, but then so did Tolstoy – thirty years Tolstoy had, if I remember correctly.'

'What?' she said, frowning hard.

'That story,' said Mann. 'My buddy here is crazy about all that kind of spy fiction.'

'It's true,' she said.

'It's literature,' said Mann. 'It's more than just a lousy collection of lies and evasions; it's literature!'

'No.'

'Douglas Reid-Kennedy joined the Communist Party when he was still at school. I guessed that as soon as I knew that his two closest buddies joined the CP and he remained aloof from that gay group of fun-loving raconteurs – am I pronouncing that right, Mrs Dean? . . . raconteurs. That's what your friend Corporal Douglas Reid-Kennedy was on his days off with these Gestapo guys and film stars? Well, as soon as I hear about a guy at school who doesn't go along and sing "The Red Flag" with his closest buddies, I think to myself either this guy isn't the kind of young amusing raconteur that everybody is cracking him up to be, or else the Communist Party have given him a secret number, and told him to keep his mouth shut. They do that when they spot a kid who has a job in the State Department, or a trade union, or has a father who makes electronic equipment for the US Army.'

Mann walked across the room and picked up the photo of Douglas being nursed by his father. 'Great kid you got there, Pop, but just watch out for that bolo punch.' He put the photo down. 'Yeah, you were right about Douglas's boxing career at school . . . too modest in fact. See, Douglas crippled three kids with that body punch – a bolo is an upper cut to the body, I guess you already knew that, Mrs Dean, or you wouldn't have used that exact technical word – and Douglas didn't give up as easy as you say he did. He was forbidden to box again, not only by the school but also by the State boxing authority. And don't let's imagine that our Douglas was the kind of guy who didn't develop his natural talents. He graduated from crippling people to killing people. The KGB spotted that more quickly than the US Army spotted it; they knew that he'd like assignments to kill people. Those murder assignments were his rewards, not his work.'

'No!' she screamed.

Mann looked at her as she poured herself another drink. I had watched her drinking all this time and thought that she was using all her will-power to avoid getting drunk. Now I realized that it was just the reverse of that; she wanted to be drunk more than she wanted anything else in the world, but in her present state of mind no amount of drink seemed to do the trick for her.

'Yes,' said Mann softly. 'While you went on your round trip to Paris, your Douglas stayed in the Emerald Isle. He went to a little farm off the highway, and hacked a German family to death with a spade. Three of them; we dug them up from the garbage. It was a wet day in Ireland, so if we're pressing decomposing tissue into your wall-to-wall pile carpet, I apologize, but you've got Douglas to blame for it.'

'No,' she said again but it was softer this time, and not so confident.

'And all that crap about that police report. In the middle 'fifties, the East Germans were using their "barrack police" as a nucleus of their new army. Let's define our terms. Those police we're talking about had tanks and MiG fighter planes, Mrs Dean. The police desk was just about the most important work the CIA did in Germany at that time. That's why Hank Dean was assigned to it and that's why he gave it everything he'd got, until he was mentally, and physically, exhausted.'

Mann paused for a long time. I suppose he was hoping that she would argue or confess or simply blow her top but she did nothing except sink lower in the soft furnishings and continue to drink. Mann said, 'Douglas Reid-Kennedy was a Communist agent, and he was wearing that cheap blue suit because he'd just come over from the East where he'd been talking to his pals about putting your husband on the rack. And your cock-and-bull story about Steiner's argument was disregarded because the man who pretended to be Steiner's brother-in-law wasn't an East German agent, he was one of Dean's best men. He was one of the German Communists who fled to Soviet Russia in 1938. Stalin handed him back over the frontier to the Gestapo in 1940 as part of the deal of slicing Poland down the middle and sharing it with the Nazis. That's the man who had his blood spattered over your rose-bushes by Corporal Douglas Reid-Kennedy. He had important things to tell Hank, and when he was delayed Hank was so worried that he went across there to help him. The agent got back but Hank went into the bag.'

195

'The inquiry didn't know anything about his being an agent for the Americans,' she said.

'You think the inquiry is going to blow a network because an agent is murdered. No, they let it go, and were happy not to inquire too far into it. And that was a lucky break for Reid-Kennedy.'

'Yes,' she said.

'And you tell us that the inquiry reprimanded Major Dean, and exonerated you. Why do you think they did that? They did it because Hank stood up and took all the shit that they were throwing at you. Sure he was reprimanded for leaving the papers unsafeguarded, because he wouldn't tell them that you and your god-damned boyfriend opened his safe and betrayed him in every possible way . . .'

'No, they said . . .'

'Don't argue with me,' said Major Mann. 'I just got through reading the transcript. And don't tell me you believed Douglas Reid-Kennedy and all that crap about returning the papers to the police authority. You saw that the file numbers were blacked out. That's the first thing an agent does with secret papers, so that they can't be traced back to the place where they were stolen. And even the police chief of East Berlin is going to have a hard time explaining why the papers in his safe have got all the file numbers blacked out. And you know that as well as anyone, so don't give me any of that stuff.'

He walked up to where she was sitting but she didn't raise her eyes to him. His face was flushed and his brow shiny. It would have been easy to believe that he was the one being interrogated, because the woman seemed relaxed and unheeding.

'But it wasn't anything to do with the papers,' said Mann. 'This was all a carefully planned caper designed in Moscow solely to compromise Hank Dean. I'd bet everything I own that he was offered every kind of chance to hush this thing up. Both when he was in the East Berlin prison, and after he got back. But Hank Dean knew that it was just the first step into being doubled, and Hank Dean wasn't the kind of man who ends up a double agent. He'd sooner end up an alcoholic. At least a lush keeps his soul. Right, Mrs Dean? It's your husband we're talking about, remember him?' He walked away from her. 'Or maybe you'd rather not remember, after all you did to him. Because wrecking his career wasn't enough for you, was it? You had to go screwing your way through the barracks. And you were no snob. You didn't stop at the officers' club, did you. You even had to screw the little creep who came delivering the official mail. Of course you didn't realize then that Douglas had drawn you as an assignment from Moscow . . .'

'What?'

'And Reid-Kennedy eventually got orders to make his relationship with you as permanent as possible: a wife isn't permitted to testify against her husband, right?'

'Hank would never give me a divorce.'

'And I think we know why. He suspected the truth about Reid-Kennedy and was not going to give him that final bit of protection.'

'No,' she said.

'You think it was your good breeding, or all that old-fashioned etiquette you gleaned from those cheap novels. Douglas Reid-Kennedy took the high ground – your bed – and he didn't have to fight all the way. I'd guess that that little conversation over the coffee and *Süssgebäck* took place, not in the kitchen, but in Hank Dean's bed. That's where you first heard that those bastards were holding your husband.'

197

'No,' she said. 'No, no, no.'

'And I'll tell you something else that Hank Dean kept to himself . . .'

He paused. She must have known what was coming, for she lowered her head as one might if expecting a blow about the ears. 'Henry Hope is Reid-Kennedy's child.'

'He is not,' she said. 'I swear it! You say that in front of witnesses and I'll sue you for every penny you possess. I'll make you pay!'

'Yeah, well, I can't prove it, but I looked up Hank's army records to find his blood group. And Henry-Hope was easy because he donates blood at the local hospital . . .' Mann scowled and shook his head.

'Did you tell him?' she asked. 'Did you tell Henry-Hope that?'

'No, I didn't, Mrs Dean, because it would be nicer for your son to grow up thinking that a great guy like Hank is his father than that a murderous creep like Reid-Kennedy might be. So we'll keep that to ourselves, Mrs Dean. On that you got a deal.'

'Poor Henry-Hope,' she said softly. Her voice was slurred: at last the alcohol was getting to her.

'You entertained on the boat last week,' I said. 'Who was it who came aboard on Monday?' She gave me a venomous glare.

She said, 'So he speaks, your friend. I was beginning to think he was one of those inflatable dolls they advertise in the back pages of the sex magazines.'

I passed to her the piece of paper on which I noted the dates of the pages missing from the boat's visitors' book.

She scowled at it and said, 'You get a tax deduction for the days when you entertain businessmen on a boat. Douglas always made people sign, so he could claim his proper deduction. He was obsessional about that.'

'Who was it?' I said.

She scrabbled to find the spectacles tucked down the side of the armchair. Having put them on, she read the dates with studied concentration. 'I couldn't tell you,' she said. 'My memory isn't so good these days, Douglas was always ribbing me about that.'

I said, 'I'd hate you to make a mistake about how important this is to us.'

'That's right,' said Mann. He pointed a finger down to the boat moored beyond where the palm trees were whipping about in the wind. 'You got a time bomb down there, Mrs Dean. At ten thirty I'm going to have to blow the whistle on you. This place will be filled with cops, reporters and photographers, and they will all be yelling at you – right?' He looked at his watch. 'So you got just eighteen minutes to decide how you play it – and the decisions you make are going to decide whether you live out the rest of your life as a millionairess, or spend it upstate in the women's prison with a "no parole" sticker on your file.'

She looked at Mann for a moment and then looked at her own wrist-watch just to check him out.

'Seventeen minutes,' Mann said.

'Douglas ran a legitimate business,' she said. 'You start thinking it was all mixed up with the other business and you will never unravel it.'

'You let us worry about that,' I said.

'You don't get these big government contracts by sitting on your butt, waiting for the phone to ring. Douglas went out of his way to look after his contacts, and they expected that.'

'Who was it?'

'People from some Senate Committee.'

'Which Senate Committee?'

'International Scientific Co-operation – or some such name. You must have heard of it.'

'We've heard of it,' I said. 'So who came here?'

'Only for fishing trips, and you wouldn't get me on that boat when they are fishing. I didn't get to meet any of them. They were just fishing cronies of Douglas. Like I told you, it was just social. Douglas only put it down as business so he could get the tax deductions.'

'Names!' said Mann. 'Names, goddamnit!'

She spilled her drink. 'Mr Hart. Mr Gerry Hart. He's helped my husband get other government contracts.'

'Mind if I use your phone, Mrs Reid-Kennedy?' said Mann.

17

They are made of marble, steel, chromium and tinted glass, these gleaming governmental buildings that dominate Washington, DC, and from the top of any one of them, a man can see half-way across the world – if he's a politician.

The buildings have no names; only numbers and initials. FOBS are Federal office buildings and HOBS are House office buildings. This rent-free luxury office suite, in which Senator Greenwood could sip Martinis and trim his toenails while watching the home-going traffic building up on the Potomac River Freeway, and still keep the other eye on the White House, was a Senate office building – a SOB.

The heavy silk curtains had been fully opened to reveal the cityscape through the picture windows. I could see the river Potomac and, farther away, the Washington Channel. Mirroring the sky, their waters were colourless, like two icy daggers sunk into the city's gut. Greenwood stood with us admiring the view for a moment.

'About this time I usually have a bourbon and ginger,' he smiled, and flicked a strand of hair from his eyes. A senator with enough hair to flick off his face has something to smile about, even without the palatial office, imported furniture and the rosewood cupboard full of hard stuff. 'So what will it be for you boys?'

'A tonic water,' I said.

'A bourbon and ginger would suit me nicely, sir,' said Mann.

'Thought you were going to say you didn't drink while you were on duty,' said Greenwood. He tossed some ice into glasses that were cold enough to whiten, and snapped the crown corks from three bottles in a row: they gave three little gasps.

'I'd never get a drink if I pursued that kind of policy,' said Mann.

'Right. Right!' said Greenwood in an absent-minded way, as if he'd already forgotten the beginning of the conversation. He set the drinks down on the antique side tables that were carefully arranged for each of the Barcelona chairs that faced his desk. It was a modern design: no more than two stainless-steel trestles supporting a sheet of armour glass. He walked round the desk, and sat in his Italian swivel chair. There was no front to the desk, and the papers arranged on the glass-top seemed to be floating in the air. Perhaps it was Greenwood's way of proving he didn't have a Derringer in his lap.

'Mr Gerry Hart,' said Greenwood, as though announcing that the courtesies were over.

'Yes,' said Mann.

'I've got the report,' said Greenwood.

'It's not a report, Senator,' said Mann. 'It's just a private memo to you.'

'Well, I'm not very conversant with the jargon of the CIA,' said Greenwood, in such a way as to discourage instruction. He smiled. Greenwood's smile used very even, very white, teeth. Like his attentive eyes, his sincere nods and pensive silences, Greenwood's smiles were those of a man who was thinking about something more important. He was a handsome man, urbane rather than backwoods, but some women like that better. He'd have to lose twenty pounds before he'd win admiring glances at the poolside, but in his carefully tailored light-grey mohair and hand-made brogues, with his manicured hands, and face talced like a freshly-baked cottage-loaf, I saw in him a possible ladies' man. Coming over here in the car we'd played 'One-word Who's Who': Mann's entry for Greenwood was 'bullshit', mine was 'showbiz', but no doubt, Greenwood's entry for himself would be 'boyish'.

Greenwood gave another of those dazzling smiles and said, 'The truth is, fellers, we politicos are too busy shaking hands to spare much time for reading.'

'Is that so,' said Mann.

'Well, maybe I'd better say in my own defence that I read about one hundred thousand words a day; and that's longer than the average novel.' That's what I like about politicians, even their self-criticism doesn't apply to them personally.

Mann said, 'Your influence and importance in the Senate has always made you a target for ambitious and unscrupulous people, Senator . . .' I saw Greenwood begin to scowl. Mann continued a little more hastily, '. . . And when you joined the Scientific Development sub-committee of the Senate Committee of International Co-operation . . .' Greenwood smiled to show that he appreciated the way Mann had got the name right '. . . you became one of the most powerful men in the whole United States, Senator.'

Greenwood gave a brief nod. 'Before you go on, Major. Maybe I should remind you that the CIA have got a Senate office that handles all contact with you people.'

'We want to keep limited access,' said Mann.

'Limited access,' said Greenwood. 'I'm hearing a lot about limited access from your people.'

'Any normal application, through the CIA Senate office, would be too likely to alert Mr Gerry Hart.'

'And you don't want to alert him?'

'No, sir. We do not.'

'Are we talking about off-the-record material, or press leaks, or are we talking about scientific data that my committee decided to publish but which you guys at the CIA don't like to see published?'

'We are talking about important secret material channelled to the USSR by means of an espionage network.'

'Gerry Hart working for the Russians?' Greenwood said. He drank some of his bourbon. 'This is a guy who used to work with you people – did you know that?'

'So he'd know how to pass it across. Right, Senator, you got it,' said Mann pretending to be grateful that Greenwood was of the same mind. 'And now we want to look at this house Gerry Hart owns, down near Brandywine.'

'And his apartment in Georgetown,' said Greenwood dispassionately.

Mann nodded. 'And . . .' he said. He waved a flattened hand in a moment's hesitation. Even through the double-glazing we heard the police sirens. It was a Lincoln limousine flying flags and escorted by three motor-cycle cops. We watched them as they went over the bridge, probably heading for the airport.

'And his office,' said Greenwood.

'And his office,' said Mann. 'Yes, that's it.'

'And yet, Major, you tell me you've no real hard evidence,' said Greenwood. He sat back in his swivel chair and kicked gently, so that he could spin far enough to see the Potomac. The water seemed very still, and there was the gentle rumble of a jet plane.

'Depends what you call hard evidence,' said Major

Mann sadly. 'We got his name when following another line of investigation.'

I felt Mann's indecision, as he wondered whether to emphasize our suspicions about Gerry Hart, or to minimize them and suggest that we wanted no more than a routine check that would eliminate Gerry Hart from our list of suspects. He decided not to elaborate on it, and sipped some of his drink, watching Greenwood expectantly.

Greenwood lifted one of his hand-made shoes high enough for him to retie the lace. 'What I mean by hard evidence, Major,' he said in a soft husky voice of the sort I've heard him use for his electioneering, '. . . what, in fact, everyone in this nation means by hard evidence, is something that can find a man guilty by due process of law.' He looked up from his shoe-lace and smiled at Mann.

There was no need to draw any diagrams; we all knew the way it was going to go. But Mann went through the motions. He said, 'We are at the preliminary stages of a complex and extremely delicate investigation, Senator. We don't have that kind of hard evidence which you define, but that doesn't mean that no such evidence exists. I'm now asking your assistance, so that we can get it, or eliminate Mr Hart from the investigation.'

Greenwood stared at Mann and said, 'Well, I thought I'd let you guys come on down here, so that I could get a close look at you. Well, now I've seen you, and I don't like what I see.' The two men were staring at each other. 'So beat it!' said Greenwood. 'And take the bag-man with you.' He looked away from Mann in order to indicate me.

Mann stood up without saying a word, and I did too.

Greenwood didn't get up. He said, 'You really thought I'd throw Gerry Hart to your wolf-pack?'

Mann gave him a cold little smile, and said, 'Into the snow, you mean? Well, Senator, you just better make sure Gerry Hart doesn't toss you off the back of the troika when he wants to whip up the horses.'

'You heard me,' said Greenwood softly. 'Get out!'

He let us get as far as the door before speaking again. When he did, his voice and manner had all the charm that had been there before. 'Oh, Major Mann,' he said, and waited until Mann turned back to face him. 'Just in case you are thinking of filing some kind of a report that says I'm not co-operative, just let me tell you again that I only deal with you CIA people if it's done in the proper way – through the Senate. So don't let me hear that you are making approaches to anyone working in my office, until you've cleared it with me through your office. Have you got that, Major?'

'Yes, Senator. You've made your position very clear.'

Mann was silent as we walked out to the car. For what seemed like hours, he drove aimlessly round the city: through the smart streets of Georgetown where Gerry Hart had his chic apartment, past the neat lawns of the White House – discoloured now by the winter frosts – and through the black ghettos and back along the Inner Loop Freeway.

When finally Mann spoke – apart from the muttered curses he'd used on other drivers – he said, 'Last week there was this Foreign Minister, from some little West African republic, lunched by the State Department . . . next day he took a ride down the freeway and was thrown out of a hamburger joint by some red-neck in Virginia.'

'Is that so,' I said politely. It was one of Washington's

standard anecdotes, and like most of Washington's clichés it was usually true.

Mann's mind raced on. 'It's a court here in Washington. It's not a government, it's a court. Know what I mean?'

'No,' I said.

'Like a medieval palace – the President brings in his own people and sweeps out the previous ones. Some are elected men . . . others are outsiders . . . courtiers: jesters, acrobats, jugglers and story-tellers . . . plenty of story-tellers.'

'Knights, knaves and Quixotes,' I added, 'chivalrous men and courtly ladies . . . well, it's one way of looking at it.'

The traffic came to a standstill and Mann cursed. One of the big government office blocks was emptying, and a great flood of secretaries washed through the stationary traffic.

'And what is Greenwood?' I asked him. 'Jester, joker, jack-in-the-green?'

'Court favourite,' said Mann. 'The ear of the king, and a whole army of people to back him up.' The traffic began moving again, pedestrians scattered and Mann hit the horn, accelerated suddenly and changed lanes with a reckless skill that made a truck-driver yell. 'Not only the people who owe him a favour, and the ones who want him to owe them one,' said Mann, 'but all those bastards who have an obsessional hatred of us. The CIA has a lot of enemies, and no one is going to thank us for mobilizing them under Greenwood's flag.'

'But wouldn't you have done what Greenwood did?'

'What did he do?'

'Stalled us,' I said. 'He doesn't want us in there taking Hart to pieces, and spattering blood and shit all over everyone in Greenwood's office. My guess is he'll tow

Gerry Hart slowly out into the middle of the ocean, and sink him out of sight of land.'

'Are you trying to cheer me up?' said Mann bitterly. 'If Hart is the kind of high-power KGB agent we both are beginning to think he might be, he could transfer the whole operation by that time. And maybe even get clear himself.'

'You're going after Hart direct?'

'Not for the moment.'

'Are you going higher?' I asked him.

Mann chuckled. 'The President, you mean? Like in those movies where some white-haired old actor you thought was dead years ago, shakes us solemnly by the hand, and says this is the last reel, fellers, go and get lined up for the soft focus. Hah. No, nothing like that, but I can make a shiver run up and down Greenwood's spine.'

'How?'

'He's frightened of getting spattered with Gerry Hart's blood? I'll rub his nose in it.'

'How?'

'He won't co-operate? Well, I'll show him a few tricks. He's frightened of what his friends might say if he's seen co-operating with the CIA? . . . Well, I'll scrawl CIA on his garden wall, mister, and I'll send him a thank-you through every postal delivery. I'll make that bastard the talk of Washington, I'll make him the famous CIA stoolie.'

'He won't like that,' I said.

Mann smiled. 'Wouldn't it be great if we could get him an official commendation.'

We seemed to be driving round in circles. I said, 'Are we staying the night here in Washington?'

Mann bit his lip. 'My wife is going crazy in that hotel

. . . It's my wedding anniversary today. Maybe I should buy her some kind of gift.'

'Does that mean you're staying?'

'If you see a candy store and somewhere I can park.'

They said it was the wettest winter in living memory but then they are always saying that. The sky had turned a dirty orange colour, and now the rain was heavy.

It was the sort of tropical shower that reminds you that Washington, DC, is nearly as far south as Tunis. Mann switched the wipers on, and there was a breath of steam rising from the metal of the car. He tried to tune in to the news bulletin but the static and the high-tension wires blotted out the transmission. Nervously Mann shook a cigarette out of the packet and lit it, using only one hand. I offered to help him but he declined.

We were on South Capitol Street, heading for the Anacostia Freeway, with Major Mann still trying to decide whether to stay in town to start fabricating angst for Greenwood, when the car phone buzzed. I took it. It was the information room at Langley. 'Car hop,' said the voice.

'Cheer Leader,' I said, 'go ahead.'

'Message from Jonathan,' said the voice. 'Fabian attempted suicide at fourteen thirty hours today. He is not in danger. Repeat: he is not in danger, but he will be hospitalized for seven or ten days. Do you read that? Over.'

'Five by five, car hop.'

'Crazy bastard,' said Mann.

Langley said, 'Jonathan asks will he tell Ambrose.'

I looked at Mann. He bit his lip. I passed the phone to him.

Langley said, 'Did you read that, Cheer Leader?'

209

Mann said, 'Loud and clear, car hop. Tell nobody. Over and out.' He hung up the phone.

Mann glanced at me out of the corner of his eye. I turned to him. 'Yeah, well I'm sorry,' he said. 'It's need to know.'

'Oh sure,' I said angrily. 'Or is it, how much can you pry loose? Who the hell is Ambrose?'

Mann didn't answer.

'Those A codes personnel are from Operations,' I said. 'We've got someone else working on this investigation – and you didn't tell me.'

'It was a dangerous assignment,' said Mann defensively. 'And a need-to-know classification means only those who must know are told.'

'So that's the way it's going to be from now on?' I said. 'OK, but just don't complain afterwards.'

'Miss Bancroft,' said Mann.

Now it was my turn to go silent for a long time. 'Red?' I said finally. 'An A code agent? It took me ten years to get that.'

Mann stubbed out the cigarette he'd only just started. 'Temporary A code. Solely with Mrs Bekuv. No decision-making . . .' he waved a hand at the telephone . . . 'no access – you heard that for yourself – no filing, except through me. Just a nursemaid job.' He put the smouldering cigarette-stub into the ashtray and closed it.

'How long has she been working for the CIA?'

'Is that still ongoing – you and the Bancroft girl?' The cigarette-stub was making a lot of smoke. Mann banged the ashtray to make sure it was closed but the smoke emerged from it just the same. 'Is it? Is it still serious?'

'I don't know,' I said.

'Yeah, well when a guy says he doesn't know if a thing like that's still serious – it's still serious.'

'I suppose so,' I admitted.

'Well, you'll have to forget her for a few days. You get down to that Norfolk nut-house, and kick shit out of our pal Jonathan. And you tell Professor goddamn Bekuv that if he wants to commit any more suicide and doesn't know how, I'll come down there and lend him a hand.'

'OK,' I said.

'And twist his arm, show him some more photos of Gerry Hart. He still knows a whole lot more than he's telling us.' Mann opened the ashtray again, and gave the cigarette-stub the *coup de grâce*.

'I could drive down to Norfolk,' I offered. 'If I started right away I could be there as fast as the plane.'

It was an exaggeration. Mann smiled. 'And stop at Petersburg en route, you mean? Stop and see Miss Bancroft.'

'Yes,' I said.

'Go by plane, kid. I told you to stay away from her. Do I have to put it in writing?'

'But . . .'

He said, 'We're friends, aren't we? Real friends I mean?'

'Yes,' I said. I looked at him, waiting for what would follow these portentous and, for Major Mann, unusually personal words. 'Why?'

Whatever he was going to tell me, he changed his mind about. 'Oh, I was just going to say, take care of yourself.' He changed lanes to get to the freeway exit. 'I'll take you to the airport,' he said.

I should have obeyed orders. I didn't, and what happened subsequently was all my fault. I don't mean that I could have influenced events, it was far too late for that, but I could have protected myself from the horror of it. Or I could have let Mann protect me, as he was already trying to do.

18

After Mann dropped me at the airport I went straight to the car rentals and asked about fast cars. I finally got a Corvette Stingray. While I was waiting for it, I bought a heart-shaped box of chocolate-covered fudge. The old lady behind the counter seemd relieved to get rid of it.

My car was gold with real leather upholstery, a V-eight motor of 200 bhp, and once on the highway I put my foot down all the way south. I told myself that I needed a fast car to pay a brief visit to Red and still reach Norfolk in time to phone Mann and convince him I'd taken the plane. But looking back on it, I realize that the flashy car was just one more part of my determination to make Red love me, as desperately as I loved her.

Red Bancroft, Mrs Bekuv and three shifts of heavies were tucked away in a house in the country, not far from St Petersburg, Florida. It was a dark night, and the place was difficult to find. My headlights picked up a sign that said 'Hook Ups for Trailers and Campers'. There were only two trailers hooked into the power line and I heard the door of the nearest one click as soon as I stopped. A man stepped down. On the other side of the road there was a small sign for 'Pederson's Herb and Fruit Farm – Private'. I parked off the road close to a billboard that advised me 'Next time fly the friendly skies'.

With hardly a word spoken, he took me to the trailer, but not before flashing a torch into the back of my car and checking the boot to be sure I was alone. There were two more of them inside the trailer, big men with heavy

212

woollen zipper jackets and high-laced boots, but their faces were soft and pale, and none of them looked the type who goes camping in the depths of winter. Behind the trailers I saw three cars and a couple of guard dogs secured to a post.

'I suppose it's OK,' he said reluctantly. He passed the card and the CIA slips back across the table to me. 'You follow the path – through the yellow gate near the sign. I'll phone the house to tell them.' He switched off the lights before opening the trailer door: he was a careful man.

'Let's make it a surprise,' I said.

He looked at me with interest. Afterwards I wondered how much he knew about what was happening there, but he wasn't the sort of man who makes free with good advice. 'Suit yourself,' he said.

I dropped the car keys on the table and then stepped down into the mud. It was a long way to the house, but as I got near there was enough light from the upstairs window to help me pick my way along the garden path, and across the apple orchard. The kitchen clock was at midnight, and I could see a tray, set with chinaware and flowers, all ready for next morning.

Softly, as if from miles away, I could hear voices, arguing loudly.

The kitchen door was unlocked – with so much security there was no fear of burglars – and I went in. I walked through the hall and into the lounge from which the voices came. There was an abandoned backgammon game in the middle of the carpet, and scatter-cushions on the floor. All was lit by the dusty blue light of the TV, and the voices were those of a TV quiz. There were a couple of chords from an electric organ and a round of applause from the studio audience. '. . . and, for ten thousand dollars . . . fingers ready on the buzzers all you nice people . . . In 1929, Douglas Fairbanks made his first all-talking movie. For this two-part question, I want, first, the name of his female star, and, for the second part, the name of the movie.'

On the air I could smell the mentholated cigarettes that Red smoked. I switched on the lights – two big Chinese vases with parchment shades – there was no one here. A log fire was dying in the hearth, and near by there was a jug of water and a bowl of melting ice. There was also a whisky bottle and two glasses; all of them empty. The TV contestants were deep in thought. It was during this silence that I heard the groans from upstairs. 'Oh my God!' It was a woman's voice – Katerina Bekuv's, and there was a shrill strangled cry.

I don't know if I made much noise running up the stairs, two at a time; or if I shouted anything, or what I might have said. I can only remember standing in the bedroom doorway and looking at them: I remember how tanned was the nude body of Katerina Bekuv against the pale skin of Red Bancroft, who was kneeling over her. The groans I'd heard were not groans of pain. The scene is burned into my memory: Katerina Bekuv spread-eagled and limp, her head lolling back so that her long blonde hair almost reached the floor. Red tense, straightening her back to sit up and look at me, her eyes wide and fearful. From Katerina came a long orgasmic whisper. I stood there numb.

'Get some clothes on, Ambrose,' I said finally. 'Come downstairs. I want to talk to you.'

When Red Bancroft arrived in the sitting-room she was wearing nothing but a silk kimono, and even that was left untied. Her hair looked more auburn than red under this light and it was still dishevelled. She wore no make-up, and her face looked like that of a young child, but her demeanour was not childlike. She strode across to the TV set. I had been sipping at a measure of brandy and staring at the TV screen with unseeing eyes but now that she was standing there I heard the master of ceremonies say 'One of the most shocking crimes of the decade took place in 1929 in Chicago . . . Now here's your question . . .'

'Are you watching this?' she asked with mock politeness.

I shook my head.

'. . . four men, two of them in police uniforms . . .' As she switched the TV off, the master of ceremonies fluttered like a burned moth and collapsed, into a small blue flame that disappeared.

'St Valentine's Day Massacre,' she said. 'Al Capone.' She tore the cellophane off a packet of Kools, took one out and lit it.

'Switch it on again and ask for your ten grand.'

She walked across to the cupboard, found a new bottle of Scotch and poured herself a generous measure. This was a different Red Bancroft to the soft sweet girl I'd fallen in love with. 'Do you realize what kind of priority this investigation has got?' she said.

'Don't talk to me like I'm one of your security guards,' I said.

She drank a little of her drink, paced across the carpet and back, and then rubbed her face as if trying to decide what she wanted to say next. 'I don't know how much you've been told,' she said, which was as good a put-down as I've yet come across, 'but Mrs Bekuv is a KGB officer of field rank. Did you know that?'

'No,' I admitted.

She drank some more whisky. 'You want a drink?' she asked suddenly.

'I helped myself already,' I said indicating the glass of brandy that I'd left on the side table. She nodded.

'When they realized that Bekuv had gone, and that we had him, Moscow panicked. They tried to kill him that night at the party. Then they changed their tactics. Mrs Bekuv was sent after him. Moscow sent her. She was sent to control him, monitor and modify what he told us.'

'The stabbing,' I said.

'It was good that, wasn't it?' It was as if she took pride in the expertise of her lover. 'She grabbed the sharp edge skilfully enough to cut herself, without doing too much damage to the ligaments. Then she did a couple of deep slash cuts into her coat.'

'A bad cut in the abdomen . . . four stitches,' I said.

'This is a professional,' said Red. 'You don't get field rank in the KGB if you're afraid of the sight of blood.' She put her glass of whisky to her face and smelled it delicately as one would an expensive perfume.

'And Gerry Hart brought her out and delivered her to us.'

She looked at me with some disdain. 'Gerry Hart has been working for the Russians for at least fifteen years. He's a senior officer in the KGB – you know how they give these people military ranks and medals to make them feel important.'

'So bringing Mrs Bekuv out of Russia was entirely a KGB operation?'

'All the way, baby. All the way.' She tied a knot in the cord of the kimono.

'Does Mann know all this?'

'I've only known it for thirty minutes,' she said.

I heard Mrs Bekuv moving on the floor above us. I

said, 'You and . . . her. Was that something that just happened? Or was that part of the plan?'

'It *was* the plan,' she said immediately. 'It was the *only* plan. You and Major Mann chasing here and there across the world were just diversionary. Holding Mrs Bekuv here, and turning her so that she'll break Hart's network, that was the real plan.'

I didn't argue with her; all agents are told that their contribution is the most important part of the plan. I said, 'But why not tell me?'

'We fell in love,' she said. 'You and me – there was no disguising it. At first I wanted to call off everything else but I pulled myself together, and got on with my job. It was then that I discovered the effect that our love affair was having on Mrs Bekuv.'

'You mean Mrs Bekuv was jealous of me?'

'Don't sound so incredulous. Yes, that's exactly what I'm telling you. She won me away from you, and she was proud of herself for doing it.'

'Well, thanks for the memory,' I said.

Red came closer to me and touched my arm. 'I loved you,' she said. 'I loved you. Remember that, won't you.'

Overhead we heard Mrs Bekuv walk across the floor. 'Just for a time I wanted out of this whole business.'

'Out of this business? Or out of that business?' I moved my head to indicate the upstairs room where Mrs Bekuv was still moving around.

'I'm still not sure,' said Red. She looked me full in the eyes and her voice was calm and level. 'Don't blame the Manns,' she said. 'They wanted the best for both of us.'

'And what was the best for both of us?'

She didn't answer. From upstairs I heard Mrs Bekuv sobbing. It was very quiet, the sort of sobbing that goes on for a long time.

'You got paint on that nice leather coat,' said Red. 'When did you do that?'

'Christmas,' I said. 'It's not paint, it's Mrs Bekuv's blood.'

I picked up the glass of brandy I'd poured, and I drank it in one gulp. Then I picked up my ten-dollar box of fudge and left.

19

After the baroque night, a rococo dawn. A boiling sky of turbulent clouds, and a sun that bored a golden tunnel right through it. It needed only a Tiepolo to paint a busty Aurora there, and surround her with naked nymphs and some improbable shepherds.

'What are you looking at?'

'You stay in bed, Professor Bekuv. The doctor says you need a complete rest.'

'This hospital food is terrible. Could you arrange for food to be sent in for me?'

'That might be difficult, Professor. You are on maximum security now. The people cooking your food may not be graduates of the cordon bleu, but they are triple-star security cleared.'

'So you think someone might try to poison my food?'

I counted to ten. 'No I don't think anyone will poison your food. It's a routine precaution that always goes with maximum security . . . .people.'

'Prisoners,' said Bekuv. 'You were going to say prisoners.'

'I was going to say patients.'

'No one tells me the truth.'

I turned to face him. I found it difficult to feel sorry for him. The breakfast of which he had complained so bitterly had been entirely eaten. He was now munching expensive black grapes from the fruit-bowl. On the other bedside table his hi-fi controls had been arranged. His condition was a tribute to modern medicine or to the circumspection of his attempt at suicide. Bekuv slotted a cassette into the player. Suddenly four giant loudspeakers, that had been arranged round his bed, filled the little hospital room with the opening bars of the *Rosenkavalier* waltz.

I walked to the table and switched the music down.

'I want to listen to the music,' said Bekuv. 'I am not feeling well enough to continue talking.'

I looked at him and considered all kinds of responses but I didn't use any of them. 'OK,' I said. I went downstairs to talk to Jonathan.

The Strauss music could still be heard. 'Tell me again about the suicide,' I said.

'He's in good shape, isn't he,' said Jonathan anxiously.

'Are you sure he took an overdose?'

'They pumped him dry and analysed it.'

'You'd better tell me everything that happened just before that.'

'I told you. It was the same routine as every other morning. He got up at six, when the alarm went. He took a shower, shaved and we sat down to breakfast at seven.'

'An hour to shave, shower and dress?'

'He listens to the news and reads his mail.'

'You let him have mail?'

'Hi-fi magazines, *Newsweek, Time*, two sci-fi magazines advertising crap from the places he bought his record-player and stuff, little notes from his wife, a Russian-language weekly from New York, all of it goes via the accommodation address of course . . .'

'You keep a photocopy of the notes from his wife?'

'And then the envelope is resealed – he doesn't know, I'm sure.'

'Let me see it.'

'Do you read Russian?'

'And hurry it along, will you.'

'You'd better come down to the microfilm reader.'

The letters from Bekuv's wife – and even all the pages of the magazines etc. – were recorded on microfilm.

'The translator looked at it. He looks at everything. He said it was just the usual sort of thing.'

The spidery writing in the labyrinth of Russian script was made even more difficult to decipher when projected in negative upon the glass screen of the reader.

My love,

I hope you are well. Don't take sleeping tablets every night or you may become dependent on them. A milk drink used to be all you ever needed to sleep, why not try that again.

Here the weather is very cold and there is much rain, but they are being very kind to me. I was wrong about Miss Bancroft, she is a really wonderful girl. She is doing all she can to arrange that you and I can have a serious talk but for the present it is better we are separate. It is important, Andrei.

Your ever loving K.

I read a rough translation aloud to the man they called Jonathan.

'Nothing there – right?'

'Nothing,' I said.

'You don't sound very convinced. You think that they might have some sort of code?' he said.

'Every man and wife talk in code,' I said.

'Don't go philosophical on me, pal. I majored in chemistry.'

'It might mean something to him,' I said.

'Mean something that would make him want to take that whole jar of goofballs?'

'Could be.'

Jonathan sighed. From next door there came the buzz of the telex alarm and the chatter of the printer. He went to answer it.

I began to see Andrei Bekuv in a new light, and I felt a little guilty at the way I'd treated him. His querulous complaints, and the studied interest in music and hi-fi equipment, I saw now as desperate attempts to prevent himself thinking about his lesbian wife, and how much he needed her. This letter would be more than enough to tell him she was in love with Red Bancroft.

Jonathan interrupted this line of thought with a telex that he'd torn off the printer. It was coded and headed-up with the arranged cipher, but the signature was in clear triplicate.

MESSAGE BEGINS MOVE FABIAN TO AIRPORT IMMEDIATELY FOR AIR MOVEMENT FOXGLOVE STOP CIA REPRESENTATIVE AT TERMINAL STOP AMBROSE WILL TAKE LUCIUS THERE STOP YOU WILL TAKE CHARGE STOP AT YOUR DISPOSAL LIKEWISE AMBROSE JONATHAN AND STAFFS STOP WAIT FOR ME AND TAKE ORDERS FROM NO OTHER PERSON STOP HOLD THIS AS YOUR AUTHORITY STOP MESSAGE PRIORITY SANDMAN OPERATION PRIORITY PRESIDENTIAL REPEAT PRESIDENTIAL MESSAGE ENDS MANN MANN MANN ACKNOWLEDGE

'Acknowledge?' said Jonathan.

'Is there anyone there at the other end?'

'Only the operator.'

'Acknowledge it. Then ask Langley to give us scrambled telex facilities at the airport and some back-up. What have you got here?'

'Two cars and fourteen men, but six are on three-day lay-offs.'

'Armoured cars?'

'Windshield and gas tanks – the usual agency design.'

'We'll need more cars. Get a couple of your people to use their own. Don't tell Bekuv what's happening.'

'What *is* happening?' he asked.

'We're moving, that's what's happening.'

'You know what I think,' Jonathan said. 'I think this is an alarm. I think the Russians are going to hit this place and try snatching the professor from us.'

'Send the acknowledge.'

'You mean don't let Bekuv know until we're ready to go?'

'I mean don't let Bekuv know. You're setting up this wagon-train, and I want you to make it look really impressive. Bekuv will be travelling with me in the Stingray and we won't be anywhere near you.'

'I'll want that in writing, you know. It's dangerous. And on your own, you might have trouble getting Bekuv to move his ass.'

'I don't see why I should,' I said. 'He's going to see his missus, isn't he?'

20

Incoming flights were being diverted and delayed. Planes were circling and stacked all the way from Chesapeake Bay to the Allegheny Mountains. Outgoing flights were hours behind their scheduled times. The terminal buildings were a noisy chaos of irate travellers but we were half a mile away, and the airport seemed very still from the service area where Mann had improvised an emergency control room. There were half a dozen phones there, constantly ringing as CIA clerks lied to the press and deflected official inquiries. A quarter of a mile along the apron an Algerian Airways Ilyushin jet was parked. It was surrounded by service vehicles, and men were topping up its kerosene, pumping its sewage, loading hundreds of plastic meals, respooling its movies, generating its electricity, removing its baggage and loading its freight.

I delivered Bekuv to a CIA man and went into Mann's makeshift office.

Mann was making monosyllabic noises into a phone when I went into the room. 'What's going on?' I said.

He indicated a chair and, when he'd hung up the phone, he said, 'Gerry Hart is out there, with a Cold Combat Magnum in one hand and Senator Greenwood's necktie in the other.'

'You're kidding.'

'Yeah, I'm kidding – it's only a Centennial Airweight.' We watched a jumbo lumber past us round the perimeter.

'You made him run then.'

He gave me a sour smile. 'He's taking the four o'clock direct flight to Algiers, and I *do* mean taking it. He wants the Bekuvs with him, and he's threatening to blow Greenwood's head off if they are not delivered to him.'

'You're going to hand them over?'

'I'm not going to call his bluff. Everything points to Hart as a long-time commie agent. He's a pro – I believe he'd do it, don't you?'

'I don't know,' I said. I pulled a chair close to where he was sitting at the desk. 'This is not an escape. A guy like Hart must have a dozen good passports under the floorboards. And using Greenwood's name he could bump his way on to any Air Force jet.'

'So why is he in there with a cannon and leaping around like a vitamin pill endorsement?' said Mann. He put his hand-made English shoes, and their overshoes, into the middle of his paperwork, leaned back in the swivel chair and blew a smoke-ring at the ceiling.

I said, 'He wants the Bekuvs – you told me that – he's waiting for the Bekuvs.'

'Moscow won't give him a medal for this circus,' said Mann. 'This doesn't fit into the détente crap that the Russians are hard-selling Washington.'

I took off my leather overcoat and helped myself to one of Mann's cigarettes. 'If Hart wants the Bekuvs, then Moscow wants the Bekuvs,' I said.

'Naw,' said Mann. 'For all Moscow knows, we've milked the Bekuvs dry.'

'Not if the Bekuvs knew something so important that we'd be sure to act on it the moment we found out.'

Mann nodded reflectively. 'And something that Moscow would know we'd acted on, the moment we did it.' He got up and went to the window to stare at the Ilyushin jet. Then he looked to where the jumbo had reached the far end of the runway; it was now no more than a speck of aluminium, glinting in the winter daylight.

'How did Hart make contact?' I asked.

'Very cool. He teletyped Langley – Operations – told them that if everyone played along this end, he'd guarantee that there would be no public mention from the Moscow end.'

'Always the politician.'

'He knew that would appeal to the brass,' said Mann. 'A chance to brush a foul-up under the carpet . . . and by going through the teleprinter he knew that one of the copies would go to the director's office . . . no chance of us losing the offer between radiator and wall.'

Mann was still looking out of the window, watching the servicing of the Algerian jet, when there was a sudden roar from the distant jumbo and it came tottering down the runway at full power. It seemed very close before the nose lifted in rotation, and it screamed across our heads with enough noise to make the windows rattle. 'Flying dancehall!' said Mann, and turned back to the table that was strewn with his problems.

'Are we following the plane?' I asked.

'To Algeria? So that Hart and the Bekuvs can line up with all those black-power refugees, hijackers and hopheads from California and thumb their goddamned noses at us as the Aeroflot connection disappears into the sunset.'

'It was just a thought.'

'What's on your mind?'

I said, 'Suppose that what makes the Bekuvs important hasn't happened yet.'

'And it is going to happen. Is that what you mean?'

'If you were Bekuv, taking up our offer to let you

defect, would you put a little insurance into the safe deposit?'

'Electronic secrets, you mean? Maser equipment?'

'Who knows what.'

'So where's the safe deposit?' said Mann.

'Somewhere south of In-Salah. Somewhere in the Sahara desert, for instance? Somewhere you couldn't find unless Bekuv himself was along to help you.'

'Jesus Christ,' said Mann. He picked up a phone and dialled a three-digit number.

'You think I'm right?' I said.

'No,' said Mann, 'but I can't take a chance that you might be.' Into the phone he said, 'I'm going to need that airplane after all. In fact you'd better get me a ship that can get to Algiers a whole lot faster than that Ilyushin.'

A man came into the room. He had a federal marshal's buzzer tucked into his top pocket and a Smith and Wesson Heavy-Duty .44 sitting under his arm, in the sort of Cuban-hitch shoulder-holster that security men wear when they are not feeling shy. He gave a military salute and said, 'Miss Bancroft wants to see you, Major.'

'Show her in,' said Mann.

'Whatever you say, sir,' said the federal marshal, and withdrew.

Mann gave me the sort of smile you give a Jehovah's Witness before telling them to go away. I realized that he had Red Bancroft's report of my visit to the house. He said, 'Mrs Bekuv wants Miss Bancroft to go along with her.' He turned and saw through the frosted glass panel that someone was waiting outside the door. 'Come in, honey,' he called.

Red Bancroft wore a mustard-coloured jersey-knit dress, with a federal marshal's badge over the heart.

Mann said, 'We were just talking about it.'

'Gerry Hart is probably taking that plane to Moscow,' I said. I looked at her. 'Do you know what might happen to you in Moscow?'

Mann said, 'Are you sure Mrs Bekuv doesn't know you are in the CIA?'

'I don't think so,' said Red Bancroft.

'That's like walking into a police station to ask the time just after you stole a million dollars,' I said. 'Not thinking so is not enough. And besides, what use would you be to us – you have no communications link, no network, not even a contact. You've no field training and you don't speak Russian – do you?'

She shook her head.

I said, 'You could get the greatest breakthrough in the history of espionage, and how are you going to tell us?'

'I'd find a way,' she said. 'I've had field experience.'

'Look,' I said as kindly and as softly as I could manage. 'Moscow isn't Montreal, and the KGB are not a freaky group of Marxist drop-outs. They won't give you a map of the city, and stamp welcome into your passport, just because Mrs Bekuv is crazy about you . . . and that will be just for starters.'

'Now, take it easy,' said Mann.

Red Bancroft was angry. Her cheeks were flushed, and she bit into her lip to hold back a torrent of protests. Mann said, 'Well, it's my decision and I figure it's worth the risk.' Red Bancroft brightened. Mann said, 'What you tell Mrs Bekuv about your connection with the CIA is entirely up to you. It's a delicate situation and I don't want to be a back-seat driver. But – and here's a big but, honey – if I tell you to get off that plane in Algiers, or any other place Hart might be taking it, I want you to move fast. And I don't want any arguments – you got it?'

'You can count on that,' she said.

'Now you can get back to Mrs Bekuv,' said Mann. 'And if you've got any doubt about the way it's shaping up, I want you out. Right?'

'Right,' she said. She picked up her handbag from the desk, and said, 'Thank you, sir.' To me she gave no more than a nod.

When she'd gone I said, 'Whose idea was that?'

'Hers,' said Mann. 'She's Psychological Directorate; you know what they are like.'

'She's over-confident,' I said. 'We put in an attractive lesbian to seduce Mrs Bekuv away from her husband, and away from her KGB duties . . . but suppose in the course of the love affair, our girl falls in love. Suppose what we are seeing is Mrs Bekuv taking our girl back to Moscow as a big fat prize – and a way of getting herself and her husband off the hook.'

'Well, don't think that hasn't crossed my mind,' said Mann. He moved his feet off the blotter and swivelled his chair to watch me as I went to the window and looked at the hard grey sky.

'Don't sacrifice the girl in order to prove that the Psychological Directorate are stupid.'

'I wouldn't do that,' said Mann. He grabbed his nose and waggled it, as if trying to make it rattle. 'She's a damned good operative. If we ever get a woman running a division it will be Red Bancroft.'

'Not if she goes to Moscow it won't,' I said.

Mann pressed the button on his phone. 'Tell Miss Bancroft to take that goddamn marshal's badge off before she goes along the corridor to talk with the Russians,' he said into the phone. 'I'm going to see Hart.' He put the phone down. 'We're giving the Bekuvs to Hart now,' he told me. 'He's not dumb enough to let us take him,

229

without Greenwood getting it first – but you never know.'
Mann sighed.

They were drinking coffee in a freight office at the far end of the corridor. At first glance it was a cosy little scene until one took a closer look at Senator Greenwood. His high-notch hand-stitched Cheviot suit was crumpled, and the silk shirt was open at the front to reveal not only a gold medallion but also a loose collar of string that was attached to an M.3 submachine-gun in such a way that the muzzle was always under his chin and Gerry Hart's finger on the trigger.

Greenwood's face was tight, and his tan had faded. As we came into the room he turned to us and began his loud entreaties. 'Get me out of here,' he said. 'I'll guarantee the departure of the Algerian plane – my word of honour as a Senator – now just let's act like reasonable human beings.' Greenwood's voice was hoarse as though he'd said the same sort of thing many times.

'You're riding with us,' said Hart.

Greenwood turned his eyes to Mann. 'I hope you're satisfied,' he said. 'This is all your doing. It was your visit that caused all this.'

'Is that so,' said Mann politely, and it was his polite indifference that infuriated the Senator.

'When I get out of here, I'll come after you with . . .'

'Shut your mouth, Senator,' said Mann.

'I won't shut – '

Gerry Hart tugged on the string hard enough to strangle his words, and said, 'Yeah, do as the man says, Senator.'

Hart was wearing a waterproof zipper jacket with an airline badge; he looked like a baggage handler.

'You're flying these people to Algiers, then?' Mann asked Hart.

'I don't know yet,' said Hart. The lack of animosity

230

between the two men bewildered Greenwood, and frightened him, but he said nothing.

'Well, you'd better know soon, if you're taking the Algerian flight-crew,' Mann said. 'They haven't got the kind of flying experience that will wing you into any place you stab on the map.'

'Why would you worry about that, Major Mann?'

'Because I don't want that airplane blundering across the goddamned airlanes and scattering Ilyushin spare parts across the countryside, or my ass will be in a sling.'

'Well, that will be a nice way for me to go,' said Gerry Hart. He smiled.

I looked out of the window. The underside of the cloud was flat and featureless, like a sheet of mirror reflecting the wet concrete of the runways. And it was cold, so that in places there was ice underfoot.

Mann had brought in a lot of local help. There were men on the roofs of both maintenance hangars, and more on the freight administration block and along the walkways. The men were in pairs: a sniper with a rifle, and a back-up man wth a radio phone. There was a large, flat, open space between us and the Ilyushin out there on the tarmac. We all knew that Hart would have to walk there – using motor transport would make him more vulnerable – and we were all hoping that he'd make a mistake.

There was a crackle from the radio phone and Mann said, 'Tell the tower to stand by. And tell all units that the party is moving out to the plane.' He collapsed the antenna and put the radio phone back on to the desk, but from it came a continuing crackle of procedure.

There was a look of relief on Greenwood's face as the CIA man brought Professor Bekuv into the room. Red Bancroft came soon after with Mrs Bekuv. The two women linked arms. It is a common enough gesture in Russia, even between men walking down the street together, but there was no doubt that Professor Bekuv saw it in another light. He smiled at his wife; it was a sad smile.

The little office was crowded now. Both groups faced each other over the tops of the bull pens, where the freight office clerks usually worked. Each of these desk-top boxes bore the graffiti of its owner: nudes, views, picture postcards, phone numbers, cartoon drawings and countless impressions of the airline's rubber stamps. The air was thick with cigarette smoke, and condensation clouded the windows. Hart unleashed his hostage so that he had free use of the machine-gun.

'Away you go, mister,' Mann told Hart. We stood at the door as they filed through. 'Stay cool, Senator,' Mann said to Greenwood. 'Even the Russians will release a US Senator unharmed. They might even put Hart on the rack to show their good will.'

'They'll stage a press conference,' said Greenwood. 'They'll put me on show. They'll make me look a fool for having a Russian agent as my assistant.' It was typical of a politician that he should look so far ahead, and typical too that he should be more concerned with how it would look to the voters, than with how his stupidity had endangered his country.

'Can't prevent you looking a fool, I'm afraid,' said Mann. 'That's your department.' He smiled at Greenwood.

As we stepped out of the door after them, the icy breeze cut through me like a rusty sabre. We kept a distance between us as we followed the party that straggled their way towards the plane.

The Algerian airliner was parked on the far side of the

heat deflectors. This series of metal scoops, which formed a castellated steel wall, caught the hot gases from the jet engines and threw them, together with their ear-splitting noise, high into the air.

The refuelling had finished, and the servicing vehicles had all departed except for the mobile passenger steps. The flight-crew were aboard and carrying out the flight checks. Their voices could sometimes be heard over Mann's personal radio.

It began when Greenwood ran. He must have decided to bolt for the protection of the deflector wall. But after he'd run only a few paces, he halted, and looked back in an agony of indecision. One of the snipers on the roof of a maintenance hangar, fired next. The bullet hit the apron, somewhere between Greenwood and the rest of them. If it was meant as a way of encouraging Greenwood to run for it, it proved a signal failure, for he stood frozen to the spot.

Hart must have thought the bullet came from either me or Mann. He swung round and fired the M.3 at us. We were about a hundred yards behind them. The M.3 had been modified for single shot, and the slugs went high, whining over our heads. Mann was half-way between me and the deflector wall. He went down on one knee, bringing out a pistol as he did so. The gun jerked but the sound of the shots was lost in the roar of the jets as the pilot opened the throttles of the airliner.

Mann got to his feet and started to run. He was an easy target, and it was inevitable that he should be shot. Hart was struggling with the bolt of the gun. He found the auto-switch and fired a short burst at Mann, who was running hell-for-leather across the icy concrete. Mann was hit. He fell, sliding on the ice and then going full length on to the hard ground. He rolled over a couple of times but he stood no chance of getting to the cover offered by the metal barrier.

By this time my gun was up and I fired, but my shots went high and I heard them hit the metal and sing away into the sky. Mrs Bekuv snatched at the M.3 in Gerry Hart's hands, and swung round to shoot Senator Greenwood. At point-blank range, those big .45 bullets tear a hole in anything, but before she had time to pull the trigger Hart was standing in front of her, grabbing at the gun to get it back.

I ran. There was ice everywhere. I heard it crack under my toes like paper-thin glass, and more than once I slid and almost lost my balance. I threw myself down alongside Mann. 'Are you hit?' I asked him. He didn't reply. His eyes were shut.

I ran a hand back along the side of his head and it came away covered in blood. I got one arm round him and dragged him towards the metal wall. The jet engine's piercing scream modulated to a roar, and I heard the cough of a gun and felt chips of concrete hit my face and hands. Mann struggled and became conscious. 'Leave me,' he said. 'Leave me or they'll get both of us.'

I knelt down, and turned to see Hart and Mrs Bekuv struggling for possession of the grease gun. He had both hands on it and was getting it away from her. I was huffing and puffing from exertion, and to steady my gun I planted my fist upon Mann's shoulder. I aimed and fired twice. Both bullets hit Gerry Hart. He flung his arms out, like a man trying to catch a ball that was too high for him, and his feet left the ground as the force of the bullets knocked him backwards full length.

Now I grabbed Mann and, half dragging him and half carrying him, I lugged him all the way to the big metal blades of the deflector and dumped him there. With both hands clamped round my pistol, I swung it round to where Mrs Bekuv was standing with the submachine-gun. But she had no eyes for me. With Hart sprawled on the ground with his eyes closed, she was able to bring the gun back to Senator Greenwood again. His eyes opened wide with terror and I saw his mouth gabbling a torrent of words that were swept away on the gases of the jet noise as the pilot brought all four engines up to full power.

Behind the noise of the jets, the cameo was mute, like some parody of a silent film. In the dim light of the overcast day, the submachine-gun made orange fire as it twisted in her hands. Greenwood cowered, holding up a slim hand in supplication, but he was torn in two by the stream of large-calibre bullets. Mrs Bekuv tightened her hold upon the gun to prevent it spraying upwards, and this tension contorted her face with a grimace of rage and hate that one would have expected only from a bad actor. Greenwood's blood spurted high enough to spatter the underside of the jet plane's wing tip. And then the Bekuvs and Red Bancroft were lost to view behind a confusion of blue uniforms as the flight-crew surrounded them.

'Run, Red,' I yelled, and half expected that she'd bring the Bekuvs back. But Professor Bekuv was pointing a gun at her. My words were lost on the wind, and anyway it was too late.

'Don't shoot,' said Mann.

I looked down and he'd rolled over to get a view of what was happening. His trenchcoat was filthy and his hair matted with mud and with the blood that was running down the side of his face. 'Hit one of the Algerian flight-crew, or even the goddamned airplane, and we'll have an international incident on our hands.'

'I thought we already had one,' I said. But I lowered my gun, and watched as Mrs Bekuv pushed Red Bancroft and her husband up the steps and into the plane. The door clamped shut and the airliner vibrated against the wheel-brakes and the lights winked. Mann's radio phone buzzed. I picked it up.

'Tower to Major Mann,' said the radio. 'The captain requests that we remove the passenger steps.'

Mann was groggy. He gave an almost imperceptible nod. 'Remove the steps,' I told them.

Mann saw the blood down the front of my shirt and realized that it was his own. He reached up to his head and touched the place where the bullet had nicked his skull. The pain of it made him suck his teeth very hard, but it was only when he turned far enough to see the airliner that he said, 'Ouch!'

'You saved me,' said Mann. 'And it was close – damned close.'

'Yes,' I said. 'Another rumble like that and I ask for a no-claims discount on my life insurance.'

'Mark-up one favour,' said Mann, and punched my arm in appreciation.

'Hart tried to protect Greenwood,' I said. 'Did you see that?'

Mann gave a grim little smile. 'Hart didn't want to lose a good hostage,' he said.

'Perhaps,' I said.

'And our Miss Bancroft wasn't working hard to jog anyone's gun arm out there, was she?' said Mann.

'Perhaps she didn't get much of a chance,' I said.

'And perhaps we've lost her to Madame Bekuv. Perhaps, instead of gaining a defector, we've lost an operative.'

I watched as the steps were driven away and the

Ilyushin released its wheel-brakes on the port side and swung round to face the feeder channel. The rising heat of the jets turned the airport buildings into grey jelly, and sent us enough unburned hydro-carbons to make our eyes water. The jets fanned over the apron, to make the puddles shimmer, and to gently ruffle the clothing of the two dead men.

I switched Mann's radio to the control frequency and heard the Algerian pilot say, 'Tower – this is Alpha double eight requesting take-off clearance.'

The reply came promptly, 'Roger Alpha double eight, cleared to runway two five, cleared for take-off. Wind two seven zero, at eight knots gusting fifteen . . .' I switched it off, and we watched the Ilyushin trundle off to the far end of the runway.

Mann was bleeding badly. 'We'd better get along to the doctor,' I said.

'You feeling sick?' Mann inquired politely.

The Ilyushin's engines came to full power, one at a time. Then, with all brakes released, it grew bigger and bigger, until, when it seemed it must roll over us, it lifted. With a brain-numbing roar it passed low over our heads.

'Yes,' I said.

21

The town of Algiers fits snugly into the curve of its massive bay. It is a city of narrow alleys and steep staircases, hovels and office blocks, secret gardens and boulevards. At its feet there is a busy port. Behind it, the roads hairpin up into the lush green hills and pine forests, climbing ever higher into the Atlas Mountains. It's an uncomfortable place. Of the whole African coastline, only the Red Sea gets hotter in summer, and few places get as much rain in winter. It was dark by the time we arrived and raining heavily.

Percy Dempsey was at the airport. He'd brought his own personal Peugeot 504. You'll not see many of those broken down along the desert tracks, polished silver by the sand. Down south in the Sahara there were only Peugeots, and Landrovers, and the smart little cars that came in by transporter. And Percy's was special; he'd taken the sump away, to provide a flat underside. The oil was pumped out of a tank in the boot. It reduced the luggage space but it was a small price to pay for a desert-worthy car.

Percy Dempsey was wearing a suit – perhaps the cable, and the CIA contact-man, had given him hopes of a long-term contract with the Americans – and a waistcoat, and a public-school tie, Charterhouse as I remember it. The grubby trenchcoat let him down, or did he think that was *de rigueur* for agents. The Algiers traffic moved slowly through the night. Yellow headlights glared through the spray and darkness.

'I sent one of my people down to Ghardaia,' said Percy. 'If they are going south to the Sahara they will have to go that way.'

'Has he got a two-way radio in the car?' said Mann.

'That would be rather dangerous, Major,' said Percy. 'Only the police are permitted such luxuries. In any of these towns and villages you can find the police station, simply by looking for the only building with a radio mast.' Percy murmured some gentle Arabic oath as the truck ahead of us stopped and signalled that it was going to turn into the docks.

'How will we know what's happening down there?'

'My man's based in a hotel, Major. We can speak to him on the phone.' A driver behind us sounded his horn, and so did another behind him.

'We don't even know they will go south,' said Mann. 'They might just transfer to the Aeroflot flight and continue through to Moscow.'

'I thought we'd have something to eat,' said Percy. 'They won't be here for hours. You made good time.' The truck turned, and we moved on into the city.

'They sold them only enough fuel to get to London. That will delay their arrival time by nearly two hours,' I told him.

'You're not worried that they might change plans in London?' Percy asked.

'That will be prevented,' I said. We stopped at a big intersection while a traffic cop twirled a baton and blew his whistle.

'Bekuv will go south all right,' said Percy. 'I had that feeling when we met him that day. He had unfinished business here in the desert.' He turned off the main boulevard into a succession of ever narrower streets.

'Where were you when we needed you?' said Mann sarcastically.

'Hindsight,' admitted Percy. 'Pure hindsight, I admit. But if you think about his indecision that day . . .' He pointed. 'This is the Kasbah,' he said. 'That's the big market.'

Mann nodded.

Percy said, 'People only go south if they have a purpose. You don't go into the Sahara to hide. Are they looking for something? Do you know what?' he parked the car in a space marked private.

'No,' I said.

'Big or small?'

'Big,' I said.

'How the hell could you know that?' said Mann.

'Deduction. Something very small and he might have tried to conceal it. Even something of a medium size would have tempted him to take it into a village post office and address it poste restante in the USA.'

'Screw it,' said Mann. 'Maybe they won't even leave the airport.'

'Big,' I said. 'It will be big.'

Percy locked the car and led the way through a maze of alleys, each one narrower than the one before it. Every third shop seemed to be a butcher, and the carcasses were displayed complete with skin and fur. 'Ughh,' said Mann.

Percy had first discovered this place during the war when he was a young officer with the First Army. He'd returned in 1955, and on and off he'd lived here ever since, right through the fighting and the restrictions and difficulties that followed it. Of course Percy spoke Arabic; not just the elegant stuff used by Cairo eggheads who came to the university to lecture on poetry, but the coarse dialects of the southern villagers and the laconic mumblings of the nomad.

The alley in which Percy lived was steep and narrow. Most of the windows were shuttered, but a café was marked by bright yellow patches of light and the ululating song of Om Kalsum, the Ella Fitzgerald of Arab pop.

This part of the old Arab quarter must have been unchanged for a thousand years. Only by common consent were the premises defined, for the rooms of one house were the upstairs of the place next door. Percy's frontage was no more than the width of his battered old door, but once inside the place opened up to become a dozen rooms, with – at the back – a view into the courtyard of a dilapidated mosque.

I heard Percy Dempsey go to the back of the house and tell the servant to fetch food. Then he returned to the front, and poured wine for some and a Jack Daniels for Major Mann. Percy had that sort of memory.

Three of the original cell-like rooms had been knocked together. The changes of level that provided a step at the entrance to each room put the dining space on a platform at the end of the living-room. Antique swords were arranged over the fireplace, where smoke rose from a log fire that was only just alight. Over the dining-table – it was too large, and the ceilings too low, for it to fit anywhere else – there was a brass chandelier that was said to have been looted from a house in Oran when the French departed. An ornate 'Chinese Chippendale' mirror provided anyone sitting at the head of the table with a chance to see into the kitchen. The floor was pine boarding, polished like glass. The carpets were brushed, the books were placed in the shelves according to size rather than subject, and the mirror was gleaming as brightly as the brass chandelier and the blades of the swords. And yet there was no cosiness. Here was obsessional cleanliness, combined with masculine orderliness in a way you seldom find, except in a lighthouse.

Mann lowered himself on to the sofa, holding his drink high so that none of it would spill. 'How do you know they will phone in good time?'

Percy said, 'Just relax for a moment, you've had a long journey.'

'Why don't you just check that your telephone is working?' It wasn't a suggestion, it was an order.

'Because I've already done so,' said Percy. He poured himself a little tonic water, and turned to look at Mann. Now that his hat was off, you could see the shaved patch of skull, the stains of the antiseptic and the large pink piece of sticking-plaster that the doctor had applied to the bullet graze. The bruising from its impact reached all the way from his discoloured eye to his stiff neck. Percy studied it with interest but did not comment.

Mann scowled and sipped at his Jack Daniels. I could tell that he approved of the high standards of hygiene that were present on every side.

Percy said, 'I hope you like Arab food.' He leaned over the dining-table to rearrange the cutlery and the glasses. I got the idea that he'd been rearranging them all the afternoon.

'I didn't come all this way for fancy cooking,' said Mann.

'But this is delicious,' said Percy.

'Look, pal. My idea of culinary exotica is hot pastrami on rye bread.'

Percy smiled, but the smile became rather fixed, and he continued to adjust the table setting in a more mechanical manner.

I walked through the kitchen to the balcony at the

242

back. It was like being in the doll's-house, the balcony was no larger than a pocket handkerchief, and it was spitting distance from here to the street. There was a wonderful view. The rain had almost stopped and stars peered through gaps in the cloud. You could see the old port and the black ocean beyond. The Grand Mosque was outlined against the night sky, and I could hear the same Arab music that I'd heard from the street.

Percy came into the kitchen whistling. He lifted the lid from a pot and brought a cooked lobster out of the water. He split it into sections with all the skills and strength of a professional chef. 'Your friend . . .' he said, still looking down at the lobster, '. . . do you think that crack on the head affected him?'

'No, he's always like that,' I said.

'Odd chap . . . and he can't sit still for a moment.' There was the sound of the front door opening. 'It's my servant with the food,' said Percy.

From the next room Mann bellowed. 'Hey, Pop. There's a waiter arrived with a mountain of chow.'

'Oh, dear,' said Percy, and sighed.

By the time I got back to the dining-table, the table was arrayed with the tiny dishes that the Arabs called *mezze*. There were miniature kebabs, sliced tomato, shiny black olives, stuffed vine leaves and bite-sized pies of soft flaky pastry. The servant was a young man. There was rain on his starched white jacket, and I guessed he'd been to some local restaurant to get the food and the strong Arab coffee that I could smell. He was a handsome youth, very slim, with carefully arranged hair and large, sad, brown eyes. He watched Percy all the time. At one time I would have been indifferent to Percy's choice of such handsome young employees – smiled even – but now I found it more difficult to write it off as just a part of the fascinating spectrum of human passion.

'I don't want a foul-up,' said Mann. He tucked a napkin into his collar, and leaned forward over the table, sniffing at the *mezze* and pushing the dishes aside until he came to the platter of hot lobster. He speared a large piece of it.

'Nothing will go wrong,' said Percy. He gave the servant the emptied tray, and indicated that he would serve the coffee himself. The boy withdrew. 'I'll drive,' said Percy. 'I know these roads. I've spent the best part of twenty years going into the desert. But the roads over the mountains are dangerous and narrow, with hairpin bends, crowded villages and bus-drivers who know only the horn and accelerator. If a man is young enough and reckless enough . . .' Percy paused, '. . . to say nothing of frightened enough, he'll outstrip any car that follows him.'

'Or get killed himself,' said Mann, with a large piece of lobster in his mouth.

'Or get killed himself,' said Percy, as he picked up a knife and fork. 'There's local beer or *ouzo*, or you can continue with the Jack Daniels.'

'And when you get over the mountains?' asked Mann. He leaned back in the delicate chair until it creaked, and then held a speared chunk of lobster aloft, chewing pieces from it and nodding approval at the flavour.

'The high plateau and then more mountains – the Ouled Nail – before you reach Laghouat, where the real desert begins: about 400 kilometres in all.'

'By that time they will know they are being followed,' said Mann.

'My dear fellow,' said Percy. He chuckled. 'He'll know he's being followed before you're in the hills, before

244

you're out of the suburbs even. If you were hoping to be inconspicuous, forget it. At this time of year there will be hardly any private cars down there in the desert. He'll see your dust for a hundred kilometres.'

Mann prodded at some cubes of grilled cheese before putting one into his mouth. They were very hot. He tried not to show his discomfort, although tears came into his eyes.

'I think Percy should drive,' I said.

Mann clamped a napkin to his mouth, nodded, looked up to see if anyone was watching him, and finally swallowed the burning-hot cheese.

'That's settled then,' said Percy and reached for the same grilled cheese cubes. He put three of them into his mouth and chewed impassively. I realized then that it was the similarity of their upbringing that made them so antagonistic. Exchange Percy's public school for the Mid-West military academy where Mann's estranged parents had sent him, and each would have become the other.

It was the small hours before the Algerian jet arrived at Algiers Airport. Mrs Bekuv must have known that we'd be waiting for her on the other side of the barrier. Whatever kind of deal the men from the Russian Trade Delegation made with the authorities, it included permission for her to leave the airport on the far side. We almost missed her altogether – but Percy's pal in Immigration tipped us off, and we gave chase.

They were in a Landrover: the two Bekuvs, Red Bancroft and the driver who had delivered the vehicle. It was that dark hour before dawn that you read about in books, and the windscreen was awash with rain and the car ahead of us no more than a blurred dribble of yellow headlights, with a couple of red dots when the driver stabbed the brakes.

We didn't speak much, the noise of the engine, the heavy rain and the thrash of the wipers made it necessary for Percy to shout. 'This bloke's damned good, and I'll tell you that for nothing!'

We were climbing. The villages were shuttered and silent. As we roared through them, there came the answering bellow of our reflected sound. All the time the rain continued. The tyres were uncertain on the steep, twisting road. Percy clawed at the steering-wheel as each hairpin revealed another hairpin, and soon the windscreen flashed pink with the raw light of dawn.

'We've got him on speed,' said Percy, 'but he's got the better traction. Damn you!' He blasted the horn as a man on a mule swayed out into our paths. 'It's like that game that children play – stones, paper and scissors – there's no telling yet what will prove the most important.'

'They know we're behind them,' said Mann.

'A driver like that,' said Percy with unconcealed admiration, 'has already calculated our tyre pressures and how much I had to drink last night.'

The sun came up very quickly, its light intermittently extinguished by the black clouds that were racing across the sky, and its almost horizontal rays shafting into our eyes, and twisting with every movement of the car. Percy slammed the sun visor fully down but it didn't help much.

They began to force the pace now, and the road became more difficult. On one side there were steep banks, pine trees and outcrops of vertical rock; on the other a sheer drop over an unmarked edge. And not all the road was hard. More than once, a sudden patch of loose surface hammered the metal underside, sent the car sliding and made the wheels spin.

Percy stared ahead, concentrating on the road's near-side edge, hitting the accelerator as soon as a curve could be seen as nothing more than a kink. He used the camber of the road too, steering up it – at an angle to the road's direction – to get maximum traction and the burst of acceleration that it provided. For one section of the road we were actually leaping into the air from one camber to the next.

'Christ,' said Mann the first time Percy did it, but the jarring crash as the car landed back on the road caused him to bite his tongue and fall sideways across the back seat.

'Hold tight,' said Percy and gave a fruity chuckle. Mann swore through his teeth.

Ahead of us, the Landrover disappeared in a fountain of spray as it hit a rain-filled ridge and was jolted up into the air. Percy pumped the brakes releasing the pressure each time the car's front dipped on its suspension. By the time we reached the ridge our speed was down to forty. The other car had spilled enough of the rainwater for us to see the ragged series of potholes. Percy flicked the steering, to hit it on a curving path and so bring the outer wheels – with the lighter loading – over the deepest hole.

In spite of all his skill we landed with a brain-shattering thump, and a terrible groan of metal. Mann clasped his hands upon his head in an effort to save himself more pain.

But the Landrover was also having problems. There were four of them crowded into it and the big bump must have shaken them up for they had slowed enough for us to be eating their spray.

'Grab her ass,' said Mann. Percy moved up close and now we could see that Mrs Bekuv was the driver. For a couple of miles we raced along together.

'It's in the soft sand where they will laugh at us,' said Percy. 'With that four-wheel drive they can crawl off into the desert and come back to the macadam again while we're still digging.'

'You brought sand-mats?' said Mann, all ready for a row.

'What are sand-mats?' said Percy, tilting his head to see Mann's reaction in the mirror. Mann gave a humourless smile and said nothing.

Although the sun was up, the rain cloud obscured it. A few yellow lights high on the road ahead of us fast became a village. The Landrover's horn echoed in the narrow street. Scarcely slowing, we followed them through the twisting alleys. A sudden scream of brakes told us that Mrs Bekuv had seen a huge desert bus, parked in the middle of the road, but the Landrover raced on, its speed scarcely checked. Avoiding a head-on collision by only the narrowest of margins, the Landrover lurched as it climbed on to the footpath and screamed through the narrow gap. Percy followed. Men and women scattered. There was a snowstorm of chicken feathers, as hens broke loose from the roof-rack of the bus, and flailed through the air, and a sickening thump as one of them struck the side of the car. Then we were through, and on the mountain road again. The surface was loose gravel and Percy dropped back as some of it hit our windscreen.

'Just hold them like that,' said Mann and for a few minutes we did. Then, after the straight stretch, with Percy pushing the needle well past a hundred, the road looped suddenly and dropped away in a tangle of hairpins to run along a short luxuriant valley.

'Jesus!' shouted Mann and I heard Percy gasp. Ahead of us the Landrover had slowed. On this straight stretch of road, that meant they were still doing well over fifty. It

248

slid sideways a little, waggled its behind and then picked up speed again as a large piece of it fell into the roadside. Percy's arm came across my chest, as he jammed his foot hard on to the brakes. We shrieked to a halt. Even so, we had to go into reverse in order to find the bundle that they had tossed out of the door.

Mann was out of the car before I was. The rain-soaked grass was high, and the twisted body of a man was tangled into it. We crouched over him and Mann picked up his limp arm and sought his pulse.

'The driver from the Trade Delegation – looks like a Russkie, eh?'

'Poor bastard,' I said. The man groaned and as he opened his mouth, I saw that his teeth were stained with blood. 'They've dumped him to lighten the weight,' I said. The boy vomited. It was mostly blood.

'Looks like it,' said Mann. To the boy he said, 'Which of them did it?' but he got only a whimper in reply.

'What kind of people are we dealing with?' I said. I wiped the boy's face with my handkerchief.

'Got to go,' said Mann getting to his feet.

'We can't just leave him here,' I protested.

'No alternative,' said Mann. 'Jesus, you know that. They are just counting on us being soft-hearted enough to stay with the kid.'

I got to my feet. 'No,' I said. 'I think they meant to slow up enough to let him out safely but misjudged things.'

'That's right,' said Mann. 'And there really is a Santa Claus – move your tail, baby.'

There was a growl from the engine as Percy flipped the accelerator pedal. The dying boy looked at me pleadingly but I turned away from him and followed Mann back to the car. Percy pulled away before the doors were closed.

'Catch up!' ordered Mann.

'That's not the problem,' said Percy. 'The problem is finding them again if they pull off the road and hide.' I realized then that both these men had the sort of honesty and devotion to duty that enabled them to disregard the dying boy. I did not admire it.

'There, there, there!' said Mann.

The dark-green Landrover was no larger than a toy and difficult to see amongst the pine trees, the scrub and mud-spattered rock. But now that Mann had pointed it out, I saw it skittering behind the trees and kicking its heels as it leaped over the hump-backed bridge that marked the bottom of the valley.

Now it was a different sort of driving; steeply downhill in places, with more and more people on the road, and horses too. At one point some soldiers tried to wave us down. Percy blasted the horn and they jumped aside.

'Was that a road block?' asked Mann.

'Hitch-hikers,' said Percy.

'Let's hope you're right,' said Mann.

We could no longer see the Landrover. It must have been a mile or two along the valley by this time. Percy pushed up the speed until we were slipping and sliding in the mud and gravel. Then the road climbed again. It climbed a thousand feet, and here it was drier, except for the rainwater that spewed across the road from overflowing gullies. We crossed the brow of the next hill to face a bleak sky, glassy like a pink-tinted mirror. Percy screwed up his eyes to see the road that twisted away along the side of a spur. We could no longer see the other car and Percy went faster and faster. For the first time in my life I felt car-sick.

Percy had an amazing technique for hairpins: he went into them at full speed, and, shortly before the bend,

250

turned the wrong way – to lose speed – and then steered the other way. The pendulum effect flicked us round the curve of the hairpin. And Percy was plunging his foot down on the accelerator even before the car had slewed far enough to face the next stretch. We were cannoning forward so fiercely that the seat-back jarred my kidneys. There wasn't room to make a mistake. To the left side of the road there was jagged cliff, and on our right a precipice. All the windows of the car were now plastered in watery mud and only the area covered by the wipers was clear.

Thin rain continued to fall but it was not enough to wash the mud from the side windows and only just sufficient to lubricate the wipers. The next bend brought a tidal wave of mud and loose grit. Percy wound his window down to provide better visibility and on my side I did the same. The cold wet wind howled through the car.

We were doing one hundred, over a blind hump, when we saw it.

The theory says that if you hit a flock of sheep at that sort of speed, you ride over them like an ice-skater in an abattoir. It isn't true. 'This is it,' shouted Percy. There was no chance of avoiding them; they were all over the road, there must have been hundreds of them, baa-baaing, running or staring at us transfixed by fear.

Percy jabbed the accelerator and steered directly at the rockface. We hit it with a spine-jarring bang that made the car body sing like a tuning-fork. Then a mess of suspension and metalwork sheared away from the rest of the car. The front dropped and chiselled into the road surface, producing a torrent of small stones that took out the windscreen, like the fire from a heavy machine-gun. We were 'rubbing off' speed and, as the car slowed, its back whipped round until we were facing the way we had come.

Percy was doing it all according to the book. He kept his foot hard down on the gas, and the spinning wheels began to slow us a little, tearing their rubber into shreds, and making a cloud of black smoke that eclipsed the world. But it didn't slow us enough, and with the engine still screaming its protest we raced backwards at seventy miles an hour.

I ripped at the door to open it but couldn't find the catch. My seat snapped, and my head hit the roof as we plunged off the edge of the world. The engine shrieked, and the earth turned askew, and we slid down the precipice with a thunderous bombardment of car components and a green snowstorm. Twice the car was almost halted by trees and scrub and twice it ripped its way through them. But now, with the suspension torn loose and a wheel missing, we were furrowing soft hillside. We slowed, lurched, tipped and finally stopped at a steep angle, embraced by a tangle of thorns, rocks and bushes. I was sprawled back in my broken seat, listening to the gurgle of escaping liquids. The air was filled with the stink of fuel and I would have gagged on it but for the way in which I was being strangled by my seat-belt.

Percy's eyes were closed, and there was blood on his face. I couldn't turn enough to see where Mann was. I tried to pull my leg free but it was trapped in the mangled metalwork, between the smashed instruments and the steering-wheel. I tugged at my leg. Someone was shouting 'fire' but the voice soon softened to a whisper and drifted away into the darkness. It was cold, very, very cold.

22

A blinding light flashed in my eyes and, as I came more
fully conscious, I saw its beam flicker across the ceiling,
and backwards and forwards over the brightly coloured
Islamic texts that were pinned to the wall. The iron
bedstead creaked as I moved under the rough blanket
which covered my legs. Only slowly did I focus on the
man. He was sitting motionless in the corner, a fat man
with an unshaven face and heavy-lidded eyes. Behind
him there was a broken clock and a heavily retouched
colour lithograph of a uniformed politician.

The fat man spoke without moving a muscle and
almost without moving his mouth. 'The man with the hat
awakes.' His Arabic was from far to the east of here;
Egypt, perhaps, where the man with the hat – *charwaja* –
is the non-believer, the infidel, the enemy.

A voice from the next room said, 'It is the will of God,'
without endorsing God's decision enthusiastically.

'Get him,' said the fat man.

I heard movements from the next room, and with
difficulty I moved my head round until I could see
the doorway. Eventually Percy Dempsey arrived. The
blinding light met my eyes again, and I saw that it came
from a small wall-mirror moved by the draught from the
door.

'How do you feel?' said Percy. He had a cup of coffee
in his hand.

'Lousy,' I said. I took the coffee he offered. It was
strong and black and very sweet.

'Your friend got another crack on the head,' said Percy. 'He's conscious but he's sleeping. You'd better come and look at him. I say! steady on with my coffee.'

I got out of bed and found I was fully dressed except for my shoes. I put them on and, as I bent down, suffered pain in a dozen muscles that I never knew I had. 'You did a good job, Percy,' I said. 'Thanks.'

'If you've got to hit anything: hit it backwards. My old dad taught me that, and he won the Monte two years running.'

'Well, he should have tried it driving,' I said.

Percy smiled politely and showed me to the little bare room where they had laid Major Mann. Someone had removed his tie and his boots, and folded his jacket to go under his head. His hair was ruffled and his face unshaven, and the bruising from the bullet nick had now turned one half of his face into a rainbow of blues, pinks and purples.

I leaned over him and shook him. 'Waaaw?' said Mann.

'Coffee, tea, or me?' I said.

'Beat it,' said Mann, without opening his eyes. 'Go away and let me die in peace.'

'Don't be a spoilsport,' I said. 'We want to watch.'

Mann grunted again and looked at his wrist-watch. He moved his arm backwards and forwards, as if to get it into focus. Finally he said, 'We've got to get on the road.'

'Get what on the road?' I asked. 'Our car is wrecked.'

Percy said, 'You want to buy a car? Eighty-five thousand on the clock, one owner. Never raced or rallied.'

'Well, rent another car,' said Mann.

'I did,' said Percy. 'I did it about five hours ago, when you were fast asleep. It should arrive any time at all.'

'Well, don't sit back waiting for a round of applause,' said Mann. 'Get on the phone and hurry them up.'

'Don't fret,' said Percy. 'I've made contact with my chap down in Ghardaia. The Landrover filled up there. He's following, and will leave messages along the route.'

'How?' said Mann.

'This isn't Oxford Street,' explained Percy. 'This is the Trans-Sahara Highway. Either they have to go south through In-Salah, or they take the other route down through Adrar, Reggane and eventually to Timbuktu.'

'The way we came last time,' said Mann. He wiped his face with a hand, and touched the puffy bruising of his chin and cheek. Then he heaved himself into a sitting position, and unfolded the jacket that had been under his head. He looked at me. 'You don't look so good,' he told me.

'And I don't feel so good,' I admitted, 'but at least my brain is still ticking over. Do you two think Mrs Bekuv wanted a Landrover because it matches the colour of her earrings? Or because they were discounted this week. I prefer to guess that she radioed Algiers from the plane, and specified that car.'

'Why?' said Mann.

'Ah. Why indeed? Why choose a car that can be outpaced by anything from a housewife's Fiat to a local bus. We've been breathing down their necks as far as this – so why didn't she ask for a tweaked-up car. Keep to the macadam and you could do the trip in a Ferrari, give or take a couple of sand filters and a sump guard.'

'But they couldn't have got past the end of the macadam,' said Percy. 'The made-up road ends in In-Salah on one route, and south of Adrar on the other. After that it's only one track.'

'Brilliant,' I said sarcastically. 'You think she's not bright enough to have a desert-worthy vehicle waiting down south. She waves goodbye and they get the best of both worlds.'

'This is not my day for riddles,' said Mann. 'Give it to me.'

'They will leave the road,' I said. 'Whatever they are going to do isn't going to be done at the poolside of some government hotel. They are going to drive off into the desert. And if she is as bright as I think she is, they will leave the road at night.'

'And that's why Bekuv came north to meet us driving that GAZ,' said Mann. 'It was such a conspicuous vehicle – that's the only GAZ I've seen in the whole of Algeria – he took it so that, before meeting with us, he could detour out into the desert and bury whatever it is they are going to collect.'

'It's too big to bury,' I said. 'I've told you that.'

'If you're right,' said Percy, 'we're going to need a Landrover too.'

'Yes,' I said.

'Or a big truck,' Percy said. 'A lightly loaded truck is as desert-worthy as a Landrover.'

Mann turned to Percy and prodded him in the chest with a nicotine-stained forefinger. 'I want to follow them across that desert wherever they go,' Mann said. 'You fix it so that we can travel across the sand, wadis, rocks – any damn where.'

23

Men become mesmerized by the desert, just as others become obsessed with the sea; not because of any fondness for sand or water, but because oceans and deserts are the best places to observe the magical effect of ever-changing daylight. Small ridges, flattened by the high sun, become jagged mountains when the sunlight falls across them, and their shadows, pale gold at noontime, become black bottomless pools.

The sun was high by the time we reached the desert. A man could stand in his own shadow, should he want to brave the heat of noon. Not many did. No goats, no camels, not even snakes or scorpions move at that time of day. Just mad dogs, Englishmen and Major Mann of the CIA.

Through the car's ventilator there came a constant rain of fine sand. I closed the vent and opened the window – the wind blew hot. I closed it again. Percy mopped his brow. Ahead of us the road shimmered in the heat. The sky was not blue; it was a hazy white, like the distant sand. There was no horizon. The glaring sunlight conjured up great lakes which disappeared only a moment before we plunged into them.

The road south is built along the edge of a sand sea as large as England. The dunes were like scaly, brown, prehistoric monsters, slumbering in the heat and breathing the puffs of sand that twisted off their peaks. And across the road writhed more sand, phantom snakes of it that hissed at the underside of the car as we sliced through them. In places the drifting sand settled on the road, making ramps that were difficult to see. We all had our seat-belts as tight as they would go but they didn't prevent us striking the roof or window when our suspension hit a big one.

'It will only need one slightly bigger than that,' I said after one particularly violent bump from a sand-ridge, 'to write us off.'

'Patrols clear them every week or so, at this time of year,' said Percy. 'It's worth a gamble while the wind stays where it is.'

'And is the wind staying where it is?'

He lifted a hand off the wheel for long enough to show me the smudge of duststorm that he had been watching. 'She's coming to meet us, I think,' he said.

'Jesus,' said Mann, 'that's all I need.' We watched it without speaking, until Mann said, 'Is that a village ahead, or an oasis?'

'Neither,' said Percy.

'Stop anyway,' said Mann. 'It's time for a leak.'

What had looked like trees were a dozen thorn-bushes, strung out in such a way as to suggest that they marked an underground watercourse, if only you dug deep enough. There was an old Renault there too, stripped of everything so that only the steel shell remained. The outside was polished shiny by the windblown sand, and the inside was sooty. It would make a convenient place for travellers to build a fire. I looked inside and found some burned chunks of rubber tyre – the nomad's fuel – and some broken bottles, the pieces scoured and white. There was a screwed-up cigarette packet too. I picked it up and flattened it – Kool Mentholated Filter Longs, the cigarettes that Red Bancroft smoked. I threw it away again, but I knew I was still not free of her.

'A leak, I said! Not a shit, shower, shave, shampoo and set.' It was Mann treating us to a favourite sample of his army witticisms as he stood by the car door, tapping his fingers impatiently. 'And I'm driving,' he said as I got in.

'Very well,' said Percy. 'We're not in a hurry.'

I stretched out in the back and dozed. Now and again there was a sudden jolt that rocketed me up to the car roof. The sun dropped and went yellow and then gold. The sky turned mauve and the dunes seemed to arch their backs as they spread their shadows. There were no flies on the windscreen now, and the air was dry and the temperature cooled enough to make it worth opening the window. The sand hissed at us and our registration plates were by now raw metal, with no letters or numbers visible, it was the mark of cars that went deep into the desert and in the villages people noted us.

I slept fitfully, awakened sometimes by oncoming vehicles that forced us off the track, and at other times by falling weightless through terrible dreams. The sun dropped out of sight and there was only the tunnel that our headlights bored through the limitless night.

'My fellow will be waiting,' said Percy. His voice was cold and distant in the manner that all men's voices assume at night. 'He'll have camels – if we need them.'

'Not for me,' said Mann. 'I'm trying to give them up.' He laughed loudly, but Percy didn't join in. Soon after that I must have gone to sleep.

'You can put both the USA and China into the continent of Africa and still have room to rattle them about,' said Percy Dempsey. He was driving.

'I know some people in Vermont who wouldn't like that,' said Mann.

Dempsey gave a perfunctory laugh. Ahead of us the road stretched as straight as a ruler into the heat haze. Only the occasional drifts of sand made Dempsey moderate the speed. 'A convoy . . . parked, by the look of it.' Dempsey's eyes seemed myopic and watery when he was reading the newspaper, or one of his favourite Simenons, but here in the desert his eyesight was acute and he could interpret smudges on the horizon long before Mann or I could see them. 'Not trucks . . . buses,' he added. 'Too early for a brew-up.'

The gargantuan trailer-trucks rolled south to Timbuktu in convoy, enough drivers in each rig to eat and sleep in relays. When they did stop, it was usually for only as long as it took to boil water for the very strong and very sweet infusion of mint tea that the desert Arab needs even more than sleep. But as we got nearer I saw that Percy was correct. These were the same giant chassis, the wheels as high as a man, but they were buses – fitted with chromium trim, and dark-tinted window-glass, and their coachwork bore the name and address of a German tourist agency. A small orange tent by the side of the track was marked with a sign 'Damen', but there was no similar facility for the men, most of whom were arranging themselves into a group for a photo.

'Don't stop,' said Mann.

'Might have to,' said Percy. 'If they are in trouble and we pass by without helping, there will be hell to pay.' He slowed as we passed the two buses until a middle-aged man in a white dust-coat waved us on with a gesture to show that all was well.

'A sign of the times,' said Percy. 'English kids come on these treks in ancient Bedford army lorries.'

It was the better part of an hour before we reached the map reference where Percy's man awaited us. It was ferociously hot as we got out of the car to inspect the place where the Bekuvs' Landrover had left the track and headed west across the open desert. The tyre tracks were still visible in the soft sand but there was a substratum of hard baked ground that in places had cracked to make pans – depressions – that were sometimes half a mile wide.

We transferred to the waiting Landrover, and Percy's man continued south with our rented car. It was better that it should pass the next police-point on time. The movements of Percy's Arab and this battered Landrover would not be so assiduously reported.

'Go slow,' ordered Mann. 'His tyres are the same as ours.'

'Less worn,' said Percy. 'And there is one that looks brand new.'

'Well, I don't want to be crawling round in the sunshine, examining tyre tracks with my vest-pocket microscope,' said Mann.

'Do you have a microscope?' said Percy. 'Some of these desert flowers are worth looking at under a glass.' There was no telling how much of it was serious and how much was mockery.

We left the flat hard ground, which the road-builders had chosen, and the going changed to the gravelly surface of the 'reg' and then to rough 'washboard', which made the suspension judder. Percy accelerated until he found the speed at which the corrugations seemed to smooth out, and we made good speed for over an hour until we encountered the first patches of soft sand. Percy sped through them to begin with, and each time found hard surface before getting bogged down; but our luck couldn't last for ever, and eventually he had to engage the four-wheel drive and crawl to safety.

The going became softer and softer until we were threading our way through a series of dunes. The tracks skirted the higher sandhills, but even so the Landrover was careering about like a roller-coaster ride. The prevailing east wind made the upward side of each dune a gentle slope but the far side was sometimes precipitous. Yet there was no alternative to accelerating over the brink. No one spoke, but it was becoming obvious that only a marginal difference of sand, or a momentary carelessness on Percy's part, would leave us stuck at either the top or the bottom of one of these dunes. We had surmounted one of the gentlest slopes as I heard the sand jamming against the underside of the Landrover and then Percy wrenched at the steering so that we slithered to the valley of the dune in a sideslip that covered us in a storm of flying sand. We stopped at a steep angle with Mann cursing and rubbing his sore head. Even through the brown swirling dust I could see what had made Percy swerve. There, not fifty yards away, was another Landrover – empty and abandoned. Even before the sand settled, Mann was out of the car and following the still visible tracks that the others had left. Red Bancroft had abandoned her shoes, and a man – Professor Bekuv – had stumbled and fallen leaving a long scar in the smooth sand.

We followed the tracks for fifty yards or so, and then they were replaced by wide shallow troughs, ridged with an even pattern of lines. Mann was the first to recognize the strange spoor. 'A dune buggy!' He hurried forward until he found a place where the softly inflated tyres had ballooned in the ridge of the next dune. 'No doubt about it – a dune buggy.' The curious little cars that Californians used for cavorting on beaches were the only vehicles that could outrun a Landrover in country like this.

'A dune buggy?' said Percy.

'Lightweight open vehicle,' I said. 'Moulded body, four wheels, specially made soft tyres with a very wide tread and a canvas top to shield you from the sun . . . roll-bar for protection, can be used to mount a heavy machine-gun . . .'

'What are you talking . . .' said Mann and then he raised his eyes to the ridge of the next dune, and he saw them too.

There were three men in the dune buggy. I studied them carefully for signs of their origin or allegiance. They had the very dark skin of the sort you see in the far south. Protecting their heads from the high sun they wore the *howli*, and their robes were ragged and dirty but had once been the *boubou* style of Mauritania far to the west. Their faces were impassive, but the man in the rear seat gave an imperious wave of the AKMS machine-pistol he was holding. Obedient to it we scrambled up the burning-hot sand.

They were patrolling, and, after walking another half hour, we caught sight of where they'd come from. It was bleached almost to the colour of the pale sand that surrounded it, a great fortress complete with crenellated walls and watch-towers. Ever since the Romans, armies had built such fortified encampments to dominate the caravan trails, wells and desert tracks. The French had built more, and used the Foreign Legion to man them. But there was no flag flying from the mast of this fort, only a tangle of shortwave aerials; dishes, rods, spirals, arrays, loops and frames, more antennae than I'd ever seen before in one place.

At first sight I had not realized the size of the fortress, but nearly an hour later, when we had still not reached its massive doors, I could see that its ramparts were as high as a six-storey building. Finally we reached it, and the Arabs herded us through the main entrance.

There were two sets of doors, and looking up I saw daylight through the sort of openings from which boiling oil was poured on to besieging knights. The second set of doors opened on to a courtyard. Parked there were more dune buggies and beyond them a helicopter. It looked like the little Kamov two-seater gun-ship that had chased Bekuv down the road on the day he defected, and shot up the car with the Arab boy in it. Now its blades had been removed, and a couple of mechanics were tinkering with the rotor linkage. But most of the courtyard was occupied by two huge radio telescopes, the dishes about sixty feet across. Bekuv was there, parading round the equipment and touching the controls and the wiring and the bowl-edge with the sort of tactile awe that most men reserve for very old cars or very new mistresses.

'Jesus Christ!' said Mann softly as he saw the radio telescopes and realized what they'd been used for. He called to Bekuv, 'Hey there, Professor. Are you all right?'

Bekuv looked at us for a long time before replying. Then he said, 'Come here.' It was a command. We shuffled over to him.

'Why didn't you tell us?' said Mann. 'Why didn't you say you'd set up this tracking station to milk the communications satellites. Was it your idea?'

Mann was unable to keep the admiration out of his voice, and Bekuv smiled in appreciation. He handed Mann a water flask that was hanging on the back of his seat. Mann drank some and passed it to Dempsey and then on to me. The water was warm and heavily chlorinated, but it was a welcome relief after our long walk through the sand.

Bekuv watched Mann all the time, studying his badly

bruised face and the plaster – dirtier now – that could be seen under the brim of his hat. Bekuv's eyes were wide and glaring, or perhaps I was just being wise after the event. 'I thought you were dead,' he told Mann. 'I thought they shot you at the airport.'

'Yes, I'm sorry about that,' said Mann. He sat down on a broken packing-case and closed his eyes. The hike through the soft sand had exhausted him.

Bekuv said, 'I was right not to trust you. My wife guessed that there was no chair at New York University . . . she guessed that you were telling me all lies . . .'

'. . . and she arranged with Moscow that you could come back here,' said Mann. 'Yeah, yeah, yeah, we know all that. But why did you *want* to come back here?'

'She said I was to dismantle the apparatus and shred all my records,' said Bekuv.

'But you're not going to do that, are you?' I said.

'No,' said Bekuv. 'I'm going to continue my work. Last night I got signals from Tau Ceti.'

'Well, that's wonderful,' I said, feigning enthusiasm.

'Who's Tau Ceti?' said Mann.

'It's a star,' I told him. 'Professor Bekuv picked up signals from it last year.'

'Is that right?' said Mann.

'So you read those books I loaned you,' Bekuv said.

'And your lectures and the notes,' I said. 'I read everything.'

Bekuv waved a hand in the air and gabbled some fast Arabic. I couldn't follow it except to guess that he was telling the guards to take Mann and Percy Dempsey away somewhere. Bekuv took my arm and led me to the main building of the fortress. The walls were a yard thick and might have been here for centuries.

'How old is this place?' I asked, more in order to keep

265

him affable than because I wanted to know. He reached into his pocket and brought out a handful of stone arrowheads of the sort that the nomad children sell in the southern villages.

'Roman,' he said. 'There must have been some sort of fort here ever since. We have water, you see. The siting leaves a lot to be desired but we have the only water for a hundred miles.' He pushed open the huge, iron-studded door. Inside, the fort was dark and even more bizarre. Shafts of hard Saharan sunlight stood like buttresses against the gaps in the shuttered windows. There was a huge staircase dappled with light that came from the broken parts of the roof, sixty feet above our heads. But the room into which Bekuv went was equipped as a modern office: a sleek desk, three easy chairs, Lenin on the wall and enough books to require the small folding step-ladder. There was another door. Bekuv walked across the room to close it but before he did so, I caught a glimpse of the gleaming grey racks of radio equipment that amplified the signals from the radio telescopes.

Bekuv sat down. 'So you have read everything.'

'Some of it was too technical for me.'

'Last night I received signals from Tau Ceti.'

'What kind of signals?'

Bekuv smiled. 'Well, I don't mean a news bulletin or a sports report. Contact would be a more scientific description. I always said that the first interplanetary exchange would be some clear suggestion of number and order expressed in electrical activity close to 1,420 megacycles.'

'Yes, I remember,' I said. 'The hydrogen atom spinning round its nucleus vibrates at 1,420,405,752 times a second. The idea of those immense clouds of hydrogen, floating through the galaxy and humming at that same wavelength in the electromagnetic spectrum . . . that captured my imagination, Professor. If I'd met someone like you when I was young, I might have chosen science.'

Bekuv was pleased with me. 'And remember, I said *near* to 1,420 megacycles. On that *exact* wavelength you can hear nothing but the hum.'

'And you sent a reply?'

'A series of binary digits – pulses and silences to represent ones and zeros – which are schematic representations of the atomic form of carbon and oxygen. At worst it will be interpreted as a sign that there is some intelligence here. At best it will tell them the environment in which we live.'

'Brilliant.'

Bekuv looked at his watch. He was excited to the point of agitation. 'We are preparing for tonight. Both telescopes will be working. One will be aimed at Tau Ceti, and the other at the open sky near to it. Both telescopes feed their reception back into the computer next door. That compares both streams of material, and cancels everything that is arriving from both telescopes. That's how I get rid of all the background crackle and the cosmic mess. Only Tau Ceti's signals are delivered to the output.' He picked up a long paper roll of computer read-out. It was a maze of incomprehensible symbols. 'This was processed only three hours ago. No matter what anyone might say, there is a regular pattern to the pulses from Tau Ceti.'

'Quite a dream, Professor.'

'Don't deny any man his dream, my friend.'

'You deserve an honest reply, Professor,' I told him. 'You don't seem to understand the dangerous position you're in. You're an embarrassment to the US Government and a threat to one of the most audacious pieces of Soviet electronic eavesdropping I've ever heard of.

You've helped Moscow set up this place to tap the US communications satellites stationed over the Atlantic. Getting material from the commercial and government satellites and, unless I'm guessing wrongly, from FEDSAT, the one that carries all the secret diplomatic material and the CIA priority data between the USA and Europe. You must have given Moscow everything from Presidential phone-calls to the Daily Yellows that Langley sends to London, Bonn and Paris.'

'It was a compromise,' said Bekuv. 'All scientists compromise with power . . . ask Leonardo da Vinci, ask Einstein. I wanted the electronic silence of the Sahara – it's the "coldest" place in the world, to use the jargon of electronics. And the only way I could sell the idea to the Ministry was by telling them that here we could get far enough west to "see" your satellites.'

I went to the window. The sun was blood-red and plunging to earth, and there came the breath of wind that so often comes with sunset. It stirred the sand, and made clouds of dust that rolled across the desert like tumbleweed. 'The party's over, Professor,' I said. 'The hijacking of the airliner, the killing of a US Senator, the treachery and death of his assistant – what kind of priority do you think this is getting in Washington . . . it's just a matter of time before they find this place. Moscow's triumph suddenly becomes a liability, and Moscow will want to snap their fingers and have this place disappear. And have you disappear with it.'

'Well, not even Moscow can snap its fingers and make a place like this disappear overnight.'

'I wouldn't be too sure of that, Professor Bekuv.'

'What do you mean?' he said. I waited a long time, watching the sun sink. The desert sky was as clear as crystal and the stars were packed together like spilled sugar. It was possible to believe him. On a night like this it was possible to believe anything. 'I mean the radio signals might be faked,' I said brutally. 'Experts – scientific experts, ready to concede their own little compromise, like Leonardo da Vinci – might have designed a series of signals that are the sort you'd like to hear. One of the Soviet Air Force's flying electronic laboratories could probably maintain the right altitude, and circle the place that would be on your direct line of sight to Mars or Tau Ceti or Shangri-La.'

'No.'

'And out there in the desert, Professor, there are a couple of big desert buses. When they stop, they put up little tents and mark them ladies' toilet, but there are no ladies to be seen anywhere. The passengers are all fighting-fit men in their middle twenties. And there is the address of a German travel agency on the side of the bus, and if you know Berlin street addresses you know it's on that side of the wall without the advertising or the voting booths. They just might be waiting to come in here and sweep up the debris.'

'What exactly are you saying?'

'I'm saying get out of here, Professor.'

'And go to America or to Britain with you?'

'For the time being, just get out of here.'

'You mean well,' said Bekuv. 'I must thank you for that . . . warning.'

'And for God's sake, don't transmit any kind of signal that an aircraft could home on.'

He wiped his nose again. He had one of those viral infections that are common in the desert; the mucous membrane is inflamed by the sand and dust in the air, and once it starts it's difficult to shake off. 'That is where I have to be, and this is what I have to do,' he said. His voice was hoarse now and his nose clogged. 'All my life has been leading up to this moment, I realize that now.'

'You have a life of achievement ahead of you,' I coaxed him.

'I have nothing ahead of me. My own people want only that part of my expertise that they can use for the military. I am only interested in pure science – I'm not interested in politics – but in my country to be apolitical is considered only one step away from being a fascist. No man, woman or child is permitted to live their life without political activity . . . and for a real scientist that is not possible. Your people were no better . . . I trusted you, and you humiliated me with the forged papers appointing me to a non-existent chair in a university that had never heard of me, and didn't wish to hear of me. My son wants to be a jazz singer and my wife has betrayed me.' He sneezed. 'Betrayed me with another woman. It's comical, isn't it? It is the true tragedy of my life that my tragedies are comical.'

'Life is a comedy for those who think – and a tragedy for those who feel,' I said.

'Who said that?'

'I don't know,' I said. 'Bob Hope or Voltaire or Eichmann; does it make a difference who said it?'

'I *must* send the signals tonight. Even if there were a million to one chance of communicating with some other worlds, it would still be a crime – a crime against science – to let it go.'

'Other worlds have waited a million million years,' I said. 'They can wait one more night. Men who want to kill you will be tuned to 1,420 megacycles tonight.'

'Yours is the voice of ignorance and suspicion. Those same thoughts and fears drag civilization back into the

Dark Ages. No scientist worthy of the name can put his personal safety before the pursuit of knowledge.'

'I wasn't putting your personal safety before the pursuit of knowledge,' I said. 'I was putting *my* personal safety before it. If you want to stay here and talk to Tau Ceti and prove me wrong – OK. But why not allow the rest of us to move off into the desert?'

'Because you will make for the Trans-Sahara Highway, and from there you will go north and get away. Don't pretend you won't.'

'I can't speak for the others,' I said. 'But speaking personally, I'll try to do exactly that.'

Bekuv frowned, got to his feet and pretended to look at his shelves of books. The daylight was fading rapidly, and the dim yellow lights in the courtyard glowed more brightly as the generators started and made the floor vibrate with a very low rumbling noise.

'Your wife drives a car like no one I've ever seen, Professor,' I said. Bekuv turned to me, nodded and fetched a packet of cigarettes out of a drawer in his desk. They were American cigarettes and here in Algeria they were precious. He offered one to me and I accepted it with thanks.

'We were both betrayed,' said Bekuv. 'Your woman, and mine . . . they have humiliated us.'

I looked at him but didn't answer.

'I'm going to kill them both,' said Bekuv.

'Your wife and Red Bancroft?'

'Yes, I'm going to kill them both. It's the only way to regain my honour.'

'How will you go about it?' I asked.

'With my own bare hands,' he held them up and made a gesture of pincers. 'And it will be a pleasure,' he added.

'You're not being scientific, Professor,' I said.

271

'You mean I'm being childish.' He turned to me and stared for a moment before blowing his nose.

'Worse – a child who has his toys stolen runs and grabs them back; he doesn't smash them.'

'I love her, I admit it.' He inhaled deeply and then let the smoke trickle out of him.

'Miss Bancroft is your problem – eliminate her and your wife will come back to you.'

'Yes, I will kill Miss Bancroft.'

'That would make your wife hate you for ever.'

'I will order one of these Arabs to kill the girl.'

'Your wife will guess you gave the order.'

'Yes,' he said. He stubbed his cigarette into an ashtray. 'It must look like an accident.'

I shook my head. 'Your wife will guess. She is a very clever woman, Professor Bekuv.'

'I must get rid of the Bancroft girl. I see that now. You are right. She is the evil one. It was the Bancroft woman who debauched my wife, and introduced her to those unnatural acts.'

'Right!' I said. 'And there is only one way in which the Bancroft girl can die, and yet leave you entirely blameless in the eyes of your wife.'

'You mean if you kill her.'

'Now you are being really scientific,' I said.

Bekuv stared at me. 'Why should I trust you?'

I said, 'If I double-cross you, you'd only have to tell Major Mann what I'd done, and I'd face a murder trial when I got home.'

'So you want me to let you go.'

'Well, you don't think I want to stay here, do you?'

'I suppose not.' Only with an effort of will could he imagine anyone so indifferent to his precious radio telescopes.

272

'I'll want a dune buggy, some water and food.'

'You can't have a dune buggy.'

'Very well, we'll go on foot, but we must leave tonight. Mann is sick. He'd not make it across the desert in the heat of day. It's a damned long way to the highway, and who knows how long we'll wait there.' He nodded. 'There's just that one thing, Professor,' I said. 'This has got to be done in such a way that Major Mann and Mr Dempsey – the old man – don't know it was me.'

Bekuv's eyes flickered as he smiled. That wariness that is ever present in the crackpot mind appreciated such caution. He held out his hand to me. 'The two men can go,' he said, 'but you will not get out of here until the Bancroft woman is dead.'

I shook his hand on it.

It was dark by the time I went up to the rooms where Mann, Dempsey and the two women were. Before his defection, this had been Bekuv's living accommodation. The two men were in the sitting-room. It was a comfortable place. There were a couple of rugs to hide the cracks in the wall, a wooden floor so new that it still smelled of anti-termite spray, leather-covered armchairs, an old crucifix, a collection of records and an elaborate amplifier and speakers. A new American air-conditioner purred gently from the boarded-up window.

Percy Dempsey said, 'We've got to get out of here.' He was sitting on the sofa. Mann was there too, but he was asleep. Percy Dempsey said, 'Your friend is sick. He should have gone back north after the car crash.'

I went over to Mann and looked at him. He looked as if he was running a temperature, but his pulse was strong and his breathing regular. 'He'll be all right,' I said.

Percy Dempsey didn't answer, but clearly he didn't agree. He pulled a bright red blanket over Mann. Mann

273

didn't awaken. I said, 'You can wake him and get him on to his feet. Take him down to the yard and leave through the main gate. Head due west – you've got a compass, haven't you?'

'Is he letting us go?'

'I made a deal with him. Where are the women?'

'Through the kitchen. There's another room. I might need your help with Major Mann,' said Dempsey.

'Prod him,' I said. 'I'll catch up with you later.'

'You've got a compass?'

'I watched the sun go down. I'll be all right. Wait for me at the highway . . .'

'He's quite a weight,' said Dempsey. He grabbed Mann's arm and shook him roughly. 'Come along,' he said.

I walked through the kitchen to find the women.

24

The still desert night was shattered by the ugly screams of Mrs Bekuv. She fought her way through the Arabs who were lounging in the doorway at the bottom of the stairs. The violent flaying arms knocked one of the boys off balance and gave another a bloody nose. They had scarcely delayed her as she ran, hysterical and screaming, across the dimly lit compound to the big radio telescopes. The great dish shapes were only faintly discernible in the light of a waning moon and a thousand stars. Only when Mrs Bekuv reached the place where her husband was standing did her garbled cries become comprehensible. It was Russian. I could pick out a few phrases here and there: 'The girl is dead' . . . '. . . who would have done it if not you . . . ? Who can I tell, who can I tell? . . . I hate you . . . why did she have to die? . . . If only it had been me . . .' many of them were repeated in that grief-stricken litany with which humans numb their minds to anguish.

'It wasn't me and it wasn't any of the Arabs,' said Bekuv, but his voice did nothing to calm her and soon he began to contract the very hysteria that he was trying to cure.

He shouted and slapped her across the face – very hard, the way they do it in old Hollywood films – but it only made her worse. She was struggling now, hitting, punching and kicking him, so that he had to hold her very close to restrain her. It was like trying to cage a wildcat. Half a dozen Arabs had come out to watch the struggle and four men at the controls of the dish –

Russian technicians – stopped their work to see what was happening. But none of them did anything to part the couple.

I turned away from the window and looked at Red Bancroft. 'She's done you proud,' I said. 'No one could have asked for a better performance.'

'She loves me,' said Red Bancroft. Her voice was matter of fact.

'And you?'

'I don't love anyone,' she said. 'My analyst says I'm bisexual. He doesn't understand. I'm neuter.'

'You don't have to hate yourself,' I said. 'You've brought no harm to her.'

'No,' she said scornfully. 'I've taken her away from her husband, she'll never again see her grown-up son. If we all get out of this alive, she'll be a KGB target for ever and ever. And what have I given her in return – nothing but a good time in bed and a lot of worthless promises.'

I looked down into the central yard. Two Arab guards were restraining Mrs Bekuv. She was still talking to her husband, but I could not hear the words. Red Bancroft came to the window and looked down too.

'She'll do it,' I said.

'Yes, she'll do it,' said Red Bancroft. 'She's incredibly clever with everyone – except with me.'

'What's the matter?' I said.

'I can't go down that rope. I'm frightened of heights . . . I get dizzy just looking down into this yard here.'

'I'll tie it round you, and lower you down. Keep your eyes closed and you'll be all right.'

'Will he come up here looking for the corpse?' she asked.

'Perhaps – but not until he's finished his transmission. And that will take hours.'

She went to the other window and looked down at the sand far below. Dempsey and Mann had left already but they were not to be seen. 'And the sentries?'

'Stop worrying,' I said. I went across to her and put my arm round her waist. It was no more than a brotherly gesture, and she did not shrink away from me as she had done earlier.

'I'm sorry,' she said. 'We both lost out – but now I'm beginning to think maybe I lost more than you did.'

'Let's get the rope round you,' I said. 'It won't get any darker than this.'

The night air was cool but underfoot the sand was warm, and soft enough to make progress slow and difficult. Even with the stars to guide, we lost our way after the moon disappeared. The sandhills, like some great rolling ocean transfixed for ever, shone in the dusty starlight.

There was no sound; it must have been flying very high. There was a flash like that of an electrical storm, and a rumble like thunder. Anywhere else and we would have written it off as a thunderstorm, put up our umbrellas and waited for the rain. But this was a thousand miles deep into the Sahara.

'Smart bomb,' said Mann. 'You put a laser beam from aircraft to target and let the bomb slide down the beam.'

'Unless you can persuade the target to put up a beam for you,' I said.

Red Bancroft said nothing. Ever since we'd caught up with Mann and Dempsey she'd been walking a few paces behind us. Several times I saw her turning round hoping to see Mrs Bekuv there.

The sound of the explosion rumbled across the empty desert, and then came rolling back again, looking for a place to fade away. I waited for Red Bancroft to catch up. She had discarded her shoes. I put my arm out, offering to help her, but without a word she limped past me, sliding sometimes in the soft steep dune. After the explosion she didn't look back again.